But He's My Grumpy Neighbor

A COZY ROMANTIC COMEDY

ANNAH CONWELL

This is for the girls who spent their lives hiding in the shadows and walking on eggshells. The ones who grew up to become women that dance in the sunlight and draw boundaries in permanent marker. In case you haven't heard it lately: I'm proud of you.

"If I loved you less, I might be able to talk about it more." -Emma, Jane Austen

Contents

Content Warning

While this is a romcom, it does deal with some heavy topics. The characters wrestle with grief and anxiety. There are depictions of panic attacks and anxious moments. There are also mentions of emotional and minor physical abuse in one character's childhood.

Also, this is a closed-door romcom, with no explicit scenes. There are some 'makeout' scenes, but the characters do not go further than kissing.

CHAPTER ONE

Juliette Monroe

It's not stalking if they're your neighbor, I think to myself as I peer through the slats of my blinds. A tall man with dark hair slides out of a sleek, pitch-black sports car. I follow his movements, my eyebrows raising in appreciation. I've heard men frown on being called beautiful, but that's exactly what he is.

He opens the door to the storage container that was delivered yesterday–I know this because I was spying then too–and lugs a large cardboard box out. He's wearing a long-sleeve black t-shirt, but I can tell by the fit that he's hiding all sorts of muscles beneath the material. The scowl on his face has me tipping my head to the side. Maybe he doesn't like moving? He does seem to be doing everything by himself. I remember doing that same thing a few years ago. I was probably scowling too.

I wish he would start moving furniture. Since I don't have x-ray vision, I can't tell what's inside cardboard boxes. But I *can* decide what kind of man he is based on his furniture, as one does.

"I bet everything he owns is modern and black," I tell Murphy, my golden retriever, while still staring out at the ridiculously attractive man stalking across his yard like he's mad at it for existing at all. Which is quite sad, considering how lovely our little neighborhood is.

Peach Hollow is a small residential community situated around a lake in Georgia. On this side of the lake, there are three two-bedroom cottages set in a row. On the opposite side are six more cottages, then there's a subdivision hidden beyond the tree line with a walking path that leads to the lakeshore. The new neighbor's home is in the middle of our row of cottages, mine is on the right, and Mr. Kipton lives on the left. Our houses are close enough that you could have a conversation from one back porch to another while watching the sunrise over the lake.

Not that I would know, because my last neighbor, Darren, worked odd hours and never spoke to me. And Mr. Kipton is a grouchy hermit who says he's too old and tired to watch the sunrise.

I gasp. "That looks like an antique end table!" My knees shift on the cushion beneath me as I try to get a better look at what he's carrying. Murphy lets out a low but loud ruff when the blinds rustle.

The man's head whips toward my house and I squeak, falling down onto the couch. The brown plaid skirt I'm wearing flops up with the movement and I quickly jerk it down as if the mysterious neighbor can see me through my walls. Murphy huffs from his dog bed and I roll my head over to look at him.

"Don't judge me. You know Peach Hollow never gets any new people. I'm desperate to talk to someone below the age of seventy-five."

Murphy seems unaffected by my plight for youthful human interaction. It's my own fault, really. I chose Peach Hollow because it embodied safety and peace at a time I needed it most. At the time I didn't care that there were no people my age, except the occasional grandkids who visited. I just cared about being in an environment opposite of what I was in before.

Now, years later, I work from home running my Etsy business selling invitation templates and stationery .... and have no friends. *None*. Well, except my best friend Caroline. She lives hundreds of miles away though, so we only see each other through video chat. I could move, but the thought of starting over again scares me, so here I stay, bored and in dire need of conversation.

The rumble of a truck makes me stiffen, memories of times past flitting through my mind for a moment before I can tamp them down. Closing my eyes, I listen and hear footsteps, then two male voices having a conversation I can't quite make out.

"I think we should check the mail," I tell Murphy, even though I know the mailman, Leonard, came and went already with nothing for me. But my neighbor wasn't here when the mail truck came by, so he wouldn't know that I'd already gone out and checked.

I run my fingertips through my hair and then smooth down my cream sweater. Even though I rarely see anyone but myself in the mirror each day, I still like to dress nice. Growing up, I couldn't wear what I liked, so now I take advantage of every freedom I have.

The bite of January air hits me as soon as I open my door and I tuck my arms around myself to brace for the cold. My outfit isn't exactly conducive to spending any more than a few minutes outside.

Murphy trots dutifully beside me as I walk to the end of my driveway. I don't look to my right even once, for fear of drawing more attention to myself. But when I get to my mailbox, I angle my body toward my neighbor's house and try to sneak a glance while pretending to check the mail.

The man from earlier meets my gaze as he walks out of the cottage and beams at me, waving as if we were lifelong friends. I blink in surprise at the contrast between his earlier scowl and now. I give a tentative wave back and open my mouth to say hello, but the greeting dies on my lips when a carbon copy of the man I'm waving to walks out of the cottage.

Twins. It's then that I begin to catalog the differences between the two. One is smiling and the other scowling. One has artfully messy hair while the other has shorter, tamed hair. They're both wearing the exact same black shirt though, which is odd. I thought most twins abandoned dressing similarly once they exited grade school. Or at least, the few sets of twins *I* know did. Scowly twin looks me over. Then, without so much as a nod in my direction, he disappears into the storage container.

"Sorry about him!" Smiley twin yells across the yard. "He gets nervous around beautiful women."

My face heats at his forward compliment.

"Grayson!" Scowly twin barks and I duck my head, giggling. "If you're here to help, *help*. If not, leave."

Grayson winks at me then goes to help his brother carry in a gorgeous apothecary cabinet. I walk slowly back to my front door, letting Murphy sniff around the yard to buy me some time. They don't seem to struggle at all carrying the large antique by themselves, made known by the fact that Grayson is chattering as if they were carrying an empty cardboard box. His brother says nothing, but I don't think it's because of overexertion.

I'm forced to walk inside when Murphy paws at the door. If I don't let him in, he'll start to whine and draw attention. My living room is nice and warm when I return, making me aware of how cold it is outside. I was too distracted by the twins to notice.

The differences between the two brothers were interesting, to say the least. My new neighbor does not seem to be a people person, but his taste in furniture was surprising and there's just something about him that makes me want to get to know him more. Maybe that's just the loneliness talking, though.

"You can do this, Juliette," I coach myself in front of my gilded mirror. "All you have to do is go over there, give him the plant, and introduce yourself. Then you can run back to your hobbit hole and overthink the entire interaction."

I pull a face and groan. I have *got* to start giving myself better pep talks. This is what happens when you live alone for too long–your awkwardness grows and multiplies like a weird fungus.

My hands tighten around the tea tin I turned into a planter and I start toward the door. He might not be a plant person, but when I made cookies for Darren to welcome him to the neighborhood he said he was allergic to chocolate. I told him that was sad, which probably wasn't the best thing to say. He didn't speak to me much after that. So, I decided to gift my scowly neighbor a basil plant.

I fling open the door and march across my yard before I can talk myself out of it. I've already done that twice in the last three days since he moved in. My brown loafers click on his driveway, the usually peaceful silence of Peach Hollow now feeling ominous. After taking a deep breath, I knock on his door, then take a step back and try to look more confident than I feel.

The door opens and every carefully crafted word I'd agonized over is burned from my brain by the piercing blue gaze of the man before me. His lips are a flat line, which doesn't bode well for my presence here, but he's also not exhibiting any other signs of anger or frustration. His arms are by his side, and his posture is relaxed. He's an intimidating man by default, but he isn't capitalizing on that. Interesting.

"I'm your neighbor," I blurt out because even though I can decipher emotions like a professional, I'm not elegant in the slightest. "My name's Juliette and I came over to welcome you to Peach Hollow."

I hold out the basil plant in front of me. He looks down at it but doesn't make any move to take it from my hands. This is not how I pictured this interaction in my head at three in the morning when I couldn't sleep.

"It's a basil plant," I explain. "See, the guy who lived here before you, Darren, well I tried to bring him cookies to welcome him to the neighborhood. But he said he was allergic to chocolate chips, so I was afraid to bring you anything food related, worried that you might be allergic to something. So I brought you a basil plant."

I pause, but he still says nothing, and then it dawns on me.

"*Oh no*, you're not allergic to basil, are you?"

I start to pull the plant back toward my chest, but his hand reaches out lightning-fast and grabs my arm. My eyes zero in on his large hand circling my wrist below where my sweater stops, warmth flooding my body from the contact. He immediately removes his hand as if my skin had turned to flame under his touch.

"I'm not allergic to basil, thank you for the plant." His voice is low and a bit gruff, different from the smooth musicality of his brother's.

I hand him the tin and resist the urge to dust the bits of potting soil from my hands on my brown suede skirt. Instead, I keep my fingers locked together in front of me and my eyes on the plant that looks much smaller in his hands than it did in mine.

"I'm Adrian," he says and my eyes spring up to meet his. They're a disconcerting kind of blue. The kind that makes you think of glaciers and frigid temperatures.

"It's nice to meet you, Adrian. If you ever need anything, me and Murphy are right next door."

"Murphy?" He quirks a brow and I smile up at him.

"My golden retriever. Don't worry, he's well-trained. He won't come in your yard or anything like that."

"Good to know."

"Well, I'll get out of your hair. I just wanted to introduce myself." I take a step back. He nods.

If I stand here long enough, would he cave and talk to me? I tilt my head to the side, studying him for a second longer before grinning. No, I think he could spend the rest of the evening in silence, counting on me to get uncomfortable before he did. His eyes dip down to my lips for barely a second, but I catch it. My stomach flips at the thought of a man this gorgeous looking at my mouth.

"Have a nice evening, Adrian," I say and turn around to leave without waiting for a response. It's unlikely that I'd get one, and for some reason that makes me like him more.

It means that if I ever do get to have a conversation with him, it'll be intentional on his part. He's probably thinking that his behavior tonight will keep me from talking to him again, but he's wrong. I'm going to get a conversation out of Adrian, even if it takes way more time and energy than most people would put into it. Something tells me he needs a friend, and lucky–or unlucky, depending on who you ask–for him, so do I.

CHAPTER TWO

Adrian Carter

Water flows from the kettle and the scent of steeping tea permeates the air. After a morning run around the lake, I'm going to soak up the tranquility and solitude of my new neighborhood while drinking my favorite Earl Grey. I moved to Peach Hollow because of the peace it emanated when I found it. After living in apartments in major cities for the majority of my adult life, this small cottage is a welcome reprieve.

My eyes catch on basil leaves in the morning light while I wait on my tea and I scowl at the plant perched on my windowsill. If only looks could make a plant wither. Every time I see it, it's a reminder of the weakness I indulged. I planned on sending Juliette back to her home, plant in hand, but she just kept talking. It was as if she was unaffected by the *leave me alone* message I was sending her. It's no good to have her thinking I'm anything more than a quiet neighbor who keeps to myself.

There is something different about her, though. Something about the combination of those innocent green eyes blinking up at me and how soft she looked with her fuzzy navy sweater. Probably more than all of that, was the secretive smile she wore as she took me in. As if she wasn't concerned with my flat look or lack of conversation skills. She seemed to find me *entertaining*.

My breath creates a white fog as I walk out onto my back deck. Maybe the below thirty winds will give the memory of her smile frostbite, so I never have to think of it again.

That secret smile has plagued me because I'm a man who picks up on cues from people. I can give someone a once over and know more about them than most people will after a full conversation. All my life, I've been the observer. But Juliette... she made me feel like I was on the other side of the magnifying glass for once. All the more reason to keep her at a distance. I don't need to be friends with some innocent but curious woman.

My brother Grayson and I left our government jobs in order to start our own private security company so that we could work less and settle down. We're both thirty now, so it makes sense to think of finding a wife and starting a family. But relationships don't come easy for me. I *like* being alone, and I don't trust easily. I was burned one too many times during my stint in the CIA. After having so-called friends use the minor details about my life I gave them against me, it's hard to trust anyone, much less become vulnerable enough to make a lifelong commitment to someone.

So as pretty as Juliette is, I'm going to steer clear of her. There's no way that someone as sweet and naive as she appears could handle all of my skepticism.

Right as I'm taking a sip of my morning tea, a loud crash pierces the air, making me startle, and my tea slosh out of my mug and onto my shirt.

"*Why me?*" I hear a familiar feminine voice whine and without thinking, I rush down my deck stairs, abandoning my mug on the railing.

I jog in the direction of the crash but stumble to a halt when Juliette comes into view. She's frowning down at my tipped-over trashcan, her arms crossed over her chest. Her beige satin pajamas shimmer in the light as she shifts from foot to foot. *Does she always look this unbelievably soft?*

A look of determination washes over her and she bends down to grab the edge of the trashcan. Her face scrunches up as she attempts to lift the mostly-full can off the ground. I bite the inside of my cheek to keep from chuckling.

"Juliette," I say and she jumps, dropping the trashcan, getting more debris on my driveway in the process.

"Adrian," she breathes out and an unwelcome tingle skips down my spine. "I am *so* sorry, did I wake you up?" Her green eyes rove over me. "Oh, you went on a run around the lake. I'm glad I didn't wake you, but I feel so bad. The trash truck is about to come and I noticed you hadn't brought yours down yet, so I thought maybe you didn't know that Friday is pickup day. I didn't want to knock on your door so early so I thought I would get it for you, but it fell over when it hit a crack in the driveway. Now there's trash everywhere, but don't worry I'll clean it up! I just can't seem to get the can upright."

She takes a deep breath after her monologue and crosses her arms over her chest again as if she's hugging herself. There are many things

I could address in what she just said, but my brain is stuck on one detail.

"How did you know I went on a run around the lake?" I ask and she blinks at me.

"What?"

"You said you thought I was sleeping, and then you said I ran around the lake. How did you know?"

"Your shoes have lake sand on them, you're wearing running clothes and your hair is mussed." I look down at my shoes, confirming that they're caked in sand. Strange how she caught all of that in one measly glance.

"Don't worry about the trash," I say instead of acknowledging the lake run. "I'll clean it up and bring it down, thanks for letting me know when trash day is."

"No, it was my fault, please let me help." She starts grabbing the trash with her hands and I don't miss the disgusted purse of her lips as she does.

"It's fine. Just let me do it." I try for a stern tone, but she continues on as if she didn't hear me. "Juliette, *stop*." My voice is hard, more of a command than a suggestion this time around. An empty takeout container tumbles from her hands and clatters against the concrete.

Slowly, she straightens to standing, her green eyes lifting. I expect to find them shining, perhaps a bit glassy, but I've braced myself for nothing. Her eyes are as serene as the surface of the lake I was just gazing upon moments ago. The silence between us is punctured only by the rustling of the wind in the trees as she regards me calmly.

"I wanted to fix my mistake," she says, and I hate how her tone has changed but I hate even more that it bothers me. Earlier she sounded like a rushing waterfall, gushing and bubbling with life. Now, she's flat as the ground beneath us. "But if that would make you more upset, I understand. I'm sorry."

"It's just that your help isn't necessary," I say, hoping that softens the blow of my earlier words.

I don't want to be friends with her, but I also don't want to be so rude that my mother would be shaking her head at me in Heaven. *Great*, now I'm thinking of my mom on top of dealing with this conversation. My fingers itch to rub the medallion that's hidden beneath my shirt, but I resist.

"Okay, sorry again." The side of her mouth hitches up in a half-smile.

She backs away from the trash can, then turns on her heel and walks across the dewy grass in her moccasins. It's then that I notice Murphy sitting patiently by the door. As soon as she steps onto the driveway, the dog walks up to her and leans into her legs. She scratches behind his ears while walking to her door. I watch her disappear inside, relief and regret battling for dominance within me.

It's good that she thinks less of you, I try to tell myself. That way, neither of us can get hurt. Trusting someone new isn't an option.

"Uncle Adrian!" My twelve-year-old niece Maddie yells as soon as she gets out of MJ's SUV.

"Hey, Mad Dog," I say with a smile and let her attack me into a hug. She's one of the limited few who get to hug me.

My sister MJ married Maddie's uncle Sebastian last year, but Maddie views both Sebastian and MJ as her parents since she never knew either of hers. When I first met Maddie, it was at her dance competition where we showed up for moral support. My brother Grayson gave her the nickname Mad Dog, and she conned us into doing a TikTok dance with her. She's had me wrapped around her finger since the moment I saw her.

"This is a nice neighborhood," MJ says, shutting her car door. "Grayson wasn't exaggerating when he said it had Hallmark movie potential."

"Since when do you watch Hallmark movies?" I ask and she spears me with a look.

MJ has always had an aversion to the overly romantic, but her husband Sebastian softened her over the past few months. He dotes on her obsessively. While I think he's a great guy, I can't stand to be in the same room as them for long. It's nauseating how much they love each other.

"I have a daughter now, she loves them."

"One time I caught Mom watching one by herself," Maddie whispers to me and I chuckle. Her whisper isn't very quiet though, as evidenced by MJ's scowl.

"I'm not going to make you hot chocolate tonight if you keep telling all of my secrets."

"Sorry, Mom," Maddie giggles as I open the door to my cottage for them.

I close the door behind us and let them explore the house, meandering behind them.

"Where's Bash?" I ask MJ, using Sebastian's nickname he got while playing football.

"He's playing poker with some of the guys. Maddie and I are actually headed over to Sophie's after this for a girls' day." MJ used to live with three of her best friends, but now that they're all married they try to get together often. Conveniently, their husbands are all friends as well.

"That's nice."

I'm not one for small talk and neither is MJ, so our conversation dwindles after that. But as Maddie is opening every drawer in the apothecary cabinet I converted to storage for tea, MJ speaks up.

"You got a plant." My spine stiffens.

The thing about my family is that our observant nature is in our blood. All three of my brothers and my sister are incredibly attentive to our surroundings. My dad is the same way, and my mom was too before she passed away. This means that rarely anything goes unnoticed.

"Yes, I did."

"You told me you didn't want any plants. We have plenty I could have given you."

"We have *a lot* at home," Maddie adds with a nod.

"I didn't buy it." I pause. "It was a gift ... from my neighbor."

MJ raises a dark eyebrow.

"The pretty blonde one?"

"Grayson told you about her," I deadpan.

"Of course he did. He tells me everything, too much, actually. So, who is she?" She crosses her arms and eyes me.

"Her name is Juliette. She's my neighbor. She has a dog."

"That's all?"

"Yes."

"Can I meet her?" Maddie asks, reminding me that she's listening to all of this.

"Maybe one day, but I wouldn't count on it," I say and she pokes her bottom lip out in response.

"I want to meet her dog, though. Mom and Dad won't let me get a puppy."

MJ sighs as if this has been a well-discussed topic in their home.

"We didn't say no, we said we would talk about it." MJ pulls her phone out of the pocket of her paint-splattered jeans. She's an artist, and it's rare she's without at least a speck of paint on her person. "Sophie says she's finishing up food. We should probably go."

"Okay, thanks for showing us your house," Maddie says and hugs me again. MJ nods to me, not being one for physical affection.

"Don't forget to water your plant." She gives me a look like she knows something more is going on before walking back through the house and leaving me behind.

But there's nothing more going on. Just a neighborly gift from a woman I plan on seeing as little as possible. That's all.

CHAPTER THREE

Juliette Monroe

"I can be there in a few hours to beat him up for you." Caroline's voice sounds through the earbud in my right ear. I'm walking Murphy around the lake and I always keep one ear free to listen to my surroundings.

The company I run sells digital wedding invitation templates, so that means a lot of my work day is spent with my eyes glued to my tablet screen while I craft new designs. So, I try to get outside at least once a day.

"It would take you more than a few hours to get here from California. And I don't need you to beat him up, he wasn't that bad. Also, there's the fact that you have no fighting skills whatsoever." I've just told Caroline about the trashcan incident and she has jumped–as usual–to physical violence as a solution.

Murphy buries his nose in a pile of orange leaves and I stop to let him sniff around. The lake and trees are bathed in golden light this evening. Sunset is my favorite time of day to walk the lake and when I time it just right I arrive back home before it's too dark out to see. I'm not a fan of darkness, so I make sure I'm safely inside before it falls.

Caroline scoffs. "Who needs fighting skills when I have a giant muscly husband who can do the beating on my behalf?"

"I thought Josh told you to stop entering him into duels."

My best friend has a tendency to let her rambunctious personality get the best of her and at times that means others get angry with her or she gets angry with them first. This leads to her yelling loudly for everyone to hear that her husband will beat them up. Josh is not fond of this little habit of hers.

"Yes, he did, but you're the exception to the rule and he knows it. You know if something was really wrong we'd be there as fast as we could." I smile as warmth spreads through my chest.

Caroline has been my best friend since we were in preschool. She was the only person I was sad to leave behind in California. She's also the only one who knows where I live now. So to have her on my side helps ease some of the loneliness that has plagued me over the last year.

The first few years after moving to Peach Hollow were full of life and joy. I relished in the weight of my circumstances being lifted. But now, I look around and see I've made few connections here. I need friends that don't live thousands of miles away. I also wouldn't mind having a boyfriend, but that seems far-fetched for someone who hasn't dated since high school.

"I know, Care. But nothing is wrong, he was just a little moody is all."

Truthfully, I'm more frustrated with my reaction to his stern voice than his gruff refusal of my help. I can't be too mad at him for telling me not to pick up trash, but I can be mad at myself for the ditzy butterflies that arose when he said *stop* in that deep, silky voice of his. I responded to him in such a bland way to manage his heightened emotions, but also to manage my own. If I remained monotone it wouldn't betray the girlish fancies plaguing my mind.

"What do your spidey senses think of him?"

I groan and the noise makes Murphy look up from his study of the grass. "You've got to quit calling it that."

"Would you rather me ask what your intense observancy and forced empathy that stems from childhood trauma revealed to you about him?"

I snort and shake my head even though she can't see me. "That *is* a mouthful."

"Exactly. So, what was his vibe?"

Murphy abandons his leaf investigation and we continue our walk again. There are a few residents that we pass who I nod to with a smile. I glance down at the watch on my wrist to be sure we're making good time. While I love letting Murphy explore, I'll haul him back to the house if it means avoiding the dark.

"He wasn't trying to intimidate me in a cruel way in either of our interactions, but he also wants nothing to do with me. Doesn't seem like much of a people person. I mean, he moved to Peach Hollow and he looks like he's around thirty. That would lend to him wanting to avoid most social interactions considering everyone here is elderly and only leaves home to go to the market or church."

"You moved to Peach Hollow and you aren't a total hermit."

"I moved here to escape, Care. That's different."

"Do you think he could be escaping something too?"

I lift my eyes and gaze across the lake at Adrian's cottage. There are no lights on inside. He's usually not home until after dark; sometimes I'm already in bed when he pulls into his driveway. I know the sound of his return well. The soft purr of the sports car's engine, he opens and shuts two different car doors, then soft footsteps as he walks inside his house. All of his movements are quiet, but in the silence of Peach Hollow they're easy for me to pick up.

"He's rarely home, so I'm not sure if this is much of a sanctuary for him. I don't think his being here is a secret, either."

I've heard people coming and going over the short amount of time that he's lived here. Bitterness has only risen up a time or two at the thought that a man so surly could have visitors while I've never had any. It's easy to tamp down those feelings though, because I know it's my fault. I could have built a different life here in Georgia, but I chose this one because it felt safer. Maybe if I would have taken more risks, I'd have a whole friend group and even a boyfriend–or maybe a husband–by now.

"Well, I know I don't have to tell you to be careful."

No, she doesn't. I've been *careful* my entire life. Even my escape from California was painstakingly cautious. Not for the first time, I wonder what it would feel like to be care*free*.

Warm air scented with cinnamon and nutmeg washes over me as I enter my favorite café, Peaches and Cream. I've visited Atlanta–or *the city* as it's called here in Peach Hollow–plenty of times, and no café there compares to this one. The pastries are delicious beyond belief and the tea selection is always rotating, making it the perfect place to try new things. It's run by Poppy Wilkes, a fifty-year-old woman with a demeanor sweet enough that you'd think she was a pastry herself.

Poppy smiles at me from behind the counter, and her warm welcome gives me a false sense of security. That security is ripped from me when I spot none other than my stoic neighbor himself at the counter. It's not like I thought we wouldn't run into each other eventually, but he's been elusive all week. I didn't expect to see him at my favorite place, to say the least.

"I'll be right with you, honeybunch!" Poppy says and Adrian glances over his shoulder. His gaze lands on me and I scan him for any clues of discomfort or anger. I notice the tightness of his jaw, but the rest of him seems to be relaxed. Without so much as a hello, he turns his attention back to the menu hanging above the counter. *Well, fine then. I didn't want to talk to you either.* Except that's not entirely true, because I'm still unbelievably curious about him.

Which is why while he peruses the menu, I peruse *him*. He's wearing fitted black pants, a black pea coat, and a cream turtleneck I can see poking out beyond the color of his coat. The darkness of his attire further accentuates his pitch-black hair and the barest hint of stubble speckling his razor-sharp jawline. It's rather annoying how gorgeous he is. Even while wearing a scowl he's the most beautiful man I've ever met. Somehow he manages to make the facial expression sexy when it should be off-putting.

"Do you have any questions about the menu?" Poppy asks him, shooting me an apologetic look. I wave my hand at her to let her know I'm in no rush. Which she knows by now, because my Saturday routine is to come in here, sample at least one of the new teas she has, eat an almond croissant the size of my head, and read whatever book I have in my tote bag until lunchtime. Then, I get a sandwich and an iced tea to go and head back home to Murphy. It's my weekly reset button. The reset I desperately need after my encounters with the man standing in front of me.

"No, thank you. I'll have a mint chocolate tea latte," Adrian replies in his smooth, deep voice.

I gape at him behind his back. Why does he have to like tea? He's gorgeous, dresses like the men on my fantasy life Pinterest boards, has antique furniture, *and* likes tea. If he wasn't so ornery, I'd think he was my future husband.

He pays with a card, then drops a few bills in the tip jar shaped like a peach and stalks over to a booth by the window. *My* booth by the window. It has the perfect view of the town square with a sliver of the lake in the distance. And he's stolen it from me. My face scrunches up in frustration and of course, this is the moment he looks over at me. He raises an eyebrow. My face heats and I whip back around to meet Poppy's knowing gaze.

"I've got your croissant in the warmer already. What tea are we thinking today?"

I study the seasonal menu and I'm instantly annoyed that the one Adrian chose sounds the best for my mood. I know I can try it tomorrow without him here, but then my routine is off even more than it already is and I'll have to deal with the post-church café traffic. The place fills up fast with a bunch of angry old sloths–aka the residents–grumbling and shoving each other in slow motion.

"I'll take a mint chocolate tea latte," I grumble and ignore Poppy's twinkling brown eyes.

Just because Adrian chose it doesn't mean I'm going to miss out on a delicious mint tea latte sweetened with homemade dark chocolate sauce. My grudge against him does not beat my love of chocolate. If it can even be called a grudge. What would I say if he asked me why I was mad at him? *I'm upset because you refused to let me pick up the trash in your driveway and also your commanding voice made my knees weak.* Yeah, that wouldn't make me sound weird at all.

"Sure thing, sugar. I'll have it out shortly."

My black Mary Janes click against the tile floor as I walk over to the booth that borders Adrian's. It's still by the window, but there's a pillar that mars my perfect view. What I should do is sit with my back facing Adrian, pull out my book, and pretend he doesn't exist for the next few hours. But something about this man makes me want to do the opposite of what I should do just to see how he reacts.

So, I plop myself down in the booth facing him and drop my tote bag on the table, the loud thump garnering his attention. His cool blue eyes watch me under full black lashes as he types away on a grey laptop in front of him. Under the weight of his gaze, my plan to unnerve him seems rather foolish, but I've already committed.

"Beautiful day, isn't it?" I ask him as I pull out my worn copy of *The Great Gatsby*. I've read it many times and it never gets old. There's something magnetic about the tragic tale.

Adrian responds with a grunt. Poppy waltzes over to deliver tea to each of us from the serving tray on her shoulder, then an almond croissant to just me. I sip my delicious drink and watch him over the rim of my mug. I prefer to drink tea out of ornate tea cups when I'm at home, but here Poppy serves them in bowl-like mugs.

"This tea is amazing, you have good taste," I comment as he lifts his mug. My eyes zero in on the movement, watching his lips graze the rim. His eyes meet mine, each of us studying the other through the steam billowing from our tea. We take a sip at the same time and it feels too intimate with our eyes locked like this. I tear my gaze away and set my cup down a little too hard on the table. Hot liquid splashes out onto my thumb and I hiss in pain.

"Shoot," I mumble, clenching my jaw and scrambling for a napkin.

The sound of movement draws my eyes away from my throbbing hand up to the counter where Adrian now stands. Poppy passes him a rag and he crosses the small shop in quick strides. When he kneels down beside me my breath catches.

"Here, this should help." His hands are gentle as he dabs at the red skin with the cool cloth.

"I'm okay," I murmur, but he continues his ministration, his brow furrowed. "Really, I think I was just caught off guard. The tea wasn't that hot."

"You should keep the cloth on your hand," he says in a low voice. "But you're right, it doesn't look too bad." He drapes the rag over my hand, then pushes up to standing.

"Thank you."

He merely nods, then returns to his seat as if nothing happened. The return to normalcy makes me wonder if I dreamt him kneeling beside me. If I didn't dream it just now, I know I will tonight.

Chapter Four

Adrian Carter

I slide out of the worn leather booth I've been occupying for the last three hours, content with the work I accomplished. My main job is to assess our clients' needs and match them with the right team to protect them. Then, while our company is working for them, I get updates from the teams to be sure everything is going well. Our clients are typically wealthy and high profile like athletes and heiresses, so managing them at a high level is important.

It's easy to spend hours in my email inbox each day, no matter the day of the week. And even though working on a Saturday makes me seem like a workaholic, I prefer to keep my work outside of my home. The boundary line between the personal and professional areas of my life helps me feel in control. So, that's how I found myself in the quaint cinnamon-scented café, Peaches and Cream.

The same café that—based on her and the owner's rapport—Juliette must frequent. A fact I will note for the future. I slide my laptop into my gray leather messenger bag and sling it over my shoulder. I'm about to head to the door when the café clerk, Poppy, bustles out from the back carrying a to-go bag and a plastic cup with what looks to be iced tea inside of it.

"Here you go, sweet girl. One turkey pesto sandwich and one peachy keen iced tea."

My eyes flick up to the menu that tells me a peachy keen tea is a southern iced tea sweetened with peach simple syrup. I have to admit, that sounds delicious. My sister MJ got me into tea when she went on a health kick in college. Ever since she introduced it to me, I've been addicted. I purchased an oversized apothecary cabinet just for tea and it won't be long before I outgrow that if I keep buying new ones.

"Thanks, Poppy! See you next week," Juliette says and Poppy gives her a one-armed hug.

I walk to the door right as Juliette is looping her bags over her arm. Her honey-blonde hair is radiant today, bathed in the sunlight cascading through the windowpane. Like everything about Juliette, it looks incredibly soft. It took every ounce of my self-control earlier to not touch her skin while handling her burn. I shouldn't have gotten up at all, but pure instinct took over when I saw the flash of pain in her bright green eyes.

The same green eyes that are watching me with too much curiosity as I stand frozen by the door. I've been caught staring, which is unusual for me. I'm used to blending into the background and being careful enough to observe from a distance. My job required it. But Juliette seems to have this uncanny ability to make me stumble.

I push open the shop door as she approaches, a gold bell tinkling overhead. Juliette smiles and glides past me out into the brisk

January air, murmuring a quick *thanks*. Since it's almost noon, the sun takes away some of the bite that this morning had, but it's still cold enough to have me tucking my hands into my coat pocket and huddling into my coat. Winter in Georgia might not compare to the northern states, but it's cold enough to make you want to be anywhere but outside.

I start off toward my house. It's a short walk, and the parking situation in this community is dismal. Everyone seems to walk everywhere instead of drive. I don't mind the exercise, though.

"Mind if I walk with you?" Juliette's soft voice comes from my right side. She's fallen in step with me, sipping her iced tea like it's not forty degrees out. Her green eyes are vibrant today, emphasized by the emerald sweater she's wearing.

I make an affirmative noise in the back of my throat then turn my attention forward. The trees are mostly barren, their golden leaves littering the path ahead of us. A car rolls past at a snail's pace and I step behind Juliette then to the right, switching sides with her. Protective instincts, nothing more. I'd do this with any woman walking beside me.

Juliette side-eyes me, an impish grin tilting her pink lips, but she says nothing. I'm honestly surprised she's gone this long in silence. I've not had many interactions with her, but all of them have been filled with words.

An old man wearing a beret and matching suspenders hobbles toward us, his face scrunched up like he just ate a lemon whole, peel and all.

"Julie!" he barks and Juliette flinches. I scan the elderly man, not noting anything threatening in his demeanor beyond his attitude. "Are you coming to the community meeting next week?"

"Yes, Mr. Kipton," Juliette says with a polite smile. She doesn't seem to be afraid of him, so I wonder why she flinched at his initial greeting.

"Good. I'm counting on you to be the deciding vote on getting rid of those pesky ducks around the lake. They are always making a ruckus when I'm trying to sleep!"

"I'll be there," she says, not giving any opinions on the duck situation.

Mr. Kipton nods and passes us, grumbling incoherently.

"You don't like him," I observe aloud as we cross the street. The lake comes fully into view now, not obscured by any of the buildings. The peace this place emits is truly amazing. I can't help but breathe a little deeper each time I take it all in.

"Mr. Kipton? He's a bit of a grouch, but I don't mind him," Juliette responds with a shrug.

"You flinched when he said your name." It's a risk to let her know I was watching her so closely, but I can't help the desire to satisfy my curiosity.

She grimaces and the expression seems out of place on her.

"He called me *Julie*, not Juliette. I don't like that nickname." There's something about the way she says Julie that leads me to believe it has more to do with her simply not liking the name. It must have a connotation attached. But I can't be so forward as to ask her.

"I see."

"It probably seems childish of me to dislike a nickname so much," she sighs. "But that name was used by someone I don't like to think about." She fiddles with her straw, twisting it in between her fingertips. Then, she shakes her head as if she didn't mean to say that out loud. "Anyway, I'd much rather be called Jules. I've always thought that was a pretty name. But you can't *ask* people to give you a nickname. They have to decide to call you it all on their own, or else it's a nickname you gave yourself."

I bite back a smile at her rambling story. Usually I find people who talk this much to be overbearing, but Juliette is different. She makes oversharing ... endearing.

"I can't comment on nicknames, since I don't have any, but I understand what you mean."

"You've never had a nickname?" she asks in a tone that says she's not surprised at all. I give her a flat look that she responds to with a wide grin.

"No."

"Don't demote me back to one-syllable answers." Her tone is that of an exaggerated plea. "I won't tease you. I'll be good."

"Somehow, I don't believe you," I reply drily. She laughs and it's like the first day of spring after a harsh winter, bright and hopeful and sweet.

Our cottages come into view, looking like a matching set. The only difference being that mine is gray while hers is a pale blue. I pause with her at the end of her driveway.

"Thank you for a pleasant walk," Juliette says with the formality of a royal.

I dip my chin in a nod. She smiles in that secretive way again, the kind that makes me feel like she knows something I don't, before turning and walking to her door. My eyes trail over her, the delicate curve of her hip, her black tights stretched over her legs. Each time she takes a step the hem of her plaid skirt lifts and falls in the most tempting way. She pauses at her front door and looks over her shoulder with a smirk. Heat burns the tips of my ears and I swiftly turn on my heel to walk to my own driveway.

I keep my head down as I stride for my front door, going inside my cottage without so much as a glance in her direction. Being around Juliette is like keeping a candy jar on your desk: you know you shouldn't reach for more, but it's *right there*, taunting you. Every interaction with her ends up with me doing something out of character. I need to stay away, but it's difficult when she lives barely ten feet away from me.

I shed my coat and throw it onto the couch, then immediately pick it up again and walk it to my closet. My muscles are twitching with pent-up energy. I scan my house, looking for anything I can clean or organize and come up with nothing. It's not difficult to keep a tidy home when it's just me.

I yank open one of my drawers and pull out a pair of joggers and a Georgia Thrashers Football sweatshirt. I'll go for a run around the lake. Surely the feeling of the cold air numbing my face and burning in my lungs will get rid of whatever *this* is.

After changing, I slip out of my back door and cast a quick glance to the right to see if Juliette is out with Murphy. Deeming the area neighbor-free, I jog down my wooden porch steps and out to the path that winds around the lake.

I run harder than usual, chasing the burn. After one lap of practically sprinting, my lungs are aching from inhaling the frigid air, but my mind is no better off than it was when I set out. I slow to a gentle jog, letting my eyes bounce around the lake.

A family of ducks paddles across the water, making me think of Juliette. I pass a couple sharing a croissant, my mind drawn once more to Juliette. Growling, I pick up my pace again. No matter how much I push my body though, Juliette's laugh won't leave my brain. In fact, I think she's made me delusional because I swear I hear it over the whipping wind.

It's only when I see her golden hair in the distance that I realize I'm not delusional, just incapable of escaping her. It seems I'd have to move to be rid of her. She waves at me from her place on the metal bench by the lake. A large blanket is draped over her legs, thankfully hiding them from view. Murphy trots around, occasionally stopping to paw at the wet sand close to the lake.

"Are you stalking me, Adrian?" she teases as I slow to a stop next to the bench.

My breathing is still ragged from my sprint, making me have to lift my hands up to my head. Cool air nips at the skin above my waistband. I don't miss the way her eyes rake over me, pausing at that exposed skin for a second too long before bouncing back up to my face. My blood heats and I drop my arms, shoving my hands in the pocket of my hoodie instead.

"I was out here before you, so I should be asking you that."

"So you looked for me on your run, then." Her eyes sparkle.

"I merely noted my surroundings."

She hums and turns her attention back to Murphy, who is rolling around in the sand and leaves. Instead of getting upset though, she lets out a playful sigh.

"Well, I'm going to go," I say, hating how awkward I sound. I'm not an awkward man. A little adverse to socializing, but not awkward.

"Have a nice run!" Juliette chirps and snuggles up under her blanket.

I take off again, wishing that I could outrun the image of Juliette warm and soft under a blanket. The kind of image that makes me want to join her there on the bench instead of what I need to do which is stay far, far away.

CHAPTER FIVE

Juliette Monroe

"Gerty, you have *got* to quit parking your scooter in the main square. It's digging tracks in the grass," Henry Hayes, Peach Hollow's community representative–an overpowered and useless position–says from his place at the front of the church. All community meetings are held in the local church on Thursday evenings.

"All the grass is dead anyway," Gerty, aka Gertrude Pines, grouses. Gerty has recently purchased a yellow motorized scooter which she drives around the community and parks wherever she pleases. She also wears a matching yellow helmet everywhere, including now. I'm afraid of what her silver hair looks like beneath it. I think she might sleep in it.

"There is a bike rack, not ten feet from where you park."

"I drive a scooter, not a bike," Gerty snaps.

"Forgive me," Henry says drily, then bangs his gavel. "All those in favor of Gerty parking in the bike rack say aye."

Affirmatives echo through the old wooden church. Henry opens his mouth to move on to the next subject when the doors at the back of the room swing open. No one is ever late to a community meeting. It's impossible to sneak in, because the large oak doors are heavy and scrape the floor when you push on them.

All of the heads in the room–including mine–swivel toward the door. You could hear a pin drop in this silence, well maybe only *I* could hear it drop since most of the people here are hard of hearing, but still.

A familiar tall and muscular form fills the doorway, making my heart skip. Adrian lets the thick door slam shut behind him, the noise reverberating throughout the sanctuary. I let out a little sigh as I take him in. I can't help it. The man is torturously attractive. He's wearing a *suit* for crying out loud. A dark navy suit tailored to perfection, with a crisp pinstripe shirt underneath. And–*goodness gracious*–the top two buttons of the shirt are undone.

"We do not tolerate tardiness, boy," Henry says, trying to stand tall at the front of the room. It's hard to look intimidating compared to Adrian though.

"The flyer said 6:15." Adrian's low voice echoing through the silent room has my pulse fluttering.

"We changed the meeting to six, it was on the community Facebook page," Henry says, haughtiness coating his scratchy voice.

"I don't have Facebook."

A chorus of gasps filter through the crowd and I can't help but giggle. Adrian's blue eyes snap to me and I bite my lip to stifle my laughter. I think I see amusement flicker over his expression, but I can't be so sure this far away. I wave him over and I feel the weight of everyone's stares as I do. He reluctantly walks toward my pew. I scoot away from the end of the bench. Something about him makes me think he's the type of man who likes to be near an exit.

He sits next to me, practically hugging the end of the pew. *Okay*, so we're not as close as I hoped after our few encounters.

Henry clears his throat. "Well, since we have pressing matters to attend to–"

"And I have to get home to feed my cat!" Burt shouts from the back row.

"And Burt has to get home to feed Snuffles, we'll proceed in spite of our interruption."

Henry starts to talk about the duck situation that Mr. Kipton is so passionate about. I've heard about the ducks a thousand times since living here, so I tune him out. The only reason I come to these events is because it gives me a form of entertainment besides reading, plus the chance to be around people.

Adrian shifts beside me, his arm splayed awkwardly on the wooden end of the pew. It looks as if it was meant to be an armrest, but it's got this odd curve that doesn't make for a nice resting place.

"You can relax, I don't bite," I whisper, leaning toward him. There's ample space between us that he seems determined to keep.

He looks down at me, something glittering in his blue eyes. I can imagine him in another life leaning down and whispering *but I do*. The thought sends a tingle down my spine–but doesn't come to fruition.

"They should vote for new pews," he mutters and shifts once more. This time, he lets the arm closest to me rest on the back of the pew, then sets his left ankle on his right knee. He looks like he belongs on the cover of a magazine, or in a board room commanding people. I know I'd listen to him.

"We only vote on pointless matters," I whisper back and the corner of his mouth quirks up.

On the outside, I'm smiling softly, but on the inside, I'm doing an awful winner's dance. There are lots of hip shaking and flailing arms, maybe even a sprinkler move or two. Because seeing Adrian even come *close* to smiling at something I said feels worthy of celebration.

The sound of Henry's gavel rapping the podium drags my attention back to the subject at hand.

"All in favor of capturing the ducks and relocating them say aye."

"Aye!" Mr. Kipton shouts, but no one else does. Not even Adrian, a fact that makes my smile grow. He might be a grump, but at least he doesn't hate our cute fowl residents.

"Once again, the duck issue will be tabled due to lack of support."

Mr. Kipton starts on his usual rant about the noisy useless birds. I lean against the back of the pew with a sigh, only to have it transform to a sharp intake of breath when Adrian's hand brushes my back through my burgundy turtleneck. He quickly moves his arm to rest on his leg, but the heat from his touch stays with me.

Henry bangs his gavel again. "That's enough, Kip. You can try to rally votes for the next meeting. Everyone is dismissed. Don't forget to grab a cookie from Peaches and Cream on your way out!"

Everyone starts to shuffle to the door, and I stand, stretching my arms above my head. Five minutes in these seats is five minutes too long. I'd rather stand for an hour than sit in these for any length of time. Not to mention I was hunched over my desk all day today working on new designs and packing orders.

"That was a fairly short meeting," Adrian comments, surprising me with small talk. I half-expected to blink and him to disappear before my eyes as soon as the meeting was over.

"Count yourself lucky," I say as I grab my caramel-colored coat and shrug it on. "The previous meeting lasted two hours."

Adrian steps out into the aisle and waits for me to walk with him. It's hard to keep my smile restrained so I don't grin like a maniac at his simple gesture. I want to be friends, not scare him away.

"What on earth could constitute a two-hour meeting?"

We bypass the horde of people crowding around the cookie table. I'd rather pay for a cookie than stand in that line. Adrian seems to share my sentiment. He holds open the large door, and a brisk wind nips at my cheekbones when we exit the building. It's nighttime, but I didn't drive here because I like to leave the spots to the residents who can't walk home.

Town meetings during the winter months always end up with a walk through the dark, holding my phone flashlight and using each streetlamp as a checkpoint. The pepper spray tucked in my right coat pocket is usually already brandished before my foot even leaves the last church step. I'd like to say I wasn't always this cautious, but that would be a lie. From the first moments I can recall I've always kept my footsteps light and been aware of my surroundings.

Growing up in a home full of chaos and uncertainty will do that to you. Suddenly you know your mother's emotions by the way she grips her coffee cup, and your father's mood by the sound of his footsteps on the stairs. When no one communicates effectively, you pick up other methods of discernment. And I used that knowledge to make myself as small of a target as possible.

After fleeing my childhood home, my roots traveled with me, planting themselves in this new soil. I know it's not abnormal to carry pepper spray at night, but when you combine it with the rest of my *quirks*, I probably seem like a paranoid freak. I feel ridiculous carrying around pepper spray in *Peach Hollow* of all places. It's not even that I feel as though I'm in true danger–my parents probably don't care enough about me to try to find me–but I can't help but worry that one day that will change.

Adrian's discerning blue eyes watch me from the bottom of the church steps. I realize I've been standing here for a moment too long … and that I haven't answered his question.

"The main cause for debate was whether we should allow a food truck to park near the lake once a month," I finally answer him and hop down the remainder of the steps.

We walk side by side toward our homes and I feel safer than I ever have. I still turn on my phone flashlight, thankful when Adrian doesn't ask me why I need one when there are street lamps. It's odd that this taciturn man could feel safe to me when many of the men I've encountered tend to feel the opposite. Maybe it's just a result of not interacting with men close to my age in years, though.

"What was the decision?"

We turn a corner and our arms brush through our coats. The meager touch makes my stomach flip. Yep, I think I need to get out more. Maybe I'll give in and try that awful dating app Caroline is always telling me about. I shouldn't feel this way over a simple occurrence. Poor Adrian is merely walking home next to me and I'm deluding myself into thinking there's chemistry between us. I don't even know what romantic tension *feels* like, so it's unlikely that I'm capable of labeling our interactions as anything more than neighborly.

"It was split for a while, hence the length of the meeting. But Poppy ended up convincing someone on the negative side to become a supporter. Now a barbeque truck comes once a month. It's not the best food, but it keeps people from having to go to the city, so they line up around the block."

"The city?" There's humor lacing Adrian's tone. "Do you mean Atlanta?"

"Yes." I let out a soft laugh, a white puff of air escaping my lips. "That's what everyone calls it here. If you stick around, you'll start saying it too I imagine."

If you stick around, really Juliette? He just moved here, *of course* he's sticking around. My nerves from being out at night are melding with the ones I get while trying to interact with Adrian like anything resembling a normal human. It's a miracle that I haven't rambled incessantly yet.

My porch light welcomes me as we close in on our row of cottages. This is the most peaceful post-meeting walk home I've had in a while. Usually, my pepper spray creates an indent in my hand from gripping it too hard and I feel queasy for half an hour; more if I don't have a cup of calming tea.

"Thanks again for the company." I look up at Adrian once we reach the end of my driveway and give him a gentle smile. He dips his head in acknowledgment and I can't help but feel like he's seeing right through my attempt at casual conversation. I wonder what he sees when he looks at me.

I turn on my heel and walk to my door, feeling his eyes on me the entire time. Once it's unlocked and I'm about to slip inside, his silken voice finds my ear.

"Goodnight, Juliette."

My stomach swoops at the sound of my name on his lips.

"Goodnight, Adrian," I say over my shoulder.

Once inside, I make chamomile tea and pet Murphy while trying to forget my neighbor's piercing gaze and the quirk of his lips. But my efforts are futile because I spend the night dreaming of those very lips brushing mine.

CHAPTER SIX

Adrian Carter

"For the last time, I'm busy," I growl at my brother Grayson and push past him into my office. He's just invited me to one of our employee's birthday parties. I'm pretty sure it involves karaoke. Needless to say, I won't be attending.

"Busy doing what? Staring at your ceiling?" Grayson falls onto the leather couch to the right of my desk and splays himself out. He has no concern for the amount of space he takes up with his body or his personality.

"Working."

"All of our clients are safe and happy," Grayson states, sliding a rubber band ball out of his pocket and tossing it toward the ceiling. On top of the many differences between Grayson and me–our style, hobbies, and overall demeanor–he's also incapable of being *still*.

"Yes, and I'd like to keep it that way. Which is why I need to *manage our company*."

While I manage the placement of our teams and their day-to-day concerns, Grayson takes care of making sure the clients are truly *happy*. He also finds us new clients by networking at events I'd never willingly attend and schmoozing people in general. His easygoing nature and ability to hold a conversation with anyone makes him perfect for that side of the job.

"The point of starting this business was to put down roots and have lives outside of work."

"I know." And if I didn't know, I'd come to realize it rather quickly with how many times Grayson mentions it in a week.

I have put down roots. My house in Peach Hollow attests to that. But Grayson thinks that my life should look like his when I'm perfectly content with working and then leaving to sleep in my peaceful home.

"Okay, you don't have to come to Kylie's party with me, but you have to leave work before six today or else I'm staying here with you."

I glower at him, but he looks unphased. That's the unfortunate part of growing up with my co-founder: he's not intimidated by me in the slightest. Even if I threatened bodily harm, he'd hold that easygoing grin while dodging my every punch.

"Fine. I'll leave before six. Doesn't it bother you that your most effective threat is your own presence?"

He throws the ball in the air and catches it.

"Nope. I know the real problem is not my personality, but that you're unsociable."

I clench my jaw and turn my attention to my computer monitor. Maybe if I ignore him, he'll leave. It hasn't worked in the past, but one can hope.

"Oh, I'm making an amendment to our agreement." I cut my eyes to him. His grin makes my scowl deepen. "You need to do something *outside* of your house after work. Shake on it or else I camp out here on this couch for the rest of the evening."

"I do this and you leave me alone about social events for at least a week," I counter, knowing I won't get him to commit to anything more than a week.

"Deal!" He propels himself up off the couch and sticks a hand across my desk. I shake it, ignoring the smug grin on his face.

It won't be hard to fulfill my commitment. I'll go for a walk around the lake then go back home and try not to pull my laptop out until it's time to fall asleep. Grayson saunters out of my office and I pinch the bridge of my nose. This is going to be a long night.

It's an unseasonably warm day for the end of January, which means that my evening stroll is far more crowded than I would like. I've been stopped three times now by people I recognize from the town meeting last night.

I shouldn't have gone to the meeting, but my curiosity got the better of me. I knew I'd see Juliette there. My steps falter when I recall her green eyes sparkling as she whispered next to me during the meeting. I wanted to do more than *talk* when I looked down at her, that's for sure. But getting close to Juliette would be a mistake. Trusting anyone but family has always been a mistake for me.

Not to mention the fact that Juliette is clearly hiding something. Her admission about her nickname, the way she's always on guard, and that haunted look in her eyes when we left the meeting all combine to make up someone with a whole slew of secrets that I have no business uncovering. Even if my protective instincts multiplied by ten looking at her last night, it would be foolish of me to try to get involved.

I pick up my speed, dodging the ambling neighbors enjoying the sunset. My main objective is to complete this run to be able to tell Grayson I fulfilled my end of the bargain. There's no need to stop to enjoy the sunset; the sunrise over the lake is better anyway.

I jog the final stretch of my usual trail, but I halt when I see Juliette outside. She's lying on her stomach on a picnic blanket by the lake. Her attention is focused on the book in her hands as she kicks her bare feet absentmindedly. Murphy is sprawled out beside her, sleeping. I swallow as I approach her, my throat feeling tight.

The warm hues of the setting sun make her look ethereal in her cream sweater and cuffed jeans. Her blonde hair resembles spun gold and it's a breathtaking view. I'm once again struck by how soft and sweet she looks. Her head turns and I've been caught staring. The sunny grin she gives me makes my heart give an odd thump in my chest.

"This is a rare sight," she calls out, not moving from where she's splayed out on the blanket. It feels awkward staring down at her like this, so I take a few steps forward and sit down in the grass beside her blanket.

Her grin widens and I feel as though I've fallen into some sort of trap.

"What do you mean?" I ask as she shuts her book. *The Great Gatsby,* the same book she was reading in the café. The spine is fraying and the copy looks like it's been bent open and folded over several times. I haven't read it in years, but I have a sudden urge to pick it up again and see what the woman beside me finds so enthralling about it.

"You're usually not home until much later, sometimes I'm in bed when I hear your car pull in."

An image of Juliette curled up in those satin pajamas of hers flits through my mind and I sink my hand into the grass and dead leaves beneath me in an effort to combat the image and the feeling it evokes.

"I decided to leave work early today, enjoy the weather."

She hums and props her chin in her hand, her green eyes scanning me. I get the feeling that she can see through my lie, but she says nothing to confirm my suspicions.

"What do you do for work?"

"I run a private security company." No point in lying to her about what she could easily find out if she googled my name.

"That's close to what I guessed," she says, smiling as though she won a secret game with herself.

"What did you guess?" I pick at the blades of brown grass, trying to look less curious than I actually am.

"I thought you might be in the CIA." My hand stills. There is no way she just *guessed* that. "Oh, or the FBI. Either one."

"Why would you think that?" I rely on the very training she assumed I've had to keep my voice level.

She pushes up onto her knees and shrugs.

"You've got this whole *I keep secrets for a living* vibe." She gestures my way as if it's obvious. Murphy stirs, lifting his head and plopping it onto her legs. She pats him with an unguarded affection that warms my chest.

There's a lot of mystery surrounding Juliette, but even so, moments like this soften me toward her. I wonder what it would be like to be on the receiving end of her affectionate ways ... *No.* I can't go there. No matter how tempting it is staring at her windswept hair and soft smile.

"What do you do?" I ask instead of responding to her observation of my *vibe*.

"I run my own stationery company," she says with a bright grin that shows how much she loves her job. "I design wedding invitations and stationery sets and sell them online."

The sun has dipped below the trees now, taking the golden rays with it. Juliette pushes the rest of the way up to standing and tugs her quilt out from under a disgruntled Murphy. He huffs and trots off toward her back deck. I stand up as well but don't make any move to leave.

"Stationery sets? Do people even write letters anymore?" I ask as she shakes out the blanket, leaves and grass catching in the breeze.

"You'd be surprised how many people buy them. Though I will admit it's a bit of a lost art." A wistful smile tips up her lips and she hugs the quilt to her chest, staring off toward the lake. "There's just something about a handwritten letter. It shows this level of care and thought that can't be captured in an email or text."

"I don't know if anyone has ever written me a letter," I say and immediately regret the admission. It sounds like I'm asking *her* to write me one. This is what I get for trying to make conversation. I'm going to blame Grayson for this, even if he's not here.

"I haven't received many myself." She folds her blanket up, still staring out at the lake. "That's partly why I started the company, to bring back something lost. But I also love calligraphy, which lends to designing invitations. Those are my most purchased products."

"If any of my brothers get married, I'll point them to you," I say and her whole expression brightens.

"That's sweet of you, thank you, Adrian."

The sound of my name on her smiling lips is addictive. It's a shot of whiskey with a honey chaser. A sweet burn that makes warmth unfurl in my chest, my heart basking in the sunshine of her presence. It makes me want to do anything to get her to smile like that again, to hear her inject pure kindness into my name in a way I don't think anyone else has. My jaw clenches. I shouldn't be having these thoughts.

"It's nothing." My voice comes out more gravelly than I intended. Her eyes search me once more, those intense emerald irises likely seeing more than I want them to. I clear my throat and take a step in the direction of my cottage. "Have a nice evening."

"You too."

I feel her watching me as I walk back to my house. My past career has made me well acquainted with the feeling of being watched, but something about this is different. For once I don't feel confident in my measured steps and pushed back shoulders. I find myself second-guessing the length of my stride and wondering if the way I'm swinging my arms seems off to her.

Once I'm behind closed doors I shrug my shoulders up and down a few times, trying to rid myself of the unnerving feeling of being *seen*. I laugh at myself, raking a hand through my hair. She's not an agent, just a mildly observant neighbor. I'm being paranoid for nothing.

Telling myself that doesn't stop me from replaying our conversation like an interrogation tape in my mind, trying to determine how much I gave away. Each time I do though, I end up getting sidetracked by the memory of her smile.

CHAPTER SEVEN

Juliette Monroe

About once a month, I convince myself I'm a better woman than I actually am. This usually occurs after watching too many self-help YouTube videos, the ones that tell me how to be *that girl*. These videos convince me that I'm the type of girl who is going to wake up before sunrise, work out, drink green juice with a smile on my face, and write in my planner everything I want to do that day ... then *do* all of those things.

So, I've decided to be that girl today, and in the dim morning light, I am already regretting my decision. Working out right now sounds about as appealing as walking over hot coals, and the fact that I drug myself out of bed at all instead of hitting snooze is a miracle. My shoulder hits my closet door, eliciting a grumble as I balance on one foot, sliding a fuzzy sock on the other.

Fuzzy socks and oversized sweaters are not workout clothes, because there will be no working out today. But I will at least stay up and watch the sunrise. I actually think the sunrise is prettier than the sunset, but I hate waking up early. Murphy doesn't even lift his head as I shuffle by him on my way to the kitchen. He doesn't do mornings either.

I yawn as I fill up my electric kettle. Tea will make this morning better. It makes everything better. While the water heats, I look for a good strong tea. Something with caffeine to help me wake up. I settle on my favorite English breakfast tea and while it steeps I gather supplies to watch the sunrise on my deck.

I nudge the sliding glass door with my elbow and carry out the mountain of blankets and books weighing down my arms. My brain feels as foggy as a bathroom mirror after a long shower, so I doubt any of the books I brought out will be read, but they bring me comfort by having them near. Icy air bites at my face with a kind of ferocity that I'm too sleepy to deal with.

"Why am I like this?" I mutter under my breath as I go back inside to retrieve my tea. Floral teacup in hand, I return outside to brave the elements and try to feel like I am accomplishing what my past self set out to do.

The wicker couch I bought at a yard sale from Gerty is nice and cozy now that I've outfitted it with the majority of my throw pillows and the comforter from my bed. I burrow down into the blankets, trying to expose as little of my body to the winter air as possible. I'm so glad I ran away to the South and not someplace like *Michigan*. I'd never leave my house with all that snow.

I lift my eyes to where the sun is beginning to rise above the treeline. Pastel pinks and soft blues tint the sky, making everything resemble a watercolor painting. The tea warms my palms and when I gingerly take a sip I start to think this early morning stuff might not be too bad. Peach Hollow has always been a place of peace for me, but in quiet moments like this, the feeling is magnified.

The sound of leaves crunching draws my eyes away from the sky. My breath catches in my throat when I see Adrian running toward his own back deck. His head is down, so he doesn't see me snuggled up here. As much as I've loved talking to him the past few days, I am perfectly okay with him not noticing my existence right now.

My hair is in a bun on top of my head that resembles the stuffed hedgehog toy I got Murphy for Christmas–the one he ripped in half so that all the fuzz spills out. And even though I have on a giant sweater and three blankets, I'm not wearing a real bra, just a thin bralette. Somehow, knowing that is embarrassing enough to have me sliding further into my cozy cocoon, keeping just my eyes out. I set my tea on the ground beside me so I don't spill it.

Adrian walks up his back steps, pausing on his deck and stretching his arms above his head. I watch, enraptured, as he does a few more stretches. In the back of my mind, I know it's wrong to watch him without him knowing, but I can't bring myself to speak up. Watching his muscles bunch beneath his tight running shirt has me incapable of speech.

His hand reaches for the hem of his shirt and my eyes get wide. He lifts it up and wipes at his forehead and ... *Oh. My. Abs.* My mouth drops open and my brain shortcircuits. It's only a partial view, he's not even fully facing me, but I'm done for. Why does he have to look like that? He belongs in a museum, on a pedestal with a spotlight and a warning sign that says staring too long will turn you into a puddle.

Suddenly, he turns my way. I let out an embarrassing squeak and duck under my comforter. I squeeze my eyes shut and hold my breath. *Don't see me. Don't see me. Don't–*

"Juliette." The warm humor lacing his tone makes my stomach do a little backflip.

Ever so slowly, I lift my very warm face out from under the covers. Adrian is leaning against his deck railing watching me with the faintest smirk on his lips.

"Good morning," I say, infusing a chipperness I don't feel into my words.

My hands shake as I lift my tea cup off the ground. I take a sip to give myself something to do besides blurt out *'You have abs!'* like a starstruck teenager.

"Did you enjoy the show?"

I inhale a sip of my tea and cough it out with burning eyes. "*What?*"

Did I just blackout and wake up in an alternate reality or did Adrian just *flirt* with me? I blink the water out of my eyes and scan him again, making sure it's him and not his brother Grayson. No, this is Adrian. His hair is the same length, he's wearing his usual running clothes, and even the way he stands is so undeniably *him*. So that must mean he really did just flirt with me.

He shakes his head, that gorgeous little smirk still toying with his lips in a way that makes me wish he would hop that railing and kiss me breathless.

"Why didn't you say anything when I walked up?" he asks and I bite my lip.

"I didn't want to bother you."

He raises an eyebrow like he doesn't believe me but doesn't comment on it.

"What tea are you drinking?" he asks.

I want to back up and ask him if he was flirting with me, but I'm too embarrassed to bring it up. I'm not used to male attention, so I don't know how to handle it whenever I think too much about it. And I tend to overthink ... *a lot*. So, I'm going to treat this interaction as friendly, or else I might hide under my blankets again.

"What if I'm drinking coffee?"

He gives me a flat look and I smile at him, laughing a little. I think I see a ghost of a smile come across his lips, but I can't be sure.

"English breakfast tea sweetened with coconut sugar and a splash of cream." I pause, then decide to take his question as an opening for a conversation. "What tea are you going to have this morning?"

"I was thinking of making a London fog, but now you have me reconsidering."

"Do you have a favorite English breakfast tea?"

He tilts his head to the side like he's thinking about it and then shrugs. "I can't say that I do."

I push myself up out of my blanket nest. My sweater falls off my shoulder and I push it back up, blushing at the thought of Adrian seeing the strap of my bralette.

"I'm about to introduce you to your favorite," I say with a smile. "I'll be right back!"

Warm air hits me as I walk inside, ensuring that after this conversation I'm going to curl up on my couch with Murphy and work from there the rest of the day. It's too cozy not to. It'll be the perfect atmosphere to design a custom invitation for a bride getting married this fall.

I grab the tin of English breakfast tea still out on my countertop and pull out two tea bags. I slide them into a Ziploc and head back outside where Adrian waits on his deck. Dew soaks through my socks as I pad down the stairs and across the short walk to him.

"Here, you should try this one, it's from one of my favorite shops." I lift the bag up to him and he reaches over the railing to take it from me. His fingertips brush mine, warm tingles cascading down my arm at the tiny touch.

"Thank you."

The look in his eyes is unreadable, and I'm worried maybe he doesn't want the tea. Maybe he wasn't flirting–or teasing as a friend–earlier. He might still be trying to keep his distance from me and now I look ridiculous for taking small talk as a cue for more.

"You don't have to take it if you don't want it," I say, hoping my voice sounds sincere enough to cover up any hurt feelings I'd have if he gave it back. Which I wouldn't, of course, because it's just a small rejection from my hot neighbor. That's all.

"No, it's not—I don't want to take and not give you something in return." He disappears into his cottage, and I wish I could see inside, but I can't from where I'm standing.

He comes back out with a bag of his own, handing it to me.

"It's a lavender Earl Grey," he says and I nod, staring at it in my hands.

The very *last* thing I should do is turn this into something it's not. I should take it for what it is, a kind neighborly gesture, and move on. But when I meet Adrian's blue eyes again my heart skips and my intentions are lost in the whirlpool of his irises.

"Thank you," I whisper and he dips his chin. "I hope you have a nice day at work." My words seem pointless, but when the corner of his mouth hitches up in a small grin I feel like maybe my social skills aren't totally lacking.

"You too." He pauses. "You should probably get inside before you freeze."

"Right." I take a step back. "I'll go then." Amusement flickers across his expression and I quickly turn around then book it back to my deck before I can say or do anything else I'll regret.

I glance over at his house once more when I slide open my door–only to find him still leaning on his railing, watching me. My hand lifts in an awkward little wave before I practically dive into my cottage.

"I have no business being around people," I tell Murphy and collapse onto my couch. Murphy harrumphs in what I assume is agreement and lays his head on my feet.

My phone vibrates in my pocket so I pull it out to see who could be messaging me at such an awful hour of the morning.

And there, blinking on my screen, is a reminder of the other awful decision my past self made last night. The little heart logo makes my stomach twist, as do the words beside it.

You've got a match! Start a conversation with Kyle.

Yep. I caved and signed up for that dating app Caroline met Josh on. My loneliness got the best of me and until ten minutes ago I thought I had no chance with my sexy, scowling neighbor. Now I have no idea what to do.

Just because Adrian *maybe* flirted with me a little, doesn't mean he's actually interested. I can't get hung up on him. It's highly unlikely a man worthy of being in a museum would want me anyway.

So, with a heavy sigh, I message Kyle. What's the worst that could happen?

CHAPTER EIGHT

Adrian Carter

"Thank you," I say to Poppy when she brings my white chocolate chai and blueberry muffin to my booth.

"You're welcome, sugar."

The bell chimes above the door and my gaze snaps over to catch Juliette pushing her way in. She rakes her hands through her windswept hair with a huff.

"The wind is brutal today," Juliette says as she unravels the deep brown scarf around her neck and then shoves it into the beige tote bag hanging from her arm.

"I know!" Poppy exclaims as she walks back behind the counter. "I was afraid of being blown away on my way here this morning."

Juliette's green eyes scan the shop, landing on me. She gives me a small smile and I shift in my seat.

"Good morning, Adrian." Her voice holds a warmth I wish it didn't.

I shouldn't have let that line slip yesterday morning. It was too tempting–*she* was too tempting–the moment I caught her staring at me. My opinions on relationships haven't changed, so even a friendship with Juliette is foolish. And yet this morning I came here. The place I knew she'd be.

I give her a nod in reply to her greeting and try not to be obvious in my perusal. She's always so beautiful. Every version I've seen of her is soft and lovely in a way that makes me want to pull her close. I hate how effortlessly she's slipped into my mind. My resolve should be much stronger than this.

"Can I get a winter spice tea and an almond croissant please, Poppy?" Juliette asks when she steps up to the counter. She reaches down to adjust one of her knee-high socks and I tear my eyes away, clenching my jaw.

"You got it, honey. It'll be right out."

"Thank you!"

I keep my eyes on my laptop until blonde curls and a tan sweater come into view. Juliette is sitting across from me, her green eyes sparkling.

"This is my favorite booth, you know," she says. "It has the perfect view of the square with the lake in the background. I've sat here most Saturdays for years."

That explains why the last time I sat here she gave me that cute frustrated look.

"I can move."

She waves a hand at me. "You were here first. I figured you might like some company though."

"What made you think that?" My words come out more teasing than gruff and she grins at me.

"Your easygoing grin, of course," she says and I can't help but chuckle.

"I'm working. I won't be good company for you."

"I'll be reading. So I think we'll make perfect company for each other," she says as Poppy walks up to deliver her tea and pastry. She thanks her then takes a sip of her tea.

"Don't expect any riveting conversation," I warn her, and she raises a brow. I stifle a grin at her reaction. "Alright, I'll work and you'll read."

She smiles and pulls out that same worn copy of *The Great Gatsby*. There's a floral bookmark placed toward the end of it. I'm itching to find out why she's read that book so many times, but I hold in my question. When she opens it I spot notes in the margins and various lines highlighted. My curiosity is overwhelming when it comes to Juliette, but I can't give in any more than I already have.

We settle into a surprisingly comfortable silence. I would have expected Juliette to attempt to start a conversation with me, but her focus has been entirely on her book. I, on the other hand, haven't gotten past the email I was writing when she walked in. My eyes keep flicking up at every clink of her teacup or flip of a page. It's hard not to stare at those pink lips and honey-blonde hair.

I force myself to look out the window, only to freeze when I notice not one, not two, but *all three* of my brothers crossing the road. Grayson spots me through the café window and a wide grin splits his face. This is terrible.

"Why?" I groan out loud when they burst into the shop.

Juliette lifts her head, a crease between her brows.

"We're here to kidnap you!" Grayson announces with his usual dramatic flair.

Juliette turns her head to see my brothers, a grin lighting up her face.

"You don't usually tell the victim that you're kidnapping them," I say and Levi—my oldest brother—snorts.

"You're making it sound like you have a lot of experience in kidnapping," Levi says and I sigh.

"I'm not going to go with you, I'm busy."

"Clearly," Maverick—the second oldest—remarks with a smirk, tipping his head toward Juliette. "Who's this?"

I watch Juliette's reaction play out on her side profile. Her cheekbones tint pink and she ducks her head. It only serves to make her prettier than before.

"Oh, hey! It's the cute blonde neighbor I told y'all about," Grayson says and I stifle a groan.

"I'm Juliette," she introduces herself in her lilting voice and stands. I stand as well, feeling the need to be ready for escape or to hit one of my brothers. Either way, standing makes me prepared.

"Nice to formally meet you, Juliette," Grayson drawls, leaning against the neighboring booth with a grin. "I'm Grayson, and these are mine and Adrian's other brothers, Levi and Maverick."

Juliette's mouth drops, her green eyes widening.

"*All* of you are brothers?"

"Yep," Grayson answers. "We also have a sister, but she's off living in married bliss."

"Grayson made it out like you'd taken to living in a cave and avoiding all human interaction," Levi says to me. "But if you're on a date, we can leave you alone."

"I'm *not* on a date." My tone is harsh, but they'll pester me if I don't nip this in the bud. Juliette's face falls for a second before she stretches her lips into a tight smile. My heart squeezes painfully in my chest at the thought of hurting her feelings.

"I crashed his work day is all," Juliette explains, tucking a strand of hair behind her ear. "But I have to go anyway. It was nice meeting you. Have fun with um ... whatever it is you're doing."

She grabs her stuff and weaves around my brothers, hurrying out the door.

"Great job, Adrian. You probably made the girl cry," Levi says, shooting me a reprimanding look.

I growl and start to pack up my things.

"Everything was fine until you showed up."

"You barely do anything other than work; we had to track you down," Maverick speaks up. I shrug on my coat and snatch up my messenger bag.

"I come to family dinners, I go to all of Maddie's dance competitions, and I text in that insipid group chat. What more do you want from me?"

"It's not about what we want from you. It's what we want *for* you," Maverick explains as we all walk out of the shop.

I don't look back or say anything to Poppy, certain that she's going to take everything to the town rumor mill. My next evening run around the lake will include more people stopping me than usual. Another reason to be mad at my brothers.

"We want you to be happy," Grayson says, throwing his arm around me. I push him off, but he just puts it back.

"I am happy, especially when my brothers don't invade my neighborhood and ruin my Saturday plans."

"Your Saturday plans of working in a coffee shop and then going home to do nothing? Forgive me," Grayson retorts sarcastically. If

I didn't think it would induce a heart attack in one of the residents strolling down the sidewalk, I'd take Grayson to the ground right now.

"Work-life balance is important, Adrian," Levi chimes in, using the older brother tone that grates my nerves.

"That's rich coming from the detective who is rarely ever home," I shoot back as I stalk toward my house.

"All of you have terrible social lives," Grayson says with a shake of his head. "But Adrian is walking around with a face identically as gorgeous as mine and not even going on a date or two. It's a crime against womankind."

"Humble," I say and Grayson squeezes my shoulder with a mischievous grin.

"Just come out with us. We're going to throw axes. You can pretend the target is Levi's face if you'd like."

"This whole thing was your idea. He should be angrier with you than me."

"I'm his twin, he can't stay angry at me."

"I wouldn't be so sure," I grumble and come to a stop in my driveway. "Fine. I'll go, but only if you promise not to come here unannounced ever again."

"What if it's for a surprise party?" Grayson asks and I glower at him. "Okay, okay, chill. I won't come without at least texting you first."

I nod. "Good. Now let's go print a photo of Levi for the target."

The next morning I walk across my yard to Juliette's front door. All night, I couldn't get her crestfallen look out of my mind. I tried to tell myself that I should leave things that way. It would be easier if she was upset with me and stayed away. But I couldn't bring myself to do it. We're neighbors, we'll have to see each other a lot, it doesn't make sense to be enemies. It has nothing to do with *liking* her, no, it's all very practical.

I knock lightly on the door three times, hearing Murphy bark once in response. The door opens and Juliette appears in the gap. Her blonde hair is in soft waves, the light strands standing out against the deep mauve of her sweater dress. The dress that is hugging her figure a little too perfectly. I swallow and keep my eyes on hers, which are wide with surprise.

"Adrian." The breathy way she utters my name has warmth pooling in my stomach. This was a mistake. I should have just let her hate me.

"I came to apologize for yesterday," I state. She blinks up at me. "I was rude and I shouldn't have said things the way that I did, even if we aren't dating."

The smile that spreads across her face steals my breath. She's unbelievably beautiful.

"Thank you for apologizing, but it's okay. I'm sure it's hard having your brothers gang up on you like that."

"I brought you something." I hold up a bag of cookies. "Maverick owns a bakery and I remembered you mentioning you like chocolate, so I brought you chocolate chip cookies."

Her eyes crinkle up at the edges as her smile widens even more. She's too sweet, too pure.

"Thank you," she says with a kind of awe that my small gesture seems unworthy of.

"It's no big deal."

She opens her mouth to respond, but the buzzing sound of a phone interrupts. When she pulls it out of her dress pocket, I take a step back.

"I'll let you take that. See you around."

"See you." She says with a smile and then answers the phone in a cheery voice. "Hey, Care!"

I walk back to my house, unsure of how to feel. For the first time in a while, I'm unhappy a conversation I was a part of was interrupted. I expected Juliette to talk to me, maybe retell that story about the guy who lived in my house before me. Now I'm left feeling bereft over missing out on her animated storytelling. My brow furrows. *What is wrong with me?*

CHAPTER NINE

Juliette Monroe

"Caroline you won't believe what just happened," I whisper into the phone, worried that Adrian will hear me through the walls on his way back to his house.

"Why are you whispering? I've told you before that Murphy doesn't actually understand you." I look over at the dog in question, who is currently gnawing on a chew toy shaped like a teacup.

"I think you're wrong, but that's not why I was whispering." I peek out my blinds, but Adrian is gone. "Adrian just came over to my house, apologized, and brought me chocolate chip cookies."

"What did he have to apologize for?" Caroline's voice takes on a protective edge.

"Nothing, it's not important." I wave the bag of cookies around even though she can't see them. "What's important is that he *brought me cookies*."

"So?"

"Caroline don't you dare *so* me! When you first started dating Josh I dissected every text he sent, even when it was only a thumbs up."

I set the cookies on my kitchen counter then begin to pace back and forth. My little cottage has an open concept living area, so I can easily walk from my front door to my back door in a straight line.

"That thumbs up meant something and you know it," she defends, then sighs. "*Fine*, he did go out of his way to do something extra for you. He could have just said he was sorry in passing."

"Exactly. He also could have not apologized at all."

"That would have been rude."

"Yes, but he would have successfully pushed me away."

Caroline snorts. "He'd have to do a lot more than that to get you to leave him alone. You're practically in love with him."

I gasp. "I am *not*. I think he's cute."

"I believe your exact words after seeing him shirtless were: I want to marry him and have his perfect babies."

My face heats and I lift my hand to my cheek to cool it down.

"You would have said the same thing."

"Not the point. The point is that you're infatuated with him and not doing anything about it."

"What am I supposed to do? Go knock on his door and throw myself at him?"

"That would be a fun start to a relationship." I roll my eyes. "But no, what you need to do is put yourself in his line of sight often. Also, it wouldn't hurt if you flirted a little."

"That would be a great plan if I was capable of flirting at all."

"You'd be great at flirting if you stopped thinking so much."

"So change the very essence of my being? I'll get right on that." We both laugh, but mine transforms into a groan. "Caroline, I can't do this."

"You don't have to, there are plenty of guys out there. There's always Kyle." The reminder of my dating app match makes me scrunch my face up. We've been messaging back and forth all week. He's nice and has made me laugh a few times with his messages, but he's not Adrian.

"That's true."

"Don't sound so excited," she teases and I sigh.

"You're right, I shouldn't get so caught up in Adrian that I don't give Kyle a chance. Even if Adrian looks like he was carved out of stone just for me."

"That's the spirit."

An icy gust of air stings my face when I walk out onto my back deck before sunrise. Adrian has turned me into a morning person. All week I've shuffled out here with my hot tea and blankets, hoping to catch a glimpse of him and maybe have a short conversation.

The first three days he merely nodded to me, murmured good morning and disappeared into his cottage. Yesterday, however, he told me he enjoyed the tea I gave him. I told him I placed an order for the one he gave me. The exhilaration I felt from that minor interaction was pathetic. Yet, I'm out here again, chasing the high.

I take a sip of my chai tea right as he's rounding the far side of the lake. It's much too cold to do anything other than curl up and complain about it, which makes his dedication admirable. My mind wanders to my date for tonight, Kyle. Is he a runner? I haven't asked him if he works out because that seems shallow and rude. Also, I'm afraid he might ask me if *I* work out and the answer would be embarrassing.

I agreed to meet him at Mama Peach's Diner for dinner tonight. My plan is to walk there and then if he turns out to be a creep, I'll run to Peaches and Cream and hide in Poppy's back office. But I think it will go well. I hope it does anyway. Maybe Kyle will be my soulmate and I'll forget about Adrian's perfect abs and sexy scowl. Because he is still very closed off and it's not looking good for us in the future relationship department.

Speaking of ... Adrian jogs into his backyard, his breath making white clouds in front of his mouth. He nods to me and I lift my teacup in greeting.

"Good morning, Adrian," I say with a smile.

"Good morning, Juliette." He surprises me by walking up to my railing. The deck is up off the ground, high enough to require steps down, but not so high that Adrian can't see over it. Though he is rather tall.

"Did you have a nice run?"

His chest rises and falls a little faster than usual, but he doesn't seem too out of breath. If I ran from here to my mailbox my lungs would be *burning*.

"Running isn't nice."

I laugh at his blunt statement. "Don't people get some sort of runner's high?"

"Endorphins rise, sure. But it's mostly miserable. Cold in the winter and hot any other time of the year."

"So why do you do it?"

He pauses, his blue eyes considering me. "To clear my head. My job can be stressful."

To most people, that sounds like a vague statement, but I know the admission means more than that to Adrian. He's essentially confessed a weakness to me, which means on some level he trusts me. His mind probably has fifty levels of security clearance and I was just given a level two pass. But I'm going to cherish my pass because I have a feeling most people don't make it this far.

"When I get stressed I take a bubble bath and drink chamomile tea, much nicer than running."

Is it my imagination or is that heat in his eyes? It occurs to me that I just talked about taking a *bath* in front of Adrian. A blush heats my face.

"I might have to try that."

"Let me know how it goes."

Adrian raises a brow at my statement.

Somebody tape my mouth shut. Or hit me over the head with a shovel. Something, *anything*, to get me to stop talking.

"I-I didn't mean it like that!" I stammer out in a rush.

"I know you didn't," he says, sounding like he's stifling a laugh. "I have to go get ready for work. I'll see you tomorrow at the café?"

I sit up a little taller, hope rising within me. He's planning on me being there tomorrow. Does that mean he's looking forward to it? Adrian isn't a man of empty pleasantries, so I can't imagine he's asking to be polite.

"I'll be there," I say, trying to keep my voice level. Between the bubble bath comment and this, my heart is going to jump out of my chest.

"Good." He taps the railing of my deck and then crosses the patch of grass between our houses.

I sit in my nest of blankets, limply grasping the handle of my teacup, staring after him. Maybe there's something between me and Adrian after all. A frown pushes my lips down. Why couldn't we have had this conversation *last* week?

CHAPTER TEN

Juliette Monroe

"Juliette?" A guy with sandy blond hair and tan skin asks me.

"Kyle?" I ask and he nods with a smile.

"Wow, you're even prettier in person," he says and I duck my head, blushing.

"Thank you, that's sweet of you to say."

When I lift my head to meet his brown eyes I'm surprised to see his smile tighter than before. His gaze has hardened too. Did I say something wrong? I shake off the feeling and gesture to the diner door.

"Are you ready to go inside?" I ask and he nods, his face softening into an easygoing grin.

He opens the door for me and I mark a tally in the pro column. We sit down in one of the worn peach-colored booths. One of my favorite waitresses, Paulette, walks up to our table almost immediately.

"What can I get you two to drink?"

"Two cokes, please," Kyle says and I blink at him in shock. Paulette shoots me a look, knowing that I don't drink soda. Even if I did, they serve Poppy's peachy keen tea here, so I always get that.

"One coke and a peachy keen tea," Paulette says as she scribbles in her peach-shaped notebook. "Coming right up."

"I ordered two *cokes*," Kyle says, sounding confused and annoyed. I try to reassure him with a smile.

"I come here a lot, Paulette knows I don't drink soda so she was just having a little fun changing up the order."

Kyle looks unamused but doesn't say anything more. Paulette gives me another look that says she's going to have a talk with me later before heading behind the counter to get our drinks.

We both open our menus, though I already know what I'm going to get. I always get the chicken tender basket with extra ranch. They make the ranch from scratch and it's so good that sometimes I get the chef, Danny, to make me my own little bottle to take home.

Paulette comes back with our drinks and flips open her little notebook again to take our orders.

"Do you need to order food or does she already know that too?" Kyle asks and I frown. The coke issue should upset *me* more than *him*, but that doesn't seem to be the case.

"I'll have the chicken tender basket with extra ranch," I tell Paulette, instead of answering Kyle.

"I'll get a cheeseburger meal."

Paulette looks like she's stabbing her notebook with her pen she's writing so hard. I know she's biting her tongue right now too.

"Is everything okay?" I ask Kyle once Paulette goes to put our orders in.

"Everything's fine. I just didn't know you were a regular here." His face morphs into a smile again. I don't like how easily he can do that.

"It's one of my favorite places." I'm careful not to say that I live around here. Right now it's looking like I'm going to be running to Poppy's office at the end of this. I'd leave now, but I don't want to be rude. He did come all the way from Atlanta.

"It's nice that you're so humble. The last few girls I've dated have been total gold diggers. I took one of them to Amelio's in Atlanta and she racked up the bill and didn't even eat all of the food."

I shift in my seat, resisting the urge to scowl. It's clear he wants me to know he has money, while throwing this backhanded compliment at me.

Paulette returns and I look up at her. Her hazel eyes are filled with pity for me. Anyone within earshot knows I'm on a terrible date right now. I dig into my food right away, hoping that I can use my mouth being full as an excuse for not talking to him.

Kyle doesn't mind talking with his mouth full. I wonder where I went so wrong. How could the app's algorithm have put us together? And why was he so much nicer over text?

At the end of our date, Kyle pays, remarking that this was just a tenth of the amount he paid on his last date. I make a nondescript noise that I think he interprets as praise by the way he grins at me.

We walk out and I grit my teeth when he places his hand on my back. *Just tell him thank you for a nice night and get to Poppy's. Fast.*

I take a deep breath before turning to face him on the sidewalk. We're across from The Fresh Peach Market, our local grocery store, and seeing various shoppers go in and out lends me a sense of safety.

"This was nice," I lie through my teeth.

"It was," he says and takes a step closer. I take a step back. I'm already standing near the wall of the diner, so it feels like he's trying to crowd me in. My hands dip into my coat pockets, one of them wrapping around the pepper spray I keep there. I don't want to assume the worst of him, but I also don't want to be stupid.

"I should probably get home," I say, and his brows furrow. Another step and he's too close. I panic when I realize my elderly neighbors probably won't even see us in the shadows here because of how dark it's gotten. I grip the pepper spray canister harder. He unfortunately grabs my arm that has the pepper spray. His grip isn't painful, but when I try to pull back it tightens.

I open my mouth to try and talk him down, but before I can say anything, Kyle is grabbed and pressed up against the wall. His hand rips from my arm and I gasp in shock. But my shock melts into relief when I see who has Kyle by the collar. *Adrian.*

"Hey man, what's your problem?" Kyle pushes Adrian's chest, but he's as immovable as stone. Kyle is taller than Adrian and has more than a few pounds on him, but this doesn't seem to affect Adrian's ability to hold him against the wall.

"My *problem* is that you're forcing yourself on a woman in the street." Adrian's voice is dangerously low.

"I barely touched her!" Kyle whines while trying to wriggle out of Adrian's iron grip.

"And you won't touch her ever again, nor will you contact her."

Kyle's face twists up in anger.

"Who are you to say what she wants?"

"Juliette," Adrian says my name, but his icy gaze doesn't leave Kyle. "Do you want this man to contact you again?"

"No," I whisper and Kyle turns his head to glare at me. Adrian presses him into the wall harder in response.

"Then it's settled. You're going to leave without so much as a glance at her, or you'll have to deal with me."

Kyle stumbles when Adrian lets him go, but he keeps his head down and doesn't look back at me as he walks to his truck. My heart is pounding in my chest and my hands are shaking.

"My car is by the market. I'll drive you home." Adrian's voice is still hard and unyielding, but I know without a doubt I'm safe with him. Even with all his gruffness, he's never given any cues that would make me feel less than secure.

We walk to his sleek sports car in silence. There's a grocery cart with a few bags inside of it near the car, and his trunk is open. He dropped what he was doing to come to my aid. My chest warms. I murmur a quiet thanks when he opens the passenger door for me.

Once he's back in the car, I assess him. His jaw is tight and his hold on the steering wheel is too tense. He's trying not to show his frustration, but it's easy to see he's angry.

"When did you know?" he asks as he backs out.

"What?"

"When did you know that he wasn't a good guy? I know you saw through him."

I tense, not liking what he's implying. "When I met him," I admit, unable to lie to him after he just saved me.

"Then why did you go out with him?"

I frown. "I didn't meet him in person until tonight. We met on a dating app. I thought I should at least give him one date before making a decision about his character."

"He could have followed you home. You shouldn't have invited him to Peach Hollow." I grit my teeth at his admonishment. He turns onto our road.

"I had a plan. I was going to go to Peaches and Cream if things went bad and wait until he left. I'm not stupid, Adrian."

"I know you're not, which is why it's baffling to me that you of all people would join a dating app. Don't you know that most of the guys on there are terrible?"

"For your information, my best friend met her *husband* on a dating app."

Usually, I would try to quell this rising tension. I'd say something appeasing and get Adrian to cool down. But knowing I'm safe to speak my mind has removed that filter.

"Your best friend is the exception, not the rule."

He pulls into his driveway and I immediately get out of the car, frustration rolling off me in waves. I was so relieved when I saw him, but now all I can see is red.

"I didn't ask for your opinion on my dating life. Thank you for helping me, but I don't need a lecture," I say when he gets out of the car.

"Juliette, you could have been hurt tonight." Childhood memories push their way into my mind like bile up my throat. I swallow them down and focus on Adrian. "I'm not trying to lecture you, I just want you safe."

"Why do you care?" The question comes out before I can stop to think.

"It's my job to protect people," he says in a cool tone. I try to read his expression in the dark, but it's hard when he's standing on the other side of the car.

"So it's not because you care about me."

He rakes a hand through his hair, the first noticeable sign that there might be something more going on. Dreadful hope rises once more. "I would have helped anyone in that situation."

It's freezing out, but even if it wasn't I'd be cold after that.

"Of course." I let out a weird, high-pitched laugh and take a step back. "You were just being a good Samaritan. I don't know why I thought any different." My foot slips off the edge of his driveway, making me wobble.

I pause, waiting for him to deny it. Or to apologize for lecturing me. But neither of those things happens, so I turn and storm across my yard without looking back.

CHAPTER ELEVEN

Adrian Carter

I shut the door to my house behind me, barely resisting the urge to slam it. My hands slide into my hair, tugging at the strands in frustration. I haven't felt this angry in ages. I haven't *felt* this much at all in a long time.

When I saw that scumbag grab her arm I almost blacked out I was so furious. It took all the self-control in my body not to rearrange his pathetic face. I growl and stalk over to my fridge, hoping some water will cool me down. Because even though we were standing in the cold, my blood is boiling.

I chug half of a water bottle and slam it on the countertop. My mind won't quit replaying the moment I spotted them across the street. Before I assessed her discomfort, an unwelcome feeling arose to the surface of my mind. *Jealousy*. I think I would have looked away from them if I hadn't felt that. It shocked me and held me in place as I watched him place his hand on her back.

It wasn't until I saw her cringe and take a step away from him that the feeling released me. Not that I felt any relief at seeing her discomfort. No, seeing her that way was like a hand around my throat. I couldn't breathe until I made sure she was safe.

Even after she was safe beside me though, I couldn't let go of the notion that it could have been much worse. Maybe I shouldn't have talked about her dating life. I groan and scrub my hands over my face.

This is why you don't get involved with people. Only bad things happen.

I should have stayed away from Juliette. She's too bright, too sweet, too soft. Now I've hurt her yet again because I don't know how to have a normal relationship. My only friends are my siblings and I haven't dated in years. All my non-family friendships have ended in bitter betrayal. I was content to spend my life alone in peace until Juliette came along with her pretty smile and starlight in her eyes. She snuck her way into my life and now I *care* about her.

My muscles are twitching and I feel like I can't sit still. I need to get away from here. Put distance between me and Juliette. So, even though the last thing I want to do is deal with his annoying optimism, I pull my phone out and call Grayson.

"Adrian!" he shouts into the phone when he answers. I immediately regret my decision.

"What are you doing right now?"

"I just got back from a date."

Of course, he did, because while I've spent my adulthood in solitude, Grayson has spent his in constant company. It's not like he has nefarious intentions or that he uses women; he just genuinely enjoys being around people for some reason unbeknownst to me.

"I'm coming to hang out."

A choking and sputtering sound comes over the line, making me lift my phone away from my ear.

"Sorry," he wheezes. "I thought you said you wanted to hang out and I choked on my drink."

I pinch the bridge of my nose. "I'll call Levi or Mav if you're going to act like this."

"Oh, you seriously want to hang out?" He whoops, the sound piercing my eardrum. "This day just got so much better. Are you on your way?"

"I am now." I grab my keys and head out to my car.

"Aren't you going to ask me why my day wasn't good?"

"You said your day got better, not that it was bad in the first place."

"Yes, but it was *implied*. Sometimes I really don't understand how your brain works."

"The feeling is mutual," I remark in a dry tone. He doesn't say anything, and I sigh as I start my car and my phone transfers to Bluetooth. "You can tell me about your day when I get there, there's no sense in having a conversation while I'm on the way to you."

"Fine, I can wait. See you soon!" He hangs up before I can.

It's a thirty-minute drive to the suburb where Grayson lives. He bought a family home in a neighborhood with a community pool and swingsets and an HOA. I told him it was weird for a single man to own a family home and he said one day he was going to have a family, so there's no sense in wasting his money on a bachelor pad.

I drive in silence on the way to Grayson's house. There's enough noise in my head tonight, I don't need anything added to it. I keep replaying every word I said, every word Juliette said. By the time I get to Grayson's, my emotions are stretched taut.

The warm glow within his two-story craftsman is a welcoming beacon after being lost in the sea of my own thoughts. That is until I notice that there are two additional vehicles in his driveway. Maverick's motorcycle and Levi's pickup truck. Groaning, I slide out of my car and trudge up the front porch steps.

The door swings open. "Brother!" Grayson grins and I shoot him a flat look.

"Why did you invite our entire family?"

"MJ and Dad would be hurt that you think they're not family."

"Did you not invite them?" I raise an eyebrow. He steps aside and beckons me in with a flourish.

"MJ is having a date night with Bash, and Dad said he'd rather watch the Thrashers' basketball game in his underwear." Sounds about right, on both accounts. My dad has always been on the antisocial side, but after Mom passed away a decade ago he basically became a hermit except for when we come to his place.

I nod in acknowledgment of his statement and walk to the stairs that lead down to his basement. It's the one area of the house that resembles the bachelor he is. With a pool table, dart boards, and a massive TV, it's a true man cave. Every time I've been over, we end up down there playing some sort of game, so I suspect that's where my brothers are now.

Maverick and Levi are playing pool when we get down there. There's money on the edge of the table, which is a mistake on Mav's part. Levi rarely ever loses at pool, *especially* if there's money on the line.

"Who's winning?" I ask, studying the table. There are a lot more solids than stripes.

"Levi," Maverick grumbles, and a smile tugs at the edge of my mouth.

"You know better, man," I tell him and he shrugs before lining up his shot. He sinks one, but he still has a long way to go if he's going to catch up with Levi.

"It's almost sad how easy it is," Levi smirks as Maverick misses his next shot.

"So, why are we all here?" Maverick asks, leaning against the wall nearby while Levi takes his turn.

"Adrian called and said he wanted to hang out," Grayson says and Levi's grip slips, making him miss the ball.

"What's wrong?" Levi asks, straightening to look me in the eye.

"Why can't I just want to hang out?"

"Because you don't like people," Maverick says and I shoot him a glare. "What? It's true. We know you love us deep down, but you're never going to be the one to make plans."

"Unless something's wrong," Levi adds.

Maverick nods. "Unless something's wrong," he repeats.

They all stare at me from their spots around the room. Maverick looks concerned, Levi is searching my face for clues–he will find none–and Grayson's eyes are dancing with amusement like he already knows.

"It's about Juliette, isn't it?" Grayson asks, confirming my suspicion. I tense involuntarily and Grayson points at me. "Ha! You tensed up. I'm right."

I rarely ever slip up like that, but hearing Juliette's name triggered something within me. Another reason I shouldn't be involved with her. She's a weakness.

"The cute neighbor girl?" Levi's brow crinkles. "Are you dating her?"

"No." They all wait with expectant faces for me to continue. I swipe a hand over my face and sigh. "We're ... acquaintances. And I offended her. I probably overstepped, but I was *right*."

"What happened?" Curiosity laces Grayson's tone.

"Not important." I grit my teeth. "I just need to figure out what to do now."

Maverick laughs. "Apologize. You're making this too complicated."

"I've already hurt her feelings once, you were there. I had to apologize after that, too." I leave out the detail that I brought the cookies he gave me to her. They would incorrectly interpret that for sure.

"Do you think you only get one apology in a friendship?" Maverick asks and bends down to take another shot. He misses, grumbles something under his breath, then faces me again. "I've had to apologize to my best friend Drew a million times."

"I'm hurt that I'm not your best friend," Grayson says, laying a hand over his heart. I roll my eyes.

"We're brothers," I remind him and he shakes his head.

"Family doesn't equal friendship. I'd like to know that we're best friends *and* brothers."

"Back to the problem at hand," Levi says with a pointed look at Grayson.

"Is it different when the friend is a girl?" I ask, hating how childish my words sound. If I didn't care about Juliette, I wouldn't even subject myself to the torture of asking advice from my brothers.

Grayson grins and he opens his mouth to say something, but Maverick speaks up first.

"No, it's not." He pauses. "Actually, I take that back, you'll probably have to apologize even more."

"That's encouraging."

"It's just the truth," he replies with a shrug. "Next time you see her, give her a sincere apology and hope you didn't screw up bad enough that she won't forgive you."

I slowly nod. "Okay, I can do that."

Grayson is practically bouncing beside me, so I look at him.

"What?" I ask and he feigns innocence by widening his blue eyes.

"Nothing."

"Go ahead and say it."

"When you marry her, can I be the best man at your wedding? I think I should get to since I'm your twin."

I narrow my eyes at him. Maverick and Levi both laugh at us.

"I'm not marrying Juliette."

Grayson's faux innocent look fades into a smirk.

"We'll see."

CHAPTER TWELVE

Juliette Monroe

I stomp down the sidewalk, taking my bad mood out on the puddles beneath my black rain boots. Some people would resent the fact that the weather matches their mood, but not me. It gives me a sense of justification. I have all the more reason to be sour when it's storming on a Saturday.

Rain pelts my clear umbrella while ice-cold air whips against every bit of skin exposed to the elements. Which isn't much, just half my face–the bottom half is buried in a forest green scarf–and the hand holding my umbrella. My fingers might fall off before I can get to Peaches and Cream, and it would be all my fault since I left my gloves on my kitchen counter.

I channel every tinge of discomfort into my frustration toward Adrian. I had all last night to stew and think everything over. It allowed me to see where he was coming from, which was unfortunate since I'd made the decision to be angry with him for the rest of time. Now, the only thing I have left to be mad about is him saying he would have helped anyone in that situation. That should be an endorsement of his character, but I can't help but be hurt by him not thinking of me as more than some random stranger on the street.

I step under the awning over the café door and shake out my umbrella. Through the window, I spot Adrian sitting at my booth and my anger intensifies. I push open the door with more force than necessary, making the bell above it ring several times in a row. Adrian's gaze lifts from his laptop, his blue eyes widening a touch when they land on me.

"Morning, sugar!" Poppy chirps, still a ray of sunshine even in this dreary weather.

"Good morning, Poppy," I reply and ignore Adrian's presence. If I'm nothing more than a stranger to him, then that's all I'll be. Mature? Not really. But my heart is a little too raw after last night to care.

Kyle grabbing me brought up a lot of ugly memories from my childhood. So, when I wasn't thinking of what Adrian said, I was reliving some of the less-than-pleasant moments I experienced growing up. My parents didn't physically abuse me often–they preferred psychological tactics–but there were a few occasions when their tempers got the best of them and they grabbed me. It was usually only to pull me to another room to yell at me, but it still left a mark on my mind, even though my body is free of scars.

That walk down memory lane sapped my strength and my more forgiving nature. If Adrian wants something more, he's going to have to do something about it, because I'm not going to be the first to say something. Not this time.

"Honey, are you okay?" I blink a few times, coming back to the present. Poppy is staring at me, concern furrowing her brow. I can feel Adrian's gaze on me even though I refuse to look at him.

"I'm fine," I say with a forced smile. "I was just trying to decide what to get. What's your current favorite?" I walk the rest of the way to the counter, keeping my eyes on Poppy.

"I have this hazelnut black tea I just got in a few days ago that I'm loving."

"That sounds really nice," I say and she rings it up for me. I take a seat at the booth opposite Adrian but sit with my back facing him.

My head hurts from lack of sleep combined with stress. Whenever I get overwhelmed, pain radiates from my head through my neck, even into my shoulder blades sometimes. I haven't had a headache like this in a while. My fingertips brush against the smooth hardback I slid into my tote bag earlier this week. A little escapism in the form of a good book wouldn't hurt. When I pull it out, I have to stifle a groan. I forgot that I put *Pride and Prejudice* in here a few days ago after I finished *The Great Gatsby*.

I love both of the books very much, but I don't think I can read about an attractive grumpy man right now. Poppy sets my tea and croissant down in front of me and I murmur a thank you. I push the book to the side and pull out my phone to scroll through Pinterest. I'm studying a recipe for a chocolate chip coffee cake when movement on the other side of the table draws my attention.

Adrian sits across from me. I blink, quite sure I'm going to wake up back in my bed after a night of fitful sleep, but no. There he sits, as real as ever in an inky black cable knit sweater, with his fingers interlaced on the table like we're about to discuss stocks. I say nothing, partly because I'm mad at him and partly because I have no idea what *to* say.

My eyes meet his and I wish I could say it was easy to hold his gaze, but it's not. His eyes have always been captivating, truly magnetic in nature, but today the glacial depths hold an intensity that makes my breath catch. If I keep staring I'll end up breaking and saying something first, trying to let him off the hook. So I avert my eyes, turning my attention to my untouched croissant.

"I'm sorry," Adrian says, his voice low and gruff. "I shouldn't have said anything about the dating app. I just care about your safety, Juliette."

"I know, side effects of your job and all," I retort, trying not to sound too bitter.

"No—well, yes it is." He sighs and I look up in time to catch the tortured look on his face before he can smooth it out. "I'm not used to this sort of thing."

"What are you talking about?"

"I don't have friends outside of my family. I'm not sure how to go about this and because of that I've hurt you in the process."

My heart aches for him. Friendship is a big step for Adrian, based on how it visibly pains him to say the word *friend*. All of my frustrations dissolve like sugar in hot tea. The fact that he sat down at this booth is probably huge for him. He could have ignored me instead, severing our relationship. So, even if I'm attracted to him, becoming his friend might be what he needs more right now. I'll just have to tamp down my feelings.

"I'll teach you," I blurt out without thinking and his mouth quirks up in the right corner.

"You'll teach me how to be friends with you?" The humor in his voice lightens the mood.

"Yes," I say in a resolute tone and sit up straighter. "The first lesson is don't butt into your friend's dating life."

He snorts and I smile.

"Based on my sister's friendships, I feel like that's not actually what friends do."

I laugh, thinking of all the times Caroline has meddled in my love life, even from a distance.

"Well, it's a rule for *our* friendship," I tell him, shooting him what I hope is a hard look. Judging by the subtle smile he's wearing, it didn't work.

"Any other lessons for today, Miss Juliette?" The teasing lilt of his voice catches me off guard and I want to throw this newfound friendship out the window. Then fist my hands in his sweater and pull his mouth down to mine.

I clear my throat and push the wayward thought out the window instead. This is not the time for fantasies. Tonight, when I'm falling asleep, however...

"I'll have to prepare a lesson plan and get back to you," I joke, then meet his eyes again. "Thank you for apologizing. And for protecting me last night. I know you said you would have done it for anyone in my position, but I still appreciate it."

Some unreadable emotion flickers across his expression, but it doesn't stay long enough for me to dissect it.

"Do you want to move to our booth?"

My heart picks up speed at the thought of anything being *ours*.

"Don't you mean *my* booth?" I ask in a teasing voice.

"I sat down first, so it's technically mine. I was just being nice."

"I didn't take you for a guy who did things just to be nice," I sass and his lips quirk up in a half-smile.

"Just move," he says, and I laugh.

We both slide out of the booth and Adrian grabs my book off the table while I pick up the rest of my belongings.

"You finished Gatsby?" he asks, and a bubbly feeling fills my chest at his noticing what I was reading.

"I did," I say as we slide into my favorite booth. "I've read it a bunch of times, but I always find something I didn't notice before. I planned on going to college for English Literature, actually, but I didn't end up able to go to college at all."

It's only after I finish speaking that I realize I just admitted I didn't go to college. I rarely tell people, because it brings up a barrage of questions that I hate answering. It's not exactly *small talk* to share how I left my parents' house at eighteen in the dead of night with a pickle jar of cash and had to start working right away to survive.

"What did you find this time?" Adrian asks before taking a sip of his tea.

I smile at him, having to hold in tears because for the first time since moving away, someone isn't interrogating me about my life choices. He studies me and I know he likely can sense my unexpected emotional response, but he doesn't ask me about it. I sip my tea and regain my composure before responding.

"You've read it?" He nods, so I continue. "Do you remember the green light at the end of Daisy's dock? Gatsby focused so much on that green light, enchanting himself to think that it was her. And then when Daisy was finally in his presence, the light lost all its meaning." I pause, tracing the rim of my cup. "I think people do that a lot. Fall in love with the idea of a life that isn't theirs and then when they step into that life, suddenly it's different than what they thought. Duller than they imagined."

I've done that, my heart whispers. I spent years dreaming of a life away from my family. My imagination concocted beautiful friendships and romance and a home filled with all the love and light I never had. But then I got here and it was like I was paralyzed by the notion of *living*. How do you function in peace when all you've ever known is chaos? So, I built a sanctuary and a fortress in one, staying safe, never risking more than I thought I could handle losing. Six years later, I'm still working through those feelings.

"I understand," Adrian says, making me lift my head in surprise.

"You do?" I don't give him a chance to respond before I ramble more. "It's a depressing thought, though, that you chase something only for it to turn out differently than you wanted."

The way he regards me, his blue eyes holding my gaze with such care, is unnerving. I don't know what to make of this thing between us, if there's anything at all.

"It's a little depressing," he agrees. "But one of the best parts of life is that you can start over each day. My mom always said that." His hand reaches up and rubs his chest and my eyes catch on a glinting gold chain poking out of the collar of his sweater.

"That's true," I say in a quiet voice.

I take another sip of my delicious hazelnut tea, watching the stoic man across from me. Maybe I can start over. The first risk I can take is becoming Adrian's friend. I'm certain that my heart couldn't handle the destruction he'd bring if I fell in love with him in the process, but maybe it's worth it. If only so I can say that I actually lived my life instead of hiding from it.

CHAPTER THIRTEEN

Adrian Carter

I finish my morning run in record time. Juliette's floodlight turned on while I was on the opposite side of the lake and I practically sprinted around the last bend. My chest is burning and I purposefully slow myself down as I get closer so I'm not out of breath when I walk up. After our time in the café on Saturday, I've been counting down until I got to see her again. And whenever I found myself looking at the time on my phone or wishing hours would move faster, I'd tell myself to stop, but it didn't work.

I ended up convincing myself that I'm looking forward to seeing her *as a friend*. That's why warmth floods my body when I see her sitting in a nest of blankets, her blonde hair in double braids, because it's good to see my friend.

"Good morning, Adrian," she says in her honeyed voice, lifting up a carafe. "I made you some tea."

I stare at her over the railing, taking in her sleepy smile and slightly puffy eyes. It occurs to me that she didn't wake up this early when I first moved here. *Does she come out here to see me?* I push away the thought, unwilling to flatter myself that sweet Juliette would deprive herself of sleeping in for *me*.

"Good morning." I clear my throat, my eyes drifting to the stairs leading up to her.

"Come sit, there's plenty of room." When I don't move, she rushes to add. "If you have time and want to, that is."

"I have time." I walk up the steps and she scoots over so that there's more space for me on the wicker couch. I move the blankets over so I don't get them dirty with sweat and sit down.

"I made a cinnamon tea. It's one of my favorites to have in the morning."

She leans out of her seat to pour the tea into a ceramic teacup with bumblebees painted onto it. I usually drink my tea out of a plain white mug, or one with a Thrashers' logo on it that MJ got me for Christmas last year, so this is new for me. It even comes with a saucer that has flowers on it. She hands it to me with a bright smile.

I'm careful to not let our hands touch, to avoid any unwanted sensations on my part. My efforts to avoid feelings are in vain though, because while moving, her sweater shifted, exposing her shoulder and a lacy burgundy strap. The urge to kiss the exposed skin hits me hard, the intensity of my attraction catching me off guard. I've known Juliette was beautiful since I saw her standing in her driveway, but this overwhelming need is new. My skin heats and I'm grateful when she pulls the fabric back over her shoulder.

Even with her skin covered, I find myself needing to avert my eyes. I focus on the ripples of tea as I drink it. The cinnamon is the perfect amount of sweetness and I can see why it's her favorite.

"Do you like it?" Juliette asks and I lift my gaze to where she's cuddled up on the opposite side of the couch, looking content as she takes a dainty sip.

"It's good."

She smiles at me, undeterred by my short answer, then sets her cup on the table.

"So," she begins, sitting up some more. That blasted sweater falls off her shoulder again, but she makes no move to adjust it. I grip my cup tighter. "I was thinking about your friendship lessons."

I raise my eyebrows. "I thought you were joking."

"I was," she says with a laugh. "But the more I thought about it, the more I think it could be fun. You said yourself you don't have many friends and I don't either, but only because there aren't any people my age here. So we're each the perfect person to practice with."

"That sounds awful."

She laughs again and I can't help the small smile that comes at the sound. She's got this infectious laugh that almost insists on you joining in.

"What would you get out of these lessons?" I ask her. "I can't teach you anything when it comes to being social."

She smiles and shakes her head. "I'll handle all the social lessons." She toys with the hem of the blanket in her lap, suddenly shy. "I've noticed you don't care about what other people think of you."

"Correct," I reply in a blunt tone and she playfully rolls her eyes.

"Well, I care probably *too* much. And if you haven't noticed, that makes me ramble and become increasingly awkward. I need your confidence."

I don't think she needs anything at all, but I don't say that. She seems sincere, so even if I think her rambling is endearing, I don't want it to seem like I'm discounting her opinions.

"Are you sure I'm the right person to help you?" Skepticism coats my voice.

"Well, you're the only one around," she jokes, shooting me a wry smile. "But you're also ... safe. I know you won't hurt me."

My spine stiffens. The way she says that makes me all the more certain that there was a time when she wasn't safe. I'm honored to be considered someone who could be, but also certain that I'm unworthy of this designation. Can I handle this kind of commitment? I know this isn't a romantic relationship, but we're going deeper than acquaintances *fast*. It's like jumping into a pool, but as soon as you hit the water you're in an ocean instead.

I drink my tea so I don't have to respond right away. If it were anyone else I think I'd say no, but there's something about Juliette that has me wanting to learn how to be her friend. Helping her in return would keep me from feeling like I owed her anything, too.

I look at her–decision made–as cold air whips at my skin. Even the warmth of the tea can't stave off the early morning chill. Juliette looks as cozy as ever though under her mound of blankets. An idea comes to mind to even the playing field further, making me smirk.

"I'll do it," I say and her face lights up. It almost makes me reconsider what I'm about to say. "*If* you go on a run with me tomorrow morning."

Her face falls.

"Why?" Her question comes out in a whine and she gives me a look that says she'd rather jump in the freezing lake.

"Because running quiets the mind, which it sounds like you need. And it makes us even because I'm sure whatever lesson you've got planned is going to be torturous."

She groans, letting her head fall back dramatically. "Fine. I will go on *one* run with you if you agree to attend Wednesday bingo night at the church."

"Bingo night," I deadpan and she pastes on an innocent smile, blinking her emerald eyes at me. "As in tonight."

"Yep! It's one of the most popular community events and the perfect place to practice talking with people. Also, friends make sacrifices, like doing things they don't want to do for their friend."

"So my first lesson is going to be talking to my elderly neighbors while they try to beat each other at a game of chance?"

"Bingo!"

"I'm starting to regret my decision."

It's almost five o'clock and I need to sneak out of the office unnoticed. This is going to be rather difficult because everyone knows I'm the last person here most nights. As many times as I've sought to remain undetected in my line of work, I know that routines are the easiest way to be noticed by others. Deviating from a routine everyone knows I follow is going to get eyes on me fast.

For the majority of my staff, a stern look should get them to stay away and not ask any questions. But there's one person here who is not deterred by my sharp looks: Grayson. He'll stop me and ask a million questions. The last thing I want to do is admit to him that I'm leaving early to go to *bingo night* with Juliette. He'll probably do some awful rendition of a TikTok dance he learned from Maddie to celebrate and then tell my entire family that I'm getting married.

So, to avoid all of *that*, I need to avoid *him*. His office is across from mine and not only is it encased in glass windows, but his door is always open. I can see him lounging in his chair, feet up on his desk, tossing his rubberband ball as he talks on the phone.

A normal person would think this means he's distracted and won't notice me slip out, but Grayson is always more observant than he appears. It's what made him a great air marshal and what makes him the best trainer for the security teams we send out. My best bet is to make myself inconspicuous and pretend to be doing something other than leaving. Which is why even though it pains me, I'm going to leave my laptop open on my desk overnight. The screen will be locked, but my entire office is going to look like I stepped out for a minute.

I keep my gait relaxed, but not *too* relaxed as I pass Grayson's office. I'm holding a file folder filled with blank paper, so it looks like I'm heading to give someone their next assignment. Once I'm out of his line of sight, I make a sharp turn toward the lobby.

"Mr. Carter!" Chloe, our receptionist, smiles at me from behind her desk. "Are you leaving early for the day?"

"Just stepping out." She'll tell the *other* Mr. Carter any information I give her, so I'm purposefully vague.

"Have a nice evening!"

I spare her a nod and barrel through the doors. There's no need to pretend to be relaxed now. I need to make it to my car before–

"Oh brother dearest!" Grayson croons out across the lot, making me growl. I was almost to my car, too. "Where might you be headed so early in the evening?"

I turn around to face him as he saunters toward me.

"Nowhere. How did you know I was leaving?"

"You were holding the folder too tight and you rarely give assignments out at the end of the day unless it's an emergency. If it was an emergency, you would have told me."

I rake a hand through my hair. It's annoying how good he is. And even more annoying how *off* Juliette makes me.

"I'm going out with a friend," I say and he raises his eyebrows.

"Okay, now for the real story."

"It's true," I grit out through clenched teeth.

"Is this friend named Juliette?" I give him a flat look and he gives me a feline grin in return. "So it's a date."

I can't help the chuckle that slips out. "No, it's not a date. It would be a terrible one if it was."

Grayson frowns at that. "Well, if she's getting you out of your fortress of solitude I guess I can't complain. Though I do wish that my own twin would want to hang out with me more."

I open my mouth to say something about us working together every day but stop. Maybe it's the way he said it, or maybe it's Juliette getting into my head about friendship, but it has me changing my intended comeback.

"We can get together sometime soon, okay?"

His grin widens. "Oh, she really is working on you. I'll have to get this girl a present!" He slaps me on the shoulder. "Have fun on your non-date, give Juliette my love."

I roll my eyes and head to my car. My mind is buzzing in anticipation as I drive to Peach Hollow. Even though I'm certain bingo will be a disaster, the thought of seeing Juliette has me tapping the steering wheel to the beat of the music.

As soon as I realize I'm doing it, I stop and grip the wheel tight. I cannot let myself feel anything more than friendship with Juliette. Nothing romantic of any kind. She has too many secrets and I don't know how to trust someone enough to love them. *It would be a disaster*, I remind myself. Then I nod in resolution and make a pact that I'll focus on all things *platonic* with her tonight.

CHAPTER FOURTEEN

Juliette Monroe

I can't stop shifting in my seat as I wait for Adrian to arrive at the church-turned-bingo-hall. Poppy eyes me from across the table like I left my brain on the church steps before entering. I've been anxious all day today. I had to redo a design seven times because I kept getting distracted and writing the wrong thing.

"You're wiggling around like you're sitting on a mound of fire ants, child. What's gotten into you? I know you're not nervous about bingo."

I fiddle with the edge of my stack of bingo cards and shake my head.

"Oh, I see now." Poppy smirks and looks above my head. "Your man is coming tonight."

I glance over my shoulder and spot Adrian making a beeline to me through the arrangement of tables. The uncomfortable church pews are pushed up against the walls and in their place is a series of plastic tables and chairs. Adrian weaves through the maze, not even sparing a glance at the people clearly trying to get his attention. We're going to have to work on that.

"He's *not* my man," I whisper to Poppy before shooting to my feet. "Adrian!" I greet his scowl with my brightest smile. His scowl softens slightly but doesn't let up completely.

"There are too many people here," he grumbles and sits in the seat next to mine.

Poppy is the only other person at our table, which is why I chose this one. Adrian already knows Poppy and they both like tea, which is an easy conversation topic. Plus, if I sat us anywhere else he'd be interrogated instead of able to have a conversation. Though with the way Poppy's eyes are sparkling, I'm not sure if she's going to stick to just *tea* in our conversation tonight.

"I'm happy you came," I say to him as I sit back down. He grunts in response. "Aw, cheer up Sunshine, tonight will be fun." My tone is teasing and without thinking, I lay a hand on his forearm.

"Please don't start calling me Sunshine," he grouses but I can see the corner of his mouth lift.

"Too late, that's your new nickname. Remember what I said about not getting to choose nicknames?" I ask with a saccharine smile. He shoots me a glare, but it has no heat behind it.

"I should have stayed at work. This was not worth dealing with Grayson."

I laugh at his sour tone and squeeze his arm. "I appreciate the sacrifice, really."

His eyes dip down to my hand on his arm and I rip it away, heat blazing across my face. *I cannot believe I did that.* I see Poppy grin wickedly out of the corner of my eye, but thankfully she stays silent.

"Attention bingo lovers!" Community Representative Henry shouts into a microphone–yes, *shouts*. "We are about to begin. Please turn off your cell phones and turn on your hearing aids. The numbers will be on the screen to my left." He gestures to a rolling projector screen. "We will not be repeating any numbers after they have been said the customary three times. Once you get bingo, you will yell it out and then I will check your card for authenticity."

"We know the rules, Henry!" Gerty squawks from her table, her yellow bike helmet bobbing on her head as she shakes her bingo dauber at him. "Let's get this thing started before bedtime." For the record, it's barely past five in the evening.

Henry looks as if he's considering retiring from his position for a moment before pasting on a smile again.

"Five minutes until the first number is called!" He forces cheer into his tone before placing the microphone back on the podium stand and stalking off to the snack table.

"Isn't bingo a form of gambling?" Adrian asks, turning my attention back to him. I think–*I hope*–my face cooled during Henry's announcement.

I shrug. "Maybe?"

"I would think the church would be against it then."

"Oh, well ten percent of the funds go to the church, so I guess they're okay with it. Did you buy a card and dauber?" The table is blank in front of him.

"Dauber?" He tries out the word, his brows drawing together. I hold up my yellow paint pen.

"It's what you dot the numbers with," I explain and he nods in understanding.

"No, I didn't know I was required to attend *and* play."

I shoot him a look and he sighs.

"*Fine*, I'll be right back."

"Thanks, Sunshine." I beam up at him.

"Don't push it."

My grin only gets bigger. As soon as he leaves the table, Poppy clears her throat.

"Don't you start," I say and pin her with a warning look. She doesn't even bat an eye.

"You like him."

"Of course I like him, we're friends."

"No, you *like* like him."

"Aren't you a little old to be using elementary terms?"

She narrows her eyes at me. "Don't you sass me young lady, or else I'm going to start passing around a rumor that you two are together. Then you'll have Georgiana at your door warning you about the dangers of holding hands before marriage."

Georgiana is Peach Hollow's morality police. When I first moved here she took it upon herself to educate me on how hand-holding leads to a baby on your hip. She has diagrams that would make even the most promiscuous of people blush. The image on page seven of her twenty-page pamphlet still haunts me years later.

"Okay, okay, I have a *tiny* crush on him. Who wouldn't? He's practically a model, except better looking because he's got this edge to him. He's definitely not a pretty boy type, he's way too brooding for that. But sometimes he smiles just a little bit and it's really something to see. He's such a Mr. Darcy and I'm a sucker for taciturn men in fiction..." I trail off when I spot Poppy's sweet smile and head tilt.

"What?" I ask, afraid of why she's looking at me like I'm a puppy who just sat for a treat for the first time.

"You've got it bad," she replies and my mouth drops. I check over my shoulder to make sure Adrian isn't near. He's still waiting on Fiona to hand over his bingo supplies. It looks like she's holding them hostage in order to get a conversation out of him.

"I do not," I protest after I turn back around. "He's attractive, that's all."

"Mhmm, whatever you have to tell yourself sugar. I bet I'll be serving almond croissants at your wedding not long from now."

I sputter, unable to form a coherent thought for a moment. "You forget there are two sides to a relationship. He certainly doesn't see me that way."

"Are you sure? He is here after all. I'm willing to bet he only showed up because it would make you smile."

I sit back in my chair, considering her words. Adrian came for me, but was it just because of our friendship lessons? Or because he cares about me on a level deeper than friendship? From what I can tell, he's not one to do something he doesn't like for another person. But he also hasn't made any moves that would suggest he's interested in me romantically. Well, aside from that flirty line when I saw his abs. My skin heats at the memory.

Adrian arrives back at our table and sits with a huff. His return drags me out of my thoughts. Probably for the best, since they aren't leading anywhere good or healthy.

"That Fiona woman is infuriating."

"She was just trying to get to know you," I say with a laugh and he scowls.

"She wouldn't give me what I paid for until I told her if I was single."

I press my lips together, fighting back another laugh.

"Fiona is always trying to find a man for her granddaughter. I keep telling her that it doesn't look good for her to be setting the poor girl up all the time, but she doesn't listen," Poppy says with a shake of her head.

A bell chimes, breaking up our conversation. Henry stands by the podium, one wrinkled hand poised on the handle of the bingo cage. He's spry for his old age, still able to get around on his own.

"Daubers ready," he says in his 'announcer' voice. He likes to lower his voice a few octaves and drawl. By the third number he loses the act because of people complaining they can't understand him, but he still tries it every time.

I–along with everyone but Adrian–lift my dauber in the air in a ceremonious manner. Adrian looks around like we're all short a few marbles. We probably are, but since we're all together he looks like the odd one out.

When I use my other hand to gesture to Adrian's dauber, his mouth turns into a thin line, but he lifts his blue dauber in the air. As if he was waiting on Adrian's participation, Henry begins to roll the cage, the sound echoing through the building.

"B52," he says into the microphone and everyone lowers their daubers to check for the number. Henry then repeats the number twice more.

I have two of that square on this sheet, so I mark them. Some people buy multiple books and have entire tables covered in cards, dotting away trying to win the jackpot. I usually just buy one book and come to get out of the house, not to win.

"What do you win if you get bingo?" Adrian asks as he presses a circle of blue paint over a square.

"All of the money is in a pot that gets split up throughout each round, except the first. The first-round winner gets a gift basket from local restaurants and stores."

He nods in acknowledgment and we fall silent, listening to Henry bellow numbers into the microphone. The first round goes by rather uneventfully, with Larry from across the lake winning the basket. The next few rounds go to various residents, with little feedback until it's time for the jackpot. I'm starting to regret bringing Adrian because we haven't spoken nearly enough to deem this a lesson in socializing.

"Bingoooo!" Gerty sings in a raspy voice from her table.

"Bingo over here too!" Georgiana calls out.

"Uh-oh," I say under my breath, and Poppy grimaces.

"What is it?" Adrian asks, looking up from his card.

"If two people get bingo, they have to split the pot," Poppy says, shooting a wary look to the front of the room. Gerty is hobbling over to Henry with a scowl on her face.

"Gerty doesn't like to share," I add. We all turn to watch what is sure to be a fiasco.

"She cheated!" Gerty points a crooked, accusing finger at Georgiana, who gasps as if someone accused her of adultery instead of bingo forgery.

"I did not, you just don't like splitting the pot."

"Check our cards, Henry, and tell Georgie here that the money is all mine."

"You know I hate being called Georgie!" Georgiana stomps one of her kitten heels with a huff.

"Both of the cards are correct," Henry says, looking as though he might be sick. "You both have won the jackpot and must split it."

"Rigged," Gerty declares. "This whole darn thing is rigged! Down with the man!" She tips the bingo cage, causing the balls to spill out all over the floor.

"Gerty, you're going to get banned if you don't quit this," Georgiana warns to which Gerty sticks out her tongue in response. If you've never seen an eighty-year-old woman in a yellow bicycle helmet stick out her tongue, you're missing out.

"This is ridiculous," Adrian murmurs beside me, but there's humor hiding in his tone.

"You mean highly entertaining," I reply.

"I fund this whole night with how many cards I buy and you know I run this neighborhood. No one is banning me. So give me my money and go find someone to give your nasty pamphlets to."

Georgiana's face turns bright red as snickers fill the room.

"They are *educational*, not nasty."

"That's enough, ladies. You may collect your winnings from Fiona on your way out. Bingo night is over."

Both women go their separate ways, each grumbling and huffing.

"He stopped them before it got good." I pout and hear one of my favorite sounds–Adrian chuckling.

I whip my head to the left and catch a half-smile that makes my heart skip. Goodness, he's beautiful. Chiseled perfection, but with a softness in his eyes that makes my knees weak. Those very eyes meet mine as his laughter fades. The room shrinks and my mouth goes dry.

"You should laugh more," I say in a quiet voice because my brain can't function properly when those lapis lazuli eyes are on me. "It's nice."

"I'll write that in my notes from tonight's lesson," he replies in a gruff voice and I smile at him.

"Good."

And it is good, *too* good. His laugh and teasing words are the kind of perfect you lose sleep over. The kind that makes your mind race, dissecting every way you could ruin it. My sleep schedule has been ruined since Adrian moved in anyway, which is rather inconvenient since I have to wake up before sunrise tomorrow to go on a run. Maybe that will ruin all of this goodness.

Adrian throws away all of our table's trash, earning an appreciative look from Poppy. My heart feels warm and fuzzy in my chest. I think that somehow, even though I hate the idea of running, I'll still enjoy tomorrow because I'll be with Adrian. And that thought is both extremely exciting and overwhelmingly scary all at once.

CHAPTER FIFTEEN

Adrian Carter

Running is my alone time. I started running for exercise in high school and I've always gone on my own. Even Grayson knew that he couldn't come with me. And yet here I am, waiting by the lake for a woman who is already putting me five minutes behind schedule. If I arrive to work late Grayson is definitely going to harass me about it for the next six to eight weeks.

By the time I spot Juliette coming out of her back door, my entire body feels frosted over. Usually, I start running right away and the heat from exercising keeps me warm.

"Sorry!" Juliette calls out as she jogs down her steps.

She's wearing brown leggings, a matching exercise jacket, and a soft pink beanie pulled low over her forehead. She looks adorable and tempting all at once and it steals the breath from my lungs. I'm attempting to regulate my breathing when she finally makes it to where I'm standing.

"I'm sorry I'm late, I woke up this morning and had to fight my inner dragon. She doesn't like running."

I bite the inside of my cheek to keep from laughing. "Inner dragon?" I ask, barely suppressing my laughter.

"Oh, yeah. She's the one I blame for my late-night online purchases and my tendency to want to hole up in a cave during the winter."

"Was she hard to beat?"

Juliette gives a sober nod. "She might still win if we don't hurry and get this over with."

I laugh, incapable of keeping it in. Juliette joins me, her giggles forming white puffs in the dim morning light.

"We better get going then," I say once my laughter subsides. Juliette's grin falls.

"I was really hoping you'd say this was all a joke and invite me up for tea."

I shake my head at her. "A deal's a deal. I had to endure bingo night, you and your inner dragon can make it through this."

Juliette whines but follows after me when I start to jog. I match her pace, which is much slower than my usual, and we settle into a comfortable silence. The only sounds shared between us are our heavy breaths and footfalls. It's ... nice. I always thought running was best alone, but it's not too bad sharing the time with someone else. It feels less lonely than usual.

After the first lap, Juliette stumbles to a stop, bracing her hands on her knees.

"You okay?" I ask her and she shakes her head, her pink beanie falling off to reveal messy blonde hair.

"Running is like dying but without the relief of death." Her words come out stilted in between short, panting breaths.

"That's a disturbing analogy."

"Disturbingly accurate," she huffs, grabbing her beanie off the paved path and straightening to stand. The apples of her cheeks are bright pink and there's a glowy sheen over her face. Even with messy hair and a tired grimace, she looks beautiful.

"You don't feel like your mind is any clearer? More at peace?"

She blinks at me.

"Any semblance of peace I possessed disappeared as soon as we started. I think my lungs are collapsing." She sucks in a breath and I chuckle, earning a glare in return.

"I know it's not fun, but you should have been able to focus on the movement and have your mind quieted."

"Your mind was quiet during that whole time?"

"Pretty much. Yours wasn't?"

"I don't even know what that would feel like." She tilts her head to the side like she's thinking. "But running is definitely *not* the way to get there for me."

"I usually run four laps." I pause when she balks at me. "*But* I guess we could call it quits for today. You held up your end of the bargain."

She smiles like I just told her she won a lifetime supply of her favorite tea. "You're the best, Sunshine," she says and I give her a flat look.

It's all I can do to hold back the smile that threatens to take hold when she calls me that. I should hate it–if anyone else said it I would–but for some reason it brings me this warm feeling whenever I hear it. Having a nickname from Juliette is a solid, real thing that shows I have a place in her life. And while I'm afraid of what having a place might look like in the future, it still feels good to have one.

"Just for that, I think we should run another lap," I smirk and turn like I'm going to run. She grabs my hand to stop me, laughing.

"Please, have mercy on my poor lungs," she begs in a dramatic tone. Her hand is cold in mine, but the touch sends tingles of awareness up my arm.

"Fine, but only because your hand feels like a block of ice."

She looks down at our joined hands as if she didn't realize she was touching me at all. I follow her eyes as well. Maybe I don't have any effect on her. I thought after I caught her staring from her porch that she was attracted to me. It's best that she isn't though. I'm learning how to be her friend right now, I'm nowhere near ready to take a title higher than that one.

When I look up, her cheeks are rosier than before. Our eyes lock and for a breath, we simply stare at each other. Until Juliette clears her throat and slides her hand out of mine.

"Sorry about that, I got a little overexcited." She tucks a stray hair behind her ear, shifting from foot to foot. When I don't say anything, she speaks up again. "Do you want to come up for tea?"

I should say no. I'll be late for work if I agree. But one look into Juliette's forest-green eyes has my reservations melting away like frost in the afternoon sun.

"Sure, that would be nice."

I'm gifted one of her beaming smiles before we start off toward her house.

After a short walk in companionable silence, we arrive back at her house. She slides open her back door, and warm air rushes to greet us like an old friend. As soon as I cross the threshold I feel as though I've stepped into Juliette's mind. Everything is so very *her*. The scent of vanilla and tea leaves in the air, all of the blankets covering her soft cream couch, the antique mirror hanging on the wall. I take in every detail as if it was my assignment, not wanting to miss a thing.

"Make yourself at home," she says as she walks into her kitchen. The layout of our homes is identical and confirming that in person carries a kind of weight I don't quite understand. It shouldn't feel intimate that I know the way to her living room because it's the same amount of steps from the back door as mine is, but it does. I already know where her bedroom is at the end of the hall, too.

I take a seat on her couch and Murphy lifts his head in acknowledgment from the large fluffy bed he was snoring on. There's no TV in the living room; instead, the wall across from the couch is covered in a collage of artwork that I'm sure my sister would appreciate. Next to me on the end table is a stack of books. I study the spines, memorizing the titles. *The Great Gatsby, Pride and Prejudice, Little Women,* and *The Age of Innocence.* All of them classics, all of them thick with tabs and worn from reading.

"I chose vanilla birch black tea. I just got it in so I haven't tried it yet, but it smells amazing." She walks into the living room holding a tray that she sets down on the weathered coffee table before sitting next to me. Teacups with golden handles and sunflowers painted on them sit in the center of the tray next to a matching cream and sugar set. The sight of the sunflowers makes my throat tight.

"I didn't know how you took your tea, so I brought cream and sugar."

I give her a stiff nod, resisting the urge to pull out the sunflower pendant hanging from my neck under my running shirt.

"Is everything okay? You don't have to stay if you're going to be late … or if you're uncomfortable."

The kindness in her voice breaks me.

"My mother loved sunflowers—they were her favorite, actually. She died from cancer over a decade ago, but they always remind me of her." My voice comes out rough from me talking around the lump in my throat.

She lays a hand on my knee, giving me a look with such intense sincerity that the backs of my eyes burn. I haven't cried over my mom in–*never*. The thought hits me like a baseball bat to the stomach. I don't know if I've ever felt this way before. Something in the way Juliette's looking at me makes me feel like she understands exactly how I'm feeling and wouldn't judge me if a tear slipped out.

"I'm sorry, Adrian. Grief is a terrible thing. It can hit you out of nowhere and steal your breath. Do you want me to get a different cup?"

I shake my head. "No, it's fine. It's a good reminder of her, it just caught me off guard." I blink a few times, clearing away the feeling of oncoming tears. "Thank you."

She gives me a gentle smile, removing the warmth of her hand to spoon sugar into one of the cups. I miss her touch as soon as it's gone.

"Of course. If you ever want to talk about her, I'm always here to listen. That's what friends do."

Friends. Right. I swallow down the remaining emotion and pour cream into my tea. There's no reason for me to want anything different with Juliette, but sitting here in her house that feels more like a home than my own makes me question my own reservations. It makes me want to get to know her more.

"What about you?" I ask.

"Hm?"

"Is there anything special that reminds you of your family?"

She tenses up for a moment, but then forces a smile.

"Not really, we're not very close. We should start drinking our tea though before it turns into iced tea." She lets out a nervous laugh.

I watch her tuck her feet under herself before grabbing her tea and taking a sip. She looks innocent, but the way she observes people isn't natural. And now she's being purposefully vague about a simple topic. Something isn't adding up and I worked in the world of secrets for too long not to notice it.

CHAPTER SIXTEEN

Juliette Monroe

"This is a terrible idea." My stomach lurches as I click the bright pink *submit* button at the bottom of the web page. "I can't believe I just did that."

"You are a rockstar!" Caroline cheers through my phone screen, doing a terrible celebration dance in her kitchen. She likes to call while cooking or cleaning or folding laundry, setting me on a stand so her hands are free. It's her way of feeling like I'm there with her in real-time.

"I am pathetic. A Valentine's Day singles' event is for pathetic people, Care." I lay my head on my desk with a groan. "I'm going to be sick."

Caroline found a few different singles' events in the city around Valentine's Day and after a week of hounding me, she finally convinced me to sign up for the least sleazy-sounding one. It's in a hotel ballroom, which already gives me hives just thinking about the awful guys who are likely to buy a room hoping to bring some lonely girl back to it.

"You are not pathetic. You are a beautiful woman making the decision to break out of her shell. I'm so proud of you."

"What if all of the guys are creeps like Kyle?" I lift my head as anxiety shoots down my spine. "What if *Kyle* is there?"

"Then you can leave. This isn't about the event itself, it's about putting yourself out there. You can do this. I believe in you."

"I'm glad one of us does," I mumble. "I wanted to sit on my couch and eat too much salted caramel gelato while watching *Emma* on my laptop."

"You can do that any day of the week. Tomorrow you're going to wear a hot dress, those heels I bought you for your birthday, and you're going to flirt your cute little tush off."

I rub my eyes, wondering if maybe this is all a nightmare and I'll wake up tomorrow, safe and alone in my little cottage. My best friend waits patiently, folding dish towels in silence.

"Okay, I'll see if Poppy will watch Murphy for the evening and I'll go. Maybe it won't be terrible."

"There's my optimistic ray of sunshine," Caroline says with her sarcastic flair.

My mind flits to Adrian when she says sunshine. We haven't had another friendship lesson since last week, or really any extended time together at all. I've been worried if he's pulling away, which is another reason I agreed to this atrocious event. It's not like he's been rude to me though, just too busy to sit and chat in the mornings after his run. Either way, he's not interested in me romantically, so an event like this is my next best route to ending my loneliness.

"Okay, I need to go to the market and hit up Poppy's before it gets too late. I will call you tomorrow when I'm panicking over if my outfit is terrible."

"Looking forward to it." Caroline grins and comes closer to the camera. "Love you, J. You deserve an abundant life, this is just the first step to grabbing it."

"Love you too, Care." I hang up before I'm tempted to tell her that this first step feels far scarier than the potential reward is worth. She'd keep me on the phone for another hour while trying to build me up.

"Okay, Murph," I sigh and ruffle his fur as I stand up from where I was sitting at my desk. "Let's hope that Poppy can take care of you tomorrow night ... or maybe not. We'll let this determine our fate."

Murphy can get a little anxious at night, so I prefer not to go too far for too long without him. Maybe Poppy will say no and then I'll have a valid excuse for Caroline. She'll probably come up with some way for me to still go. I grimace before leaving my home office and heading out the front door.

After a quick trip to the market, I march over to Poppy's, dragging the wagon I use to bring my groceries home behind me. I leave my wagon outside–perks of small-town life–and rush through the door. The bell chime usually sounds like an old friend calling, but today it resembles a funeral toll. Poppy is going to question why I need her to take care of Murphy on Valentine's Day. I'm not ready to admit that I'm heading to a lonely hearts convention.

"Juliette." Adrian's voice makes my head lift. I was so entangled in my own web of thoughts that I didn't see him at the counter.

"Oh, hey," I say, proving that my conversation skills are not ready for an event based on mingling. The sick feeling returns, twisting my stomach into tight knots.

"I was on my way to see you, actually." My eyes widen in surprise when he gives me his signature half-smile. "I got you a croissant."

My eyes search his expression for any clues as to why he would do this. There's no regret in his eyes as if he'd done something wrong, no mischief as if he's toying with me. All I find are soft blue eyes and a hint of affection. I'm probably imagining the affection, though.

"Aw, Sunshine, you shouldn't have." I take the paper bag from him with a smile.

He shrugs. "I thought it would make you smile."

My heart stutters in my chest and I have to bite my lip to suppress a lovestruck grin.

"Thank you, I needed the smile today." When he frowns I realize my mistake. Heat flares in my face, already embarrassed by what's to come.

"What's wrong?"

"Nothing. My friend Caroline just convinced me to do something I don't want to, but it's not a big deal."

His frown deepens. "Friends shouldn't push you into something you don't want to do. Even I know that. So?"

"So what?"

He raises a brow. "What's she making you do?"

I let out a sigh. "You're going to make me tell you, aren't you?" He stays silent, waiting on me to continue. "I signed up for a singles' mixer for tomorrow night." I wince.

Something dark crosses over his expression, but it clears so fast I don't know if it was truly there. He's stoic once more.

"Caroline says it will help me build my confidence even if I don't like it. So, I'm going to go. I just have to find someone to watch over Murphy tomorrow night. I'm hoping that Poppy can, but it's Valentine's Day so she could be busy."

Poppy is currently making a latte behind the counter but judging by the tilt of her head and the smirk on her lips, she's listening to our conversation.

"Do you really not want to go or are you just nervous?" he asks, his eyes not judging, but assessing.

"I'm nervous," I admit, sinking in on myself. "Terrified, actually."

His expression softens. My heart does too.

"Two white peach oolong lattes," Poppy calls out before Adrian can reply. He turns and grabs both of the paper cups, handing me one. A hesitant smile stretches my lips.

"Come on, let me walk you home."

Relief seeps into my bones. I always feel safe when Adrian is around, so I'll get to walk home without paranoia chipping away at the edges of my mind.

"I need to ask Poppy about Murphy," I say, though I want nothing more than to leave.

"I'll watch him tomorrow so you can go."

The offer is a bittersweet one. Half of me is overwhelmed that he would even do that, but the other half is wishing he would have said: *Come over to my house tomorrow night instead. I'll feed you gelato in between kisses.* But this is reality and in reality, Adrian is warming up to friendship, not falling in love with me.

"Thank you," I say to him as he opens the door for me.

"You're welcome. Now, tell me why you're nervous."

He grabs the handle of my wagon before I can and starts to drag it behind him. If he keeps being so nice I'm going to end up blurting out that I like him. And based on how hard it was to become friends, he would *freak out* if I did that. We'd probably never speak again. My heart sinks at the mere thought of losing Adrian's company, even if it's semi-torturous to be around him and be attracted to him.

"I don't have much dating experience, first of all. Or any experience in interacting with men in general. I'm worried I'm going to ramble like I do with you and then all of the guys are going to think I'm awkward and weird."

Confessing that makes my face hot, but Adrian keeps his eyes ahead and his expression neutral. After a beat, the tension releases in my chest. Admitting that out loud felt kind of good. Someone other than Caroline–the one making me do this–knows how I'm feeling.

"I could help you if you want."

"What do you mean?"

"We can have a trial run. That way you're not as nervous for tomorrow."

My stomach has apparently become a gymnast in the last hour because it is doing all sorts of backflips. Just a few minutes ago I was daydreaming about dating Adrian and here he is–offering me that same experience ... more or less.

"Like a practice date?"

"No, not a date." He makes the clarification fast, his voice clipped. "A trial run. Like a mock trial for court."

My romantic heart deflates a little, but not entirely because even if he doesn't want to *call* it a practice date, that doesn't mean that's not what it is. What else could it be?

"Comparing a singles' event to court is oddly accurate, though it does not soothe my anxiety in the slightest." I twist the paper sleeve on my to-go cup.

We pause at the end of my driveway. Adrian stares down at me, the sunset now faded, leaving behind a pale blue light that makes his irises look almost indigo.

"You told me you felt safe with me." His voice is low and it sends goosebumps across my skin.

"I do," I whisper. The moment feels heavy, holding something I can't quite name within it. Everything is quiet, even the ducks Mr. Kipton scolds aren't making a sound.

"Then I'm the perfect person to do this with. I'm not going to judge you. We made a deal when I agreed to those friendship lessons. You wanted me to help you with your confidence. I don't back down on my agreements." He says all this with solid certainty as if he's just stating a fact. But there's an undercurrent of tenderness too that makes me feel secure and cared for.

I pull in a deep breath, then let it out in a *whoosh*. I told myself I'd start taking more risks. What's riskier than a practice date with the guy I have a crush on?

"Okay, I'll do it."

"Put away your groceries and meet me over at my place when you're ready for court." His full lips lift into a teasing grin that stops my heart.

All of this emotion isn't good for me. I'm going to need to see a doctor. After years of nothing but safe and calm, I don't know if my heart can take all of this excitement.

CHAPTER SEVENTEEN

Juliette Monroe

"Don't overthink this, Juliette," I murmur to myself as I shove a box of pasta in my cabinet, only to look up and realize I put it next to my soup bowls. I retrieve it and walk it over to its rightful place.

I'm going to have to reorganize my entire kitchen if I keep this up. Or I'll spend so long putting my groceries away that Adrian will give up on me. I almost hope that happens, because I don't know if I can handle this. My heart is trying to escape my chest and I feel too warm, my skin too tight. Murphy's head lifts at the sound of cereal shaking in the box I'm holding. I set it down, closing my eyes, and focusing on my breathing. *In for four, hold for four, out for four.*

I shouldn't feel this anxious over a practice date, no not even that, a *trial run*, as Adrian so kindly put it. Disappointment accompanied his clarification at first, but now relief swoops in. If he isn't viewing this as a date, then I don't need to either. It's not that I'm afraid of Adrian, I wasn't lying when I said I felt safe with him. I'm more afraid of showing just how inept I am at romance, all the while falling for him like the foolish woman I am.

Even accounting for his gruff nature, I'm certain Adrian has been on his fair share of dates. He's too gorgeous not to have, plus there's the solid confidence he radiates at all times. I'm convinced he's never cared what anyone thought of him his entire life. Meanwhile, I spent my childhood doing only things that would elicit pride in my parents and softening my tone so that I never sounded disagreeable. Having an *attitude* only made things worse in their house.

After a few rounds of measured breaths, my heart rate slows and the shaking in my hands dulls to a gentle tremor. Adrian isn't like my parents, he's not like anyone I've ever met. He said he wouldn't judge me, so I should believe him until he proves otherwise. My lips lift into a faint smile. *Innocent until proven guilty.* If all else fails during the event, at least I'll entertain myself with court comparisons.

With my cold groceries put away, I abandon the pantry items and rush to change. When my anxiety is high, I find being in comfortable clothes helps. Besides, it's not like Adrian hasn't seen me in pajamas before. He's seen half my pajama drawer at this point. My skin flushes with heat at the thought. It's strange that he's seen me so vulnerable, even coming inside my house.

All of our boundaries are drawn in strange overlapping circles instead of one hard line. He's had tea in my house, seen me in my pajamas, bought me things, and we've even–sort of–held hands. But we're placed firmly in the friend category still. Though, I suppose only the hand-holding would bring us out of the friendzone. I'm probably confusing myself more than our situation warrants, but this is what I do best. Overthink until I spiral.

I blow out a sigh as I tug on my most-loved sweatshirt. It's from California–as the bold letters across the front suggest–a gift from Caroline. She sent it to me in a care package years ago filled with teas from my favorite local shops over there. It had been hard to give up the comfort of familiarity for the necessity of freedom. I think Caroline knew that, so she sent me something from home to help balance out those warring emotions.

After changing into leggings and pushing my feet into my moccasin slippers, I stop in front of Murphy.

"We should probably take you over to Adrian's so you get used to where you're going to stay tomorrow night," I tell him. He looks up at me with lazy eyes. "Come on, let's go outside." This changes his tune fast. He hops up, wagging his fluffy golden tail.

We walk out the front door together and cross the yard to Adrian's front porch. My anxiety rears its head again, making it hard to knock properly on the door with my shaking hands.

Adrian opens the door and suddenly I regret my choice of attire. He's still in his clothes from earlier–a grey suit with a white button down underneath. The only thing he changed was the removal of his tie and an undoing of the top two buttons of his shirt. My mouth goes dry. He looks like a debonair spy, while I look like the girl in the romance movie who's given up after being broken up with.

"I feel underdressed," I say and his eyes rove over me. His assessment is cut short though when his eyes catch on Murphy. "I thought it would be good for him to get acquainted with your house before tomorrow. If that's okay?"

"Of course, come in." His tone is all business, reminiscent of when we first met. The teasing warmth from just minutes ago has left his expression. I follow after him, wanting to indulge my curiosity about his home but end up studying his body language instead.

I don't know what kind of training he's been through, but the man is good at concealing his emotions. He's not perfect though, which helps me decipher him. His movements are a tad too stilted and when he sits down, he doesn't look comfortable at all. One of his arms is draped over the back of his couch, but it's stiff instead of relaxed. *He's nervous too.* That knowledge helps ease some of my own torturous thoughts. If this awkwardness isn't one-sided then maybe I won't descend into total embarrassment by the end of it.

"You can sit down," he says.

"Right." I sit down in an abrupt manner, leaving a cushion of separation between us. Murphy investigates the living room with his nose, the soft sound of his sniffing the only thing breaking our silence.

I let my eyes follow Murphy, investigating along with him. Everything in his home is beautiful and well-crafted. All of the furniture is carved out of dark wood that feels masculine, but there are ornate touches of design that balance out the harshness. There's a TV hanging above a bookshelf. I study the spines, my eyes catching on a few familiar titles of classics I know and love. The rest have titles that lend to mystery or suspense–something I stay away from.

The kitchen light is on, illuminating the gorgeous apothecary cabinet I saw him and Grayson carry in. On top of it are a collection of white diner-style mugs and an expensive-looking electric kettle. He uses the cabinet as tea storage, that's brilliant. I have the urge to go open every single drawer.

Adrian clears his throat, dragging my attention back to him, but not before I notice the plant I gifted him sitting in his windowsill. It looks bright and green, so he must take care of it.

"Sorry," I blurt and tuck one of my legs underneath me in an effort to relax. A burgundy blanket falls off the back of the couch into my lap, wafting a sultry scent of amber and spices.

"I've been curious about your house so I was taking it all in," I admit. It would be wonderful if I could learn how to filter myself around this man. Next I'm going to blurt out that I dreamt of kissing him.

"What do you think of it?" he asks, nothing in his tone betraying what he might be feeling.

I scan the space once more. "It's very ... you." He huffs out something reminiscent of a chuckle.

"What?"

"Nothing." He pauses, but before I have time to demand he elaborate, he speaks up again. "Does this event you're going to have a structure?"

Prickles of anxiety dance across my skin. The event is the reason I'm here, but I'd much rather snuggle up under this delicious-smelling blanket and read the copy of *Emma* I saw on Adrian's shelf. What does it say about him that he owns multiple Jane Austen novels? Is he secretly a romantic? Are they just for show?

"Juliette." The velvety way he says my name pulls me out of my thought whirlpool.

"Sorry, just nervous."

"New rule: don't apologize so much. It's okay to be nervous."

"Sorry," I say again and then cringe. The look he gives me is soft though, easing the pain that usually comes when I mess up around someone else.

"It's okay."

After a beat of silence, I answer his initial question. "There's not really a structure. You check in, get a name tag, then wander around the hotel ballroom *mingling*." I can't help but twist up my face on the last word.

"Okay, then we can just practice conversation."

I toy with the blanket in my lap, trying to go through my breathing exercises in a manner that doesn't alert him to something being wrong.

"I genuinely don't know what to say if a guy were to approach me." The blood rushes out of my face as a realization occurs. "What if *no one* approaches me? That would be so embarrassing. I can't do this."

I cradle my face in my hands, all too aware of the rising tension in my chest. I haven't had a panic attack in months, so it figures one would come up in front of Adrian. As if the man didn't have enough reason to distance himself from me.

My mouth goes dry and I can't manage to suck in a full breath. Tremors begin to shake my hands. I worry that the feeling will spread to my whole body soon if I can't get myself under control. But thinking about controlling my anxiety only serves to make me *more* anxious.

Suddenly, warm fingers are around my wrist and light fills my eyes once more as Adrian tugs my hands away from my face. He's closed the distance between us and is staring me down with a tenderness that yanks the breath out of my lungs. This isn't exactly helpful considering my heart is beating so fast I can hear it in my ears. I should probably breathe, but my thoughts are rushing so fast that I can't recall *how*.

"Name five things you can see," he says in a tone that leaves no room for rebellion. I blink at him.

"Your eyes," I murmur and he gives an encouraging nod. He's *so close* to me. I have to turn my head away to be able to name anything else. "Murphy, your apothecary cabinet, my plant, a white mug. I-is that five?"

"Yes, good job. Now name five things you can hear."

"Murphy's snores," I say and strain my ears for something more. Panic inflates in my chest once more. "I can't–"

Adrian cuts me off, rubbing circles on the inside of my wrists.

"Shhh it's okay, I shouldn't have gone with that one. Too quiet here. Name five things you can feel."

I suck in a shuddery breath.

"The couch cushion, the blanket, my sweater, my socks ..." I meet his eyes as the tension eases some. "Your hands."

The pattern of circles stutters for a moment before he continues. I focus on the navy rim around his cool blue irises and the comfort of his touch. My breathing returns to normal and my muscles relax.

"I'm okay," I whisper, but his hands don't leave my wrists and his eyes are still on me. "Thank you. I can usually just breathe through it, but it didn't work tonight. That's a good trick."

"I learned it to help someone I care about," he says, not elaborating on who. "I'm glad it helped. You don't have to go to this event tomorrow if it causes this much stress, Juliette."

There's a wrinkle between his brows that makes my lips tip up. He's concerned for me.

"I just got a little overwhelmed. I think if I can practice some I'll have gotten over the worst of my anxiety."

"If you're certain." He looks like he wants to say more–probably tell me not to go–but he doesn't. It's sweet that he's concerned, but mere concern isn't going to keep me from going. If he were to lean down and kiss me, however ...

My eyes flick down to his lips, then back up to his eyes. There's a chance my senses are dulled from all of the stress, but I swear his eyes drop to my lips too. I'm pretty sure that's the *kiss me* cue. Except, no kiss occurs.

Adrian lets go of my wrists and scoots backward while clearing his throat.

"So, do you want to practice what to say when a guy comes up to you?" he asks, not really looking at me, more above me.

"Yeah, that sounds good."

Not really, though. I know that tomorrow night–even if it's not terrible–is going to be spent thinking of Adrian's strong hands circling my wrists. Wondering what it would be like if he wouldn't have let go and had kissed me instead. Imagining what it would be like to spend a Valentine's Day with a man who buys me my favorite dessert and knows how to bring me down from a panic attack.

Yes, even if tomorrow isn't a tornado of awkward, it's going to be torturous nonetheless because Adrian won't be by my side. And I've come to like it far too much when he is.

"I do not need to know how to leverage a guy's weight to *body slam* him. This is a singles' event, not an MMA tournament." My head falls back laughing, Adrian's chuckles intermingling with the sound like a perfect harmony.

"You never know when you'll need to defend yourself," he says through his laughter.

We've spent the past hour going over various small talk options. So far I've learned that we both hate small talk and I'd much rather sit with him and drink tea than be anywhere else. But I do feel more confident about tomorrow, so that's something.

"Now every time a guy comes up to me I'm going to think of this conversation and end up in hysterics. I'll scare everyone away."

"You couldn't scare anyone away, which is why you need to know self-defense."

Even though he's teasing me, the mirth in his usually gruff voice makes me feel like a cloud or a swirl of cotton candy, all light and fluffy. I hated going through my panic attack in front of him, but I feel as though that moment shifted something between us. Before it, our relationship was a rock, all rough around the edges, but now it's been cracked open to reveal a sparkling geode.

"I do know self-defense, thank you very much," I say and bask in the glow of the impressed look he gives me.

"Good. If anyone lays so much as a finger on you and you didn't welcome that touch, I expect you to break something of theirs."

I fall into giggles again. "That's a bit extreme. Just a touch?" Maybe it's the dim light of his cottage or the aftermath of all we've gone through, but boldness overcomes me and I reach out and brush a fingertip along his exposed forearm. Around thirty minutes ago he shed his suit jacket and rolled up the sleeves of his white dress shirt.

I've been dying to touch him since (okay, before that too, but no one needs to know that).

"Is that really so reprehensible?" I ask, my voice coming out soft when I notice his eyes darken.

"Anything you don't want is worthy of punishment. You deserve respect." His words come out gravelly and rough, those deep blue eyes boring into mine.

"That's kind of you to say."

"It's not kindness, it's basic human decency." His words snap me out of the romantic haze I was enjoying. He's right, but it brings back flashes of painful memories where I wasn't treated with respect at all.

"Is there a nice way to shut a guy down before that happens? I can usually tell if they're sleazy pretty fast."

"Who cares about being nice? If they're a jerk then just tell them you're not interested and walk away."

I roll my eyes. "I don't want to be rude, *Sunshine*," I say with a pointed look. "Your not-caring-what-people-think attitude isn't always the best. I'll have to ask Caroline what she would do."

"Yes, ask the woman who encouraged you to sign up for a dating app and attend a mixer on *Valentine's Day*, of all the awful days." He shoots me an apologetic look. "Sorry, I'm breaking a friendship rule I guess."

I bite my lip to hold in a smile, shaking my head. "You already broke it when you offered to help me with this. It's okay, I know this is all kinds of pathetic. There's just not a good way to meet people." I sigh, resting my head on the back of his couch and watching him. He takes a sip of the chamomile tea he made for us to help soothe my nerves, his throat bobbing as he swallows. "I wish I lived in the Regency era. I could lock eyes with a gentleman across a real ballroom, not a carpeted hotel one."

"I'm sure you'll have a nice time. Maybe it'll be more like an Austen novel than you think."

Murphy makes a groaning noise as he stretches nearby. His movement is the excuse I need to leave. If I stay any longer I'll end up confessing feelings that I don't think Adrian is ready to hear, ruining the one friendship I've managed to forge since moving to Georgia.

"I hope you're right. I should probably head home, can I bring Murphy by around seven tomorrow?"

"Sure, that sounds good." His eyes rove over me as I stretch my arms above my head. Heat flushes my skin.

"Thanks for helping me, Adrian."

"It was no big deal."

Except it was, in more ways than one. I think I'm beginning to trust Adrian, which means this innocent little crush is blossoming quickly into something I've never had. The urge to guard my heart from any pain is fierce, but I also don't want to regret never opening myself up. Maybe falling for Adrian is going to get me hurt, but at least the scar on my heart will be one I chose instead of one someone foisted upon me. If it all goes down in flames, I'll know I walked into the fire willingly. That choice alone is more than I've ever been given in life.

CHAPTER EIGHTEEN

Adrian Carter

Grayson: When's your next date with Juliette? Are you taking her out for Valentine's Day tonight?

I glare at my phone. On today of all days, I can't handle my siblings messing with me about Juliette.

Maverick: NEXT date? Does that mean there was a first?

Adrian: No.

Grayson: Yes

I rake a hand through my hair and sigh.

Adrian: Bingo night with a bunch of elderly people is not a date.

MJ: No, definitely not.

Grayson: Anything can be a date if you kiss at the end.

I stare at my screen, contemplating blocking my twin.

MJ: I don't think that's true...

Grayson: What sad dating lives y'all must have.

Maverick: I'm worried on behalf of all the women you date if your only requirement is that you kiss at the end.

Grayson: You don't have to worry. The women I date are always happy ;)

I'm about to respond when I hear Juliette cooing to Murphy outside. My stomach twists. Why did I agree to this? I run a hand through my hair again. There's no lying to myself about my attraction to her, but I know that I'm not ready for a relationship. Juliette deserves lifelong commitment, someone to protect her and cherish her. I haven't had what could be classified as a serious relationship in years. Not to mention the fact that she's keeping secrets, I'm sure of it. I made myself a promise when I left the agency that I wouldn't trust as easily as I did before. The bitter taste of betrayal still lingers in the back of my throat.

Adrian: There haven't been and won't be any dates. No more talk about my dating life.

I silence the group chat and tuck my phone into my pocket as a knock sounds at the door. I need to get it together. Juliette is too observant for her own good and the last thing I need is for her to notice something she shouldn't.

I open my door and all of the air is sucked out of my body–along with any common sense. Juliette is *stunning*. Desire smothers the logical part of my brain with alarming ease. A dress made of burgundy crushed velvet clings to her body, fanning out from the waist and stopping at a spot that my eyes keep returning to. Her legs are lengthened by the heeled boots she's wearing and covered by sheer black tights that still reveal the creamy skin beneath.

"Adrian?" My name draws my attention to the lips that said it, the ones wet with some kind of gloss and stained a color that reminds me of mulled wine. Would they taste the way they look? Heat flares in my chest and climbs up my neck. I have to clear my throat twice before I manage to form words.

"You're early," I rasp out, trying to save my delay. "I wasn't expecting you yet."

She looks at me like she doesn't quite believe me, one of her brows raising slightly over her expressive jade eyes.

"I'm a little antsy," she explains with a nervous laugh.

"That's understandable." I pause, finally noticing the bag she's carrying and Murphy by her side. "Come in, you can get him settled and then be on your way."

She brushes past me, the scent of cinnamon and vanilla following her, tempting me further.

"He's pretty low maintenance," she says, setting the tote bag on my kitchen counter.

She moves around with a familiarity that feels too intimate. It reminds me of her last night, her in her oversized sweatshirt, snuggling on my couch and running her fingertips over my arm. The playful glint in her eyes after the raw vulnerability she shared just moments before almost broke me. I was tempted to draw her into my lap and kiss her until she forgot about any ridiculous singles' event.

"His food is in this bag, he'll need to have dinner in an hour or so. His collar and leash are in there too if you want to take him on a walk. Otherwise, you can just let him walk around my backyard area. He shouldn't run off, he's well-behaved."

I nod, pretending that I haven't been imagining kissing her.

"Do you want to exchange numbers?" I ask. "In case there's an emergency for either of us."

"Sure, that would be great," she says with a smile and pulls out her phone.

She rattles off her phone number and for a reason I can't–or maybe don't want to–name, I enter her into my phone as *Jules*. I send her a text in response so she has my number. I think she's the only woman I'm not related to in my contact list.

"I should probably get going. I don't know what the parking is going to be like in the city."

A faint smile stretches my lips when she calls Atlanta *the city*. I haven't started calling it that yet, but it's entirely too adorable when she does. I force my face into something more neutral. I shouldn't be thinking of her as adorable or beautiful or *anything*.

"Okay, text me when you get there so I know you're safe." The words come out without thinking. I'd tell MJ the same thing, even my brothers if I thought they were going somewhere potentially unsafe.

Juliette gives me a warm smile. "Thanks for all this, Sunshine. I'll text you."

She tells Murphy bye as if he were a person and not a dog, then heads for the door.

"Have fun," I say to her back, then cringe. *What is wrong with me?* Something about this whole situation has me floundering.

"Thanks, I hope I do," she says, laughter hiding in her tone. Quiet settles over the cottage once she's gone.

My stomach sinks like a rock to the bottom of a lake. Trying to ignore it, I open up the bag she sent for Murphy to see if she gave him a bowl or if I need to find one for him to eat out of.

When I open the bag, pink cellophane glints in the light. A small package of tea bags and what looks to be biscotti greets me, with an envelope labeled *Sunshine* in elegant script attached to it by way of curly red ribbon.

Dear Sunshine,

Thank you for taking care of Murphy tonight, and for taking care of me last night too. It's not easy for me to open up to others, but you're helping me with that whether you've realized it or not. I'm happy you moved in next door. You're way better than Darren (though I guess it's not his fault he can't have chocolate, but he could have told me in a nicer way). Anyway, you're a good friend and I'm grateful to have met you.

Happy Valentine's Day,

Juliette

Nerves skate down my spine. Not from the letter though. No, it's the wide smile I feel on my lips that makes my anxiety flare. I shouldn't be smiling so much over a little gift like this, but here I am, grinning like a fool at the letter in my hands. At least no one but Murphy is here to see it.

After an hour and a half of cleaning my already clean house and trying not to picture Juliette giggling next to another man, I set Murphy's bowl down to feed him. Once he's happily crunching the food Juliette left for him, my phone starts to buzz on my kitchen counter.

Grayson's name and face light up my screen, making me frown. It's Valentine's Day, Grayson should be out eating fondue with some random woman he met, not calling me. I answer the call, worry pricking at my conscience.

"Hello brother dearest," he says in a way that sounds like he's pulling a prank on me.

"What?" I bark out, not wanting to deal with his games. He tortured me enough through the group text. Plus, I'm already going to spend most of my evening worrying about Juliette—even if she did text me that she was safe and sound at the hotel—I don't need to add Grayson's antics into the mix.

"I'm just wondering why your cute neighbor is sitting at the bar on Valentine's Day instead of with you."

My brows scrunch together. "Why are you at a singles' mixer? You always have a date for Valentine's Day."

"You know our in-house accountant, Jeremy? He told me he was nervous about coming tonight so I offered to be his wing man. And he needs my help big time, there's probably ten guys to every girl in here. So, I'm trying to set some conversations up for him."

"That's decent of you," I grumble and he laughs.

The image of Juliette in a room full of mostly men is a serrated knife on the thread of my last nerve. I should have told her not to go.

"I try. Circling back to Juliette, though. Why have you not asked her out yet?"

"What if I have and she said no?"

"We share the same face, there's no way she said no." If he was in front of me right now, I'd hit him.

"Is she okay?"

"She's a lamb in a pack of wolves, but she seems to be holding her own."

"I'm going to need more than that. What's her body language?"

"If you care so much, why don't you come down here and find out?"

"I'm watching her dog," I say through gritted teeth and he laughs out loud. The sound pierces my eardrum and I'm regretting not investing in that punching bag for my spare room.

"Let me get this straight, you're at home watching the woman you like's dog on *Valentine's Day* while she's chatting up strangers at a mixer."

"You can make fun of me later–"

"Oh, I will. This is going in the group chat too."

"Just please tell me if she's okay. She fiddles with things when she's really nervous, but sometimes if her gaze is flicking around the room that's a sign she's looking for an escape but is likely trying to be polite."

I don't care if I just gave away how much I've been watching her, I need to know she's not sitting in discomfort for the sake of being cordial.

"She's fiddling with her straw. The guy she's talking to looks like a wannabe hotshot with too much hair gel and not enough respect for personal space."

I grip the counter in front of me, holding myself in place to keep from going after her. Crossing that boundary wouldn't be good, and there's still Murphy to think about. I have no idea how he'd fare in my house or the back of my car.

"Can you please watch out for her? I should have told her not to go, but her best friend convinced her it would be a good idea."

"Sure, I got her. I'll fend off the worst of them."

"If I had to bet, no guy in there deserves Juliette."

"I'm hurt on behalf of myself and Jeremy."

"If you wanted to date Juliette you would have already and Jeremy cowers every time I walk past his cubicle. Juliette needs someone who can protect her."

"Both fair points, though what I still don't understand is why you aren't here growling at anyone who so much as glances in her general direction or better yet, reading to her by a fire or whatever your idea of romance is. I wouldn't know, since you never date anyone."

I sigh, swiping a hand over my face. "Please just go over there and save her from her own politeness. You can hound me about my dating life at the next family event, I won't even put you in a headlock for it."

"Wow, you must really care about her."

I do, too much.

"She's my friend."

"I hear friendship makes a great foundation for marriage."

CHAPTER NINETEEN

Juliette Monroe

"I'd love to take you out on my yacht sometime. I bet you'd look great in a bikini," Reece–the guy I'm about to run away from–says with a smirk.

I open my mouth to politely excuse myself and speed away as fast as my little black booties will take me when a large hand comes down on Reece's shoulder. My eyes follow the arm attached to that hand all the way up to a very familiar face. For a split second my stomach swoops, thinking Adrian came to be my knight in shining armor, but then I realize it's actually Grayson.

"I think your time is up," Grayson says to Reece with an easygoing grin that doesn't match the way his fingers are digging into Reece's shoulder.

"This isn't a timed thing," Reece chuckles, but when he sees Grayson's grin transform into a look of warning, he scampers off toward a blonde in the middle of the ballroom.

Grayson takes Reece's place on the barstool next to me, lounging against the counter in a way that resembles a cat–but not a housecat, more like one of those big jungle cats that could eat you in a few bites. I knew Grayson worked with Adrian in private security, but I guess I didn't realize he'd have the same dangerous edge as Adrian, since he has the personality of a golden retriever. I'm glad they choose to use that edge for good.

"Thank you," I sigh while stirring my watered down coke. They didn't have any tea here, unfortunately. "I was about to escape, but you made it easier on me."

"You've been dodging guys left and right for a while. I figured I'd give you a break." Grayson's lighthearted nature soothes my anxiety and I find myself smiling in spite of how terrible tonight has been so far.

"I didn't take you for a guy who comes to singles' events," I say, hoping I don't come off rude. It's just that there's no way a man who looks like him and has the confidence he oozes has trouble getting a date on Valentine's Day–or any day for that matter. But maybe he's less self-assured than our previous interactions would lead me to believe.

"I'm playing wing man tonight," he replies and gestures toward a guy talking to a woman a few feet away. The guy keeps adjusting his glasses and shifting on his feet as he talks to her, but she doesn't seem put off by his lack of confidence. They make a sweet couple.

"That's nice of you. Your girlfriend isn't sad you're missing out on Valentine's Day?" I ask and he grins, that feline nature coming back into play.

"I thought you had a crush on my brother, but now you're flirting with me?"

My eyes get big and I blink a few times, trying to understand where I went wrong. "N-no I don't- I wasn't–"

He cuts me off with a wave of his hand, laughing. "I'm messing with you, Juliette. The way you phrased your question sounded like you were fishing to see if I was single."

My cheeks heat and I shake my head. "I just figured you probably had a girlfriend. I didn't mean it like that."

"If you weren't my brother's girl, I'd tease you a lot more, but I'll have mercy on you for his sake." He winks and I laugh.

"I'm not anyone's girl, hence why I'm here." I gesture toward the room with a grimace.

"Even if that's true, you don't need to be in a place like this."

I look out at the various attendees scattered about the ballroom. It's mostly men here, which I thought was good at first because it gave me more options, but now I realize it's just more opportunities to be creeped out. The whole place reeks of desperation and bad buffet food.

"This isn't what I imagined my love life would look like," I admit. "But I live in a community of mostly elderly people and I work from home, so there's not a good way for me to meet people."

"You met my brother. I know he acts like a grumpy old man, but he's only thirty."

I smile at Grayson's joke. "Your brother and I are *friends*."

"Adrian doesn't have friends."

"I know, I volunteered to be the first one." I keep my tone light, but deep down my heart squeezes for the stoic man who lives next door. At least he has his family, that's more than I can say. Somehow, his loneliness bothers me more than my own.

"Well, could you take one for the team and be his girlfriend too?"

I shoot Grayson a flat look that has him laughing. "There are two sides to a relationship. Your brother has to be willing, too."

"Ah, so that's how it is, you're waiting on him."

I shrug, avoiding his sparkling blue eyes. While Grayson is nice, looking at him only makes me wish I was with Adrian. Grayson's charisma and openness is fun to be around, but there's something about the thrill of winning a smile from Adrian that feels better than the ones Grayson freely gives everyone.

He makes a contemplative noise, drawing my attention back to him. One of his hands drags through his hair and he bites his lip like he's considering something, then he shrugs.

"He might get mad at me for telling you this, but Adrian told me to check on you." I almost knock over my drink in shock. "I called to bug him about you being here and he went into protective caveman mode. He almost sounded like he wanted to drive down here himself."

"Seriously?" I squeak out. My thoughts are racing too fast for me to grab onto any of them.

"Yeah, he told me to make sure you were okay and no guys were taking advantage of your kindness."

My heart warms like hands around a hot mug of tea. It's hard to keep my feet on the ground after hearing that, even though it could just be him being protective over me like a friend.

"Is he naturally protective?"

Grayson eyes me, considering. "Only over people he really cares about."

"So it's not a side effect of his job, then?"

"That might play a factor, but it's certainly not the main one."

"Okay, he cares about me. But is he attracted to me as more than a friend?"

He gives me a look like it's obvious, making me blush.

"Then why won't he make a move?" I ask.

Grayson drums his fingers on the bar counter as he studies me. "It's not my story to tell," he finally answers.

"There *is* a story though?" I pry, not able to stop myself. "It's not about me, then," I whisper to myself and then stiffen when I realize I said it aloud.

"No," Grayson says and my brows furrow. But then I realize his eyes are fixed over my shoulder. I glance behind me to find a guy stomping away.

"You can't scare *everyone* off."

"I've seen him around. He's ... handsy."

I shudder. "I think I might be ready to go home." I pull out my phone to check the time and my heart skips when I see that I have messages from Adrian.

Sunshine: I think he likes me.

Attached to his text is a photo of Murphy next to him on the couch. He has his arm slung around Murphy and there's a faint smile on his lips. As if I wasn't already hopelessly falling for him, he has to go and win over my dog too. Not that Murphy is difficult to win over or anything, but still. It's hard to beat the image of a beautiful man snuggling a puppy. Can I make this my lock screen without anyone noticing?

"I can walk you to your car," Grayson offers and I snap my head up.

I briefly consider showing him Adrian's photo for fun, but some part of me wants to keep it between us, even if Grayson seems to be supportive of us becoming more than friends.

"That would be great, thanks, Grayson."

We walk in amiable silence through the parking garage to my little silver Mazda. It's held up over the years, but it's nothing compared to Adrian's sleek sports car. I'm assuming Grayson drives something similar.

"Drive safe," Grayson says as I unlock my car. "Be sure to push all of Adrian's buttons and give him a hard time about everything for me."

I laugh, the sound echoing through the concrete garage.

"Will do. Thanks again, Grayson."

I slide into my front seat and close the door. Grayson walks in the direction of the hotel. I buckle my seatbelt and start my car. Right as I'm about to respond to Adrian's text, a tap on my windshield makes me jump. Grayson smiles at me as I roll down my window.

"Hey, sorry if I scared you." He shifts from one foot to the other, looking nervous for the first time since I've met him. "I just wanted to say, don't give up on Adrian." He cringes as if he regrets his words. "I mean, if he's being a jerk you don't have to stick around–" His hair falls in front of his eyes after he rakes his hand through it. "You know what? Forget I said anything. Have a nice night."

He taps the top of my car and turns on his heel, walking away at a pace too fast to be relaxed. I roll my window back up, not sure what just happened. Shaking my head, I turn my attention back to my phone.

Juliette: You two look like you've had a better night than me. I'm heading back now, see you soon.

Adrian's reply comes instantly.

Sunshine: I'll make some tea and you can tell me about it. Be safe.

Juliette: I will! Thanks, you're the best.

I bite my lip as I press send. Maybe my Valentine's Day won't be so bad after all.

CHAPTER TWENTY

Adrian Carter

I keep my steps light as I walk around my kitchen. Rays of morning sun filter in through my back door and windows, creating a soft halo on a certain head of blonde hair resting on one of my throw pillows.

Juliette stayed on my couch last night. She got in from the event late and after two cups of chamomile tea and a relay of her night, she dozed off while I was telling her how Murphy chased a duck on our walk. I didn't have it in me to move her, even though I should have. So, I went to bed and stared at the ceiling most of the night, unable to fall asleep knowing Juliette was in the other room.

Eventually, my body gave in and I got a couple hours of sleep. Now I'm up and have no idea what to do. Murphy is dozing on the rug nearby, not helping me by waking her up to go out. I walk over to her, trying to think of a way to wake her that won't feel incredibly awkward. Not that I have any reason to feel weird, but I know Juliette well enough by now to know that she'll open her eyes and start apologizing.

Her honey-colored hair is splayed out across the rust-colored throw pillow, the curls from last night loose and wild. The blanket I laid over her is tucked under her chin and her lips are parted, still stained that sweet berry color. She looks ethereal in the hazy glow of the morning. I want to let her stay here all day in this peaceful state, but I know the longer she sleeps, the more apologetic she'll be when she wakes up. I can't stand the thought of her feeling like an inconvenience, which is why I'm taking far too long to consider my way of waking her.

I reach out to touch her shoulder when there's a knock at the door. Juliette stirs, but her eyes don't open. My socks brush the hardwood floor as I pass a still dozing Murphy. He's not much of a guard dog, that's for sure.

I swing open the door and my stomach drops. Grayson and Levi are waiting for me on my front porch. I immediately step out and close the door behind me, hoping they didn't see Murphy or Juliette in the seconds the door was open.

"What are you doing here?"

"We're here to take you to the cookout," Grayson answers. I can feel Levi analyzing me, likely wondering why I stepped outside so fast. But as long as I can get them out of here before they start asking too many questions I'll be in the clear.

"I have a car, I can drive."

"When you drive, you also leave early," Grayson says and I give him a flat look.

"That's the point."

My family takes cookout days quite seriously. They spend the entire day there together eating, playing games, watching whatever sport is in season. I prefer to drive later in the day closer to the time to eat and then leave whenever I'm tired of being around people. That usually doesn't take very long.

"Yeah well you've been avoiding everyone so we've been sent to make sure you stay longer than an hour," Levi says.

I cross my arms over my chest and glower at them. "I haven't avoided anyone. I'm going to go by myself and leave when I want."

Grayson heaves a sigh, but there's a grin on his face. "Guess that means we have to use force."

"Guess so," Levi smirks.

I try to take a step back to brace myself, but there's nowhere for me to go since my back is to the door. My foot catches on the lip of the doorframe. Grayson lunges at me, trying to grab my shoulders first. I'm attempting to fight him off when Levi knocks my legs out from under me, lifting them off the ground while Grayson is holding my upper body. I swing my arm around Grayson and pull him into a headlock while twisting and kicking at Levi to get him to let go of my legs.

"This is absurd," I grit out and squeeze Grayson's neck tighter.

Levi is laughing like we're all back in grade school, while Grayson is wheezing in my ear. All the commotion almost makes me miss the door opening. We all freeze in place when a gasp sounds and I tilt my head to find Juliette standing in my doorway with disheveled hair and wide eyes.

"Nice to see you again, Juliette," Grayson rasps. I loosen the headlock a little so he can breathe better, but make sure I keep what little advantage I have.

Levi nods to her. "Juliette, didn't expect to find you here."

Her skin flushes red from her neck up. It's clear what this looks like. This is the worst possible way for Juliette to wake up.

My brothers look at me then back to her. I use the distraction of her presence to kick out of Levi's grip. Once I have my feet under me, I keep Grayson in the headlock.

"You look lovely this morning," Grayson pants, his voice somehow still laced with humor as he gazes up at her in a headlock.

Juliette seems stuck, her mouth opening and closing like she doesn't know what to say.

"She fell asleep on my couch last night," I explain for her, knowing that she's probably in shock.

"Sounds like a plausible explanation." Levi's voice is a little too teasing for my liking. I shoot him a look that shows my distaste.

"I'm going to go now before I pass out from embarrassment," Juliette finally speaks and Grayson laughs. I tighten my grip, cutting off his laughter.

She bolts across the lawn, Murphy on her heels.

"I feel like every time I've seen her she's running away," Levi–unhelpfully–comments. "Do you think it's us?"

"I think it's Adrian," Grayson rasps.

"It's definitely you two," I growl, letting go of Grayson and pushing him away from me. "Stay," I order then go after Juliette.

My socks are wet and freezing as I cross the damp grass and I add it to the list of things to be angry at my brothers about.

"Juliette, wait," I say as she starts to unlock her door. I step close to her, blocking her from my brothers' sight with my body. She smells like vanilla and chamomile and even though they're bleary, her green eyes are captivating.

"I'm so sorry, Adrian. I didn't mean to fall asleep and now your brothers think we–" she cuts herself off, squeezing her eyes shut. "I'm *mortified*," she whispers.

My fingers twitch with the desire to draw her in, to attempt to soothe her. I shouldn't do anything of the sort, especially with my brothers watching, but my protective instincts win out. I tug her into my arms and rub her back over the soft velvet of her dress. She immediately wraps her arms around my waist and I feel the tension slowly dissipate from her body. My chest warms with the knowledge that my touch did that. It's a heady feeling I want to bask in.

"You don't have anything to be embarrassed about. They take me at my word, but even if they didn't, you don't need to care about anyone else's opinions."

She tilts her head back to look up at me while in my arms. I can't remember the last time I've been this close to a woman–can't remember the last time I wanted to be either. But after we separate I know I'm going to begin to crave this. I should pull away now, try to minimize the damage, but I don't. Instead, I calculate every detail of her facial expression and the way her soft body feels wrapped up in my arms. I note every sensation and file it away in the most important cabinet of my mind, so it's easy to find and reminisce if this all goes down in flames.

"I'm not like you, I can't turn off the part of my brain that cares what people think. Ten years from now when I can't sleep, I'm going to remember this moment in vivid detail and replay it over and over again until I'm nauseous."

"If you're going to replay this moment, then let's change the ending." My voice comes out unexpectedly gruff.

Her gaze flicks down to my lips then back up to my eyes. Heat washes over me and I consider throwing caution to the wind and kissing her, but I can't. She deserves more than an impulsive kiss, but I don't know that I can open up enough to give her what she deserves.

"How do you suggest we do that?" Her low, silky voice sends a tingle down my spine and a deep ache forms within me. The kind of ache that tells me I'm already in too deep.

"Come with me to my family's cookout."

She blinks up at me, tilting her head to the side in confusion. "What?"

"Grayson and Levi are here to get me, but I'll tell them to leave and we can go together. You can meet my sister and her family and spend the day with us."

"As much as I'd like to meet them, how is that going to help me with my embarrassment? I don't want to see your brothers again for a *long* time. Long enough for them to forget that situation ... or the fact that they ever met me."

I chuckle. "Think of it as another confidence lesson. I'll help you see that it doesn't matter what anyone else thinks in a relaxed setting."

"I'll have to change."

She looks down, drawing my attention to her curve-hugging dress ... and the fact that we're still pressed together. We both take a step back at the same time. She smooths her dress skirt and avoids my eyes.

"Take your time. I'm going to kick my brothers out and whenever you're ready we can head over."

"Okay," she says in a quiet voice.

"It's going to be okay, Juliette," I tell her and she musters a soft smile. "If anyone says anything you don't like, I'll hit them. Unless it's a woman, then we'll have a stern talk."

She giggles at my words and nods. "Okay, I'll see you in a little bit."

I wait for the door to close behind her and Murphy before storming across our shared lawn to where my brothers are waiting with Cheshire cat grins on their faces.

"Now, wasn't that a fun surprise?" Levi asks, leaning against the front door.

"If either of you mention this to anyone–*including* Juliette–I will punch you in the stomach so hard you won't even want to eat whatever dessert Maverick makes."

"I thought Grayson was exaggerating when he talked about you being gone for this girl, but you really are."

"She's a *woman* not a girl, and I'm not gone for her, she's my friend." I cross my arms over my chest again. "I'm bringing her to the cookout, so I'll be driving. You can leave."

"That's even better than us taking you. Everyone is going to go crazy that you brought a *woman* home," Levi says with a grin.

I glare at him and try to take deep breaths through my nose, feeling on the edge of raging like a bull.

"Come on, Levi. Let's go before he starts swinging."

"Your first intelligent decision of the day," I grit out.

"I really hope your girlfriend cheers you up before you get to Dad's house. Because right now you're looking like a storm cloud." Grayson's cheeky smile sets me off.

I reach for him, but he dances away from my swing, laughing. He rushes to the truck with Levi, then waves like some kind of parade member as they back out of the drive.

I already regret inviting Juliette.

CHAPTER TWENTY-ONE

Juliette Monroe

I can't believe I agreed to do this. My brush snags in my hair, making me wince. After coming face to face with three of the Carter brothers while sporting raccoon eyes and bedhead, all I want to do is crawl under my comforter and not come out for at least seven business days. But here I am, raking my messy hair into a ponytail so that I don't take too long getting ready.

I'm not sure what kind of family starts a cookout this early in the day, but if this is how they do things I don't want to be the reason Adrian is late. Even if Adrian's brothers know that I didn't wake up anticipating an invitation to a family event this morning.

Once my hair is in a–rather messy–ponytail, I scrub my face with a makeup wipe. I've likely ripped out half my eyelashes in the process, but I need this melted smokey eye off my lids *fast*. All the estheticians in the world are shuddering at my treatment of my skin for sure as I immediately dab on my foundation over my barely clean skin.

Tonight once I'm home I'll do a face mask and pretend that will save the damage I'm doing, but right now I just need to look mildly presentable.

I want to make a good impression on his family. Adrian clearly loves them–in his own grumpy way–so if I want any chance with him, they need to like me too. It would have been nice to have had time to prepare and agonize over my appearance and what I'm going to say ... but maybe this is for the best. Now I quite literally don't have time to overthink. I'll have to save that for the car ride over there.

Once my makeup is passable, I tug on a pair of high-rise jeans and a sage green turtleneck sweater. I'm going for classic and cozy, so I add some faux pearl earrings and call it done. A knock sounds at the door, making me fall to the side as I'm shoving my left foot into one of my boots.

"Not trying to rush you," Adrian's deep voice flows through the door. "Just wanted you to know you can bring Murphy. My niece wants to meet him."

A sweet, fluttery feeling takes hold of my stomach, like leaves in the wind. *He told his niece about me.*

I get my other shoe on and open the door. Adrian is leaning against the beam that supports my porch overhang, looking far too debonair to be going to a barbecue. His outfit is simple–fitted charcoal pants and a pale gray sweater–but because it's *him* wearing it, it looks like he belongs on a billboard selling cologne or an expensive watch.

"I'm ready to go," I tell him. "Are you sure you want me to bring Murph? I know you don't like for other people to drive, and he'll probably shed in your car."

His eyes rove over me and I bask in the approval I find in his gaze. He might not be ready to say what's on his mind, but his body language is telling me all that I need to know. When he held me in his arms earlier I got *plenty* of confirmation that he's attracted to me too. You don't hold a woman with such strength and tenderness when you don't have any feelings for her. Not to mention the delicious rasp his voice took on. I could have sworn he was going to kiss me right then and there.

"How do you know I don't like for others to drive?"

I bite my lip, realizing I said one of my private analyses out loud. It's a theory I hadn't proven yet, so I should have kept it to myself.

"You just seem like the type," I reply with a casual shrug.

He narrows his icy blue eyes at me, and I turn on my heel to get Murphy's leash before he can study my facial expression any longer. It's only when I get a few steps into my living room that I realize I left all of Murphy's stuff at Adrian's this morning in my rush.

"Everything he needs is in my car. I laid down a few towels to protect the seats too. He could probably use some more food though," Adrian says from behind me.

"Thank you," I say over my shoulder and rush to fill up a Ziploc of his food. Murphy follows me through the house, likely hoping I'll drop him a treat–which I do, because I'm a sucker.

"What type am I?" Adrian asks when I return to my front porch to lock up.

He bends down and ruffles Murphy's fur, like it's the most natural thing for him to do. Murphy responds like they're best buds, leaning into him and getting golden fur all over his dark pants. Adrian doesn't complain, which throws off my assessment of thinking he's more of a neat freak.

"It was foolish of me to think you'd let my statement go," I say and he chuckles as he opens a door for Murphy, who jumps in and lays down on the towels like he's done it a million times before. Then, Adrian opens the passenger door for me, which turns my skin into a ripe strawberry. "Thank you," I murmur as I slide into the buttery leather seats.

Adrian gets in on his side and starts the car, immediately adjusting the temperature and turning on the heated seats for both of us. No matter how gruff he is, his default seems to be caretaking. I tilt my head to the side, watching him as he shifts the car in reverse. He reaches an arm over the backseat, turning to look out the back window as he leaves the driveway instead of using the screen in front of us. Not surprisingly, he doesn't even trust the car he bought to do what it's supposed to do.

Once we're out of the driveway, he turns back around and catches me staring. A dark brow lifts in question.

"You don't trust the backup camera," I state.

"It could lag or miss something. I prefer to look for myself."

"That's why I said you don't like for others to drive." I pause, hoping my words don't come out the wrong way. "You like to be in control."

Another eyebrow raise. Panic bubbles to the surface and I rush to explain myself.

"I don't mean it in a *bad* way! I just meant you think you can do things better than others–" I cut myself off with a cringe. "That's not right either." I take a deep breath and try again. "You want things to be done right and you feel more secure in your abilities than someone else's. Ugh," I groan. "I'm saying everything wrong. This is why I shouldn't be let out of my house."

Adrian's laughter fills the car and my eyes widen in shock. The smile on his face is breathtaking. I want to take a photo or a video and memorialize this moment. I thought he was attractive when he scowled but *wow* his smile is something else. I'd give away my entire tea collection just to see him smile like this all the time.

"You're right," he says through his laughter. "You're right about everything you said. I'm not sure if anyone but my family has called me out like that. And you did it so nicely too." He keeps laughing and I can't help but join in.

"I didn't want to hurt your feelings," I say with a giggle.

He brakes at a stop sign and shoots me a playful look. "I'm not a man whose feelings are easily hurt."

I roll my eyes. "That's quite obvious, but even if you don't care what I think about you, I care about you too much to be mean."

His smile fades into a somber look, catching me off guard. "I care about what you think, Juliette. The list of people who get to have opinions on my life is admittedly short, but you're on it."

Warmth spreads through my chest down into my limbs. This is what I imagine it feels like to get accepted into an elite club or make the Dean's list in college–only better. Adrian cares about what *I* think. I want to thank him, but instead, I dig my fingernails into my palms to try and keep from wiggling in excitement in my seat. I need to stay calm so I don't scare him off, but oh how I *wish* I could show him how important this is to me.

For the first time in a long time I have a friend that's not hundreds of miles away. One that cares for me and what I think. I can't help but feel like I'm floating in a river of champagne–all bubbly and deliriously happy. I'm going to hold onto this feeling while it lasts, hopefully it won't ever go away.

"Adrian!" Grayson shouts when we walk in the front door. "Everyone, Adrian and Juliette are here!"

"Thank you for that unnecessary announcement," Adrian grumbles.

"Everyone has been anxiously awaiting your arrival."

"Joy."

I fight back a smile at Adrian's attitude clashing with his brother's exuberance.

Grayson winks at me and slings an arm around Adrian then myself, walking us into the large living area. Murphy trots behind us, sniffing his way through the open-concept home where the kitchen, living, and dining area is one big shared space.

The back wall catches my eye immediately, sporting several windows to show off the gorgeous yard. I spot a firepit, garden, and a pool that I'm sure will feel amazing once the Georgia heat comes back. Smoke curls from a large grill as a man with a backwards hat tends to it. Murphy plops down by the back door, watching a squirrel scamper around.

"So this is the infamous Juliette," a guy with dark hair and a charming smile greets me first. "I'm Sebastian, Meadow's husband. Our daughter Maddie is around here somewhere, probably with a camera attached to her face."

"Meadow is our baby sister, MJ. Sebastian is in love with her and likes to make it weird by calling her by her full name," Grayson explains before removing his arm.

"I think that's sweet. It's nice to meet you." I fiddle with the sleeves of my sweater and Sebastian grins at me. There are a lot of people here, each of them unbelievably gorgeous too. I feel plain in the midst of them.

"MJ, come meet Juliette." Grayson waves over a beautiful woman with long black hair that almost reaches her waist.

She walks over and gives me a small smile that reminds me of Adrian before tucking herself under Sebastian's arm. He looks down at her with such unbridled affection it almost feels inappropriate to look at them. Her smile grows when she meets his gaze.

"I said meet Juliette not make eyes at your husband."

I laugh at Grayson's feigned exasperation.

MJ gives him an acidic look that juxtaposes the one she was giving Sebastian moments before. Grayson merely grins back at her. My eyes travel up to Adrian's face to find him watching his siblings with guarded amusement.

"It's nice to meet you, Juliette. I've been curious about you since I saw your gift to my brother. I loved the idea of planting in a tea tin," MJ says and I keep my eyes on Adrian for his reaction.

He keeps his expression neutral, so I decide to goad him a little.

"You seem to have told your family a lot about me. Careful Sunshine, someone might think we're friends." I tease and he meets my eyes. He's fighting to control amusement like he always does when I call him his nickname.

"It's not so much me telling them about you as it is them being nosey."

I laugh and his lips twitch.

"Did you just call him *Sunshine*?" Grayson asks. A wicked grin takes over his expression. "Oh, I'm so using that."

"No," Adrian growls, but Grayson doesn't even flinch. I didn't think that Grayson would take the nickname and run with it–*I should have known better*–I just wanted to tease Adrian a little.

"It has a nice ring to it," MJ muses and earns a glare from Adrian.

"It's kind of a personal nickname," I blurt out. The entire group zeroes in on me. I look up at Adrian again for help. Thankfully, he takes control of the situation.

"Only Juliette gets to call me Sunshine." His gruff order makes those around us share knowing looks. I'm prepared to write them off when Adrian wraps an arm around my shoulder and steers me away from them.

"Where are we going?"

My heart is beating out of my chest. Too much is happening all at once. Grayson's words at the singles event, falling asleep on Adrian's couch, our hug this morning and now a public display of affection? I don't know if I can handle much more.

"I want you to meet my dad."

My stomach plummets. Images of my dad's face twisted up in anger flash through my mind's eye. I can almost feel his hands gripping my upper arms, bruising his fingertips into me as he yelled about another mistake—about me being a mistake.

Adrian's fingertips tracing circles on my shoulder bring me back to reality. His dad won't be like mine. Adrian has never harmed me and has always fought to protect me. *I'm safe here.* I take advantage of Adrian's open affection and snuggle into his side to soak in the steady feeling he brings.

My heart slows from a gallop to a trot as we near the man with the backwards hat flipping burgers on the grill. Adrian calls out to him, and he turns around to grin at us. *Yes, I'm safe here.*

CHAPTER TWENTY-TWO

Adrian Carter

"She's not going to up and disappear if you take your eyes off her," Levi says, coming to stand beside me in the backyard.

We ate lunch not long ago and this is usually the time I'd be planning my escape, but instead I'm watching Juliette pose with Murphy while Maddie takes photos of them. For the first hour or so I kept Juliette nearby. I could tell she was uncomfortable and overwhelmed. But now she's warmed up to everyone and I don't have a good reason to keep her close. So I'm watching her from a distance as she lights up the backyard with her blinding smile.

I ignore Levi, my eyes glued to Juliette and Maddie as they laugh at Murphy rolling on his back. Their happiness makes warmth flood my chest.

"Are you going to lock her down or what?" Levi asks, pushing his way through my bubble of peace once more.

"Did you really just use the phrase *lock her down*?"

I look over at him and he cringes.

"I did. Not the best word choice, but you know what I mean. It's clear you have feelings for her."

"She's my friend, my feelings coincide with that label." As long as I ignore the number of times a day I think about kissing her.

"I know I can't force you to make a move. No one has ever gotten you to do something you don't want to do, except maybe Maddie." *And Juliette.* Both of whom are looking over at us and then back at each other with conspiratorial smiles. I'd do just about anything for either of them. It hasn't been easy realizing that Juliette has become important to me. I can't lose her, but I can't have her as mine either.

"But?" I ask, knowing there's one coming.

"*But* I want to pull the older brother card and tell you not to let her get away. Even if she's shy, a woman like Juliette isn't going to stay single forever. You don't want to be staring at your ceiling five years from now wishing you would have told her how you felt." There's a certain intensity to his words that make this feel like more than casual brotherly advice.

"Are you speaking from experience?"

He shrugs in my peripheral. Juliette and Maddie begin walking toward us hand in hand. "I might have let someone walk away, yeah. And now I'll never know what would have happened if I would have held on instead of letting go."

I can't pry any longer since Juliette is in earshot, but his words have my curiosity piqued. Levi is fairly organized and straight-laced. He's always had a specific plan for his life and even though he likes to have a good time, he's not one for impulsive acts or romantic whims. The most impulsive thing he's ever done is get a tattoo a few years back without telling anyone. So for him to be waxing poetic about a lost love means that this woman really affected him, especially since he keeps that side of his life private.

"Uncle Adriannnn." Maddie drags out the last syllable of my name while batting her eyelashes. At twelve years old, she's already a mastermind at getting what she wants. From all of her uncles, at least. MJ and Sebastian have an easier time telling her no.

"What do you want?" I ask and she giggles along with Juliette.

"Juliette said you'd ask that." A grin threatens to break my stern façade when I see Juliette smirking at me.

"Well?" I prod and Juliette gives Maddie an encouraging nod.

The way that they're already best friends speaks to each of their sugar-sweet characters. It baffles me that Juliette wonders if people like her. She brightens every room she walks into.

"Can I take some photos of you and Murphy? Juliette said he likes you."

I hate the idea of having my photo taken, but it's hard to say no to the two sets of puppy dog eyes being presented to me. They don't even need Murphy to aid them, they've got it down pat.

"Five minutes," I say and Maddie cheers, hugging Juliette.

"Come on, I'll tell you how to pose. You have to listen to me though, or else the minutes don't count."

"Yes ma'am," I say with a smile and Juliette laughs.

For the next few minutes, I listen to Maddie's instructions. *Put your arm around him, tilt your chin up, and now smile, no like* actually *smile, Uncle Adrian.* I'm about to tell her that her time is up when she grabs Juliette's hand.

"Now you pose together with Murphy! It will be so cute."

Juliette's eyes are wide as Maddie drags her over. Murphy sits dutifully beside me, content with the treats Maddie has been bribing him with behind the camera.

"You sit on the other side of Murphy and hug him. It'll be so adorable," Maddie squeals then bounds off to set up her shot.

Juliette kneels on the other side of Murphy, shooting me a nervous look.

"You could have told her no," I say and she lets out a laugh.

"Says the man who is in *multiple* TikToks with her."

"Did you watch them?" I ask and she smirks at me.

"Every. Single. One."

"I'm going to throw her in the pool," I say and Juliette laughs.

"Okay, Juliette you put your arm around Murphy," Maddie calls out, looking at us through her viewfinder. Juliette follows instructions, our arms pressing together. Her breath catches at the contact and our eyes meet.

For a moment, everything slips away. There's no camera clicking, no family watching us, nothing but her green eyes and raspberry lips. The very lips I almost kissed this morning ... and the same ones parting in what seems like anticipation now.

"Perfect!" Maddie shouts, snatching us back into reality. "Now both of you look at me, lean in close, and smile."

Juliette blinks a few times like she's coming to and then turns her head. We press in close, our faces almost touching above Murphy's head.

"We're going to look like one of those cringey couples on the cover of an L.L. Bean catalog, except without the flannel," Juliette murmurs, coaxing a laugh out of me.

"Murphy, look up here," Maddie coos and shakes the treat bag above her head. Murphy looks up, but he also charges forward. Juliette falls into me as a result and I wrap my arms around her on instinct. Her sweater rides up and my pinky brushes her warm skin as my hand splays across her back. I wonder if she can feel my pulse with her face pressed into my neck like this. She starts to giggle, her breath below my ear making me shiver.

"I don't think this happens during professional shoots though," she says as she pulls back to look up at me. Her green eyes are shining with joy. A full smile stretches my lips as I take in her beauty.

"You never know."

"Hey Sunshine, the game's on!" Grayson yells out, making my smile fall into a scowl. "Oh, sorry, you seem busy."

Juliette's porcelain skin tints pink.

"You could throw *him* in the pool," she suggests. I grin down at her.

"I like the way you think. Get Maddie to film it. This is one TikTok I don't mind being in."

We pull apart and after helping her up, I make my way over to Grayson. Because he's so observant, he catches on right away and bolts. I chase after him, the sound of Juliette's laughter filling the afternoon air. I've never been one for music, but her giggle might just be my new favorite song.

Chapter Twenty-Three

Juliette Monroe

"If you're not in the hospital right now I'm going to kill you for calling me this early," Caroline whispers through the phone speaker.

"Don't even. I know you haven't even gone to sleep yet, you insomniac. What show are you watching?"

She huffs. "*My Deadly Bus Driver.* It's a show about bus-driving serial killers."

Lovely. Can always count on Caroline to find the most obscure crime shows.

"Sounds terrible. Pause it and help me through my crisis, please."

She sighs like I'm a huge burden, but she's the one person I've never actually felt that way with. Well, her ... and Adrian.

"What kind of crisis are you having that has you up this early?" It's five in the morning here, which means it's two in California where Caroline is.

"I'm a morning person now, I forgot to tell you." She snorts and I frown. "It's *true*, but anyway, I'm about to see Adrian for the first time since the party at his family's house and I'm freaking out."

"Oh, you're a morning person so you can see *him*. That makes more sense." She pauses and I hear some shuffling in the background. "Okay, I walked outside to talk that way I don't wake Josh up. So if someone kidnaps me I'll shout out every characteristic I see and you'll have to hunt them down."

"Will do. Now, can you help me?" I peek out the window facing the lake and spot Adrian jogging up toward his back deck, right on time. "Hurry, please."

"You can't rush an expert." I roll my eyes. "I know you just rolled your eyes at me, but you're calling me for help so that makes me an expert."

"No, it makes you my only friend."

"Semantics." I laugh at her brushing me off. "My advice–condensed down for your weird time crunch–is that you should be bold. If he shows any indication of wanting to kiss you, just go for it."

"What if I misread him?"

"When have you ever misread someone?" I bite my lip. She has a good point, but I don't know that my spidey senses–as Caroline lovingly refers to them–are as reliable as she thinks. I'm not a superhero or a wizard, just someone who had to learn to be observant.

"It could go wrong and I'd lose the first friend I've made since moving here. His family was wonderful to me too. I think I could be friends with his sister, but not if I'm the weirdo who tried to kiss him."

"Or it could be amazing and his sister becomes your sister when you marry him."

Adrian jogs up his back steps, glancing over at my deck, where I'm supposed to be. My heart warms at the sight of him looking for me. I imagine a life of him kissing me good morning after his run, having tea together and watching the sunrise, and going and visiting his family. I'd talk about plants with MJ and laugh at his brothers' antics. For once in my life I'd be a part of a family that loves and wants to be around each other. Maybe the reward is worth the risk.

"If he gives me a sign, I'll do it. I'll lean in." My stomach drops at the thought.

"Good. Now go see him. I'm going to go back inside and turn on all my lights in case someone is hiding in my house. Say a prayer that I don't wake Josh up again."

Caroline loves true crime documentaries and podcasts, but they always end up making her lose even more sleep than she already does. Since we were kids she's been a night owl, but on the nights when we watched Investigation Discovery she'd keep me up talking about theories and then make me walk with her to the bathroom. Now that she lives with her husband Josh, he has to deal with her nocturnal habits. I feel bad for the guy.

"Why do you watch those shows if they freak you out?"

"I like to live on the edge."

I laugh and shake my head even though she can't see me. "Try to get some sleep, Care. I'll update you if anything happens."

"You better. I love you, J."

"Love you too."

I hang up, then inhale a shaky breath. *You can do this.* And then, when those feeble words don't work: *Maybe he won't even give you a sign to go off of.* I can't decide if I want him to give me a sign or not.

If he doesn't, then I don't have to make a move myself. But that also means I was wrong and he doesn't see me as more than a friend.

The cold handle of my sliding glass door shocks my skin as I push it to the side. I just have to go out there and talk to him. He might not even come over to see me. We could share a few words across the yard and then go about our days, no risks to be taken. No limbs to walk out on.

"Ah!" I squeak when I find Adrian standing on my porch. "You scared me," I breathe out, placing a hand on my chest over my pounding heart. I was already worked up before this, but now even more so.

"Sorry, I was coming to check on you."

"What if I was sleeping in?"

He scratches the back of his neck, looking—dare I say—sheepish. The expression makes me smile. There's something here between us, I'm sure of it. Maybe if I lean into it, quite literally, then we can cross that line together. It's clear Adrian would make an amazing boyfriend, an amazing husband, actually. He's protective, caring, honest, and unbearably gorgeous.

"I would have woken you up by knocking, I suppose."

"I probably wouldn't have gotten too mad, since you cared enough to check on me. Sorry for making you concerned though."

He nods in understanding, letting his eyes travel first over the porch, then over me. Heat bathes my skin at the feeling of his blue eyes drinking me in. I'm wearing an oversized sweater and leggings, but he makes me feel like I'm on a red carpet. I take a brave step toward him, spurred on by the desire burning in his gaze.

"I meant to say thank you for inviting me to hang out with your family." I look up at him, willing myself to be confident. My experience in romance is limited, but I've been reading people's emotions my entire life. Surely I can't be mistaking the tension between us.

"I'm happy you came. They all loved you."

His words break up my nerves. *His family loves me, maybe he can too.* Maybe he's already on his way there like I am for him. With another deep breath of cold air, I step so I'm toe to toe with him.

"And how do *you* feel about me?" My question is bold and his eyes widen a touch. But then they drop down to my mouth. And when my lips part I see his pupils dilate. *He wants to kiss me.*

I wet my lips then lift my arms to rest around his neck. Just when I start to push up on my tiptoes to brush my lips against his, he steps back, gently pulling my arms from around him. Confusion threads my brows together.

"Juliette, I–" He rakes a hand through his hair. "I'm not interested in a relationship. I'm sorry." His tone is soft, but his words sting like a whip against bare skin.

"I thought–" I cut myself off, shaking my head and taking a step back.

There's no way I was wrong. *He wants me.* I look up to study his expression once more but he's smoothed it of all emotion. A sob crawls up my throat, but I fight it down. Voices from my childhood twist around me like a tornado. *Why would he want you? Your own parents didn't love you.*

"I'm sorry," I whisper. I can't help but recall Adrian's rule for unnecessary apologies. It makes the ache in my chest stronger.

Another step back and I'm at my door. I rush inside, ignoring Adrian's pleas to wait. The latch clicks and my first tear escapes.

The walk to my bedroom is a blur. I stumble to my bed and curl up in a fetal position. It's stupid to cry over him not wanting to kiss me, but it feels like so much more than that. I spent my whole life assessing my parents' emotions in order to please them and be wanted by them. It never worked, which is why I ran away.

Adrian is one of the few people I felt like I could be myself around. Being fake around him wasn't even an option because he'd see right through me. His rejection is so painful because he's the first man I've opened up to. He helped me through a panic attack. He's been in my home and I met his family. Since leaving California I haven't been vulnerable with anyone the way that I have with him.

I don't know if I can ever face him again. The embarrassment of it all is going to haunt me forever. How can we be friends when I tried to *kiss* him? I risked our friendship and lost. It's clear now I should have played it safe like I have my whole life. My heart is barely healed from childhood, I shouldn't have opened up to more pain. At least when I was lonely I didn't feel like this.

CHAPTER TWENTY-FOUR

Adrian Carter

I've never been the guy who takes his frustrations out on a punching bag or in a ring–that's Maverick's thing–but I've run out of ideas. My fist smacks against the leather bag hanging in Maverick's garage. The throbbing ache in my knuckles does nothing to deter the pain in my chest, checking this method off the list of things to distract me from Juliette.

In the past week I've ran several miles everywhere but the lake, deep cleaned my house, gone to MJ's house and spent time with them, watched basketball with my dad, and worked way too much on managing our security teams. Through all of it, my mind found a way to bring up Juliette. It's like she's in the air. Every breath I take is a reminder of her. But all my breaths feel like I'm dragging my lungs over a gravel road.

I swing and jab harder, trying to escape my emotions, but every time I close my eyes I see her face crumpling. Sleep has eluded me like a master criminal: every time I try to catch it I grab ahold of a memory instead. Juliette pouring tea for me, her fingertips brushing over my arm, her curves pressed against me in a hug.

"Okay, that's enough," Maverick says over the sound of my fists hitting the hard leather. I pause, my chest heaving and sweat dripping down my temples. Maverick stands in the garage opening, watching me.

"I'm not done." The words scratch against my throat. "Give me a little longer, then you can have it back to yourself."

Maverick extends his hand, giving me a towel. I take it and wipe my face and neck.

"You're done. Whatever you're running from isn't going to go away just because you bloody your knuckles."

I bite back the cruel words I want to spew at him. He doesn't deserve for my baggage to be thrown at him. Even if he is a hypocrite since I know after his fiancée cheated on him he broke his hand doing this.

"Fine. I'll leave." I throw the towel on a nearby chair and grab my bottle of water before walking toward him.

He presses a hand against my chest to keep me from pushing past him. "You know you can talk to me."

"The same way you talked to me?" The words come out before I can stop them, but I'm tired of everyone asking me to be vulnerable when they aren't themselves.

I shrug his arm off of me and step around him, walking to my car.

"I talked to Grayson," he says, making me stop. "Neither of us are the best with emotional stuff, but he is. That's why I didn't talk to you. But I've gotten better and I figured talking to me is better than you bottling it up, so I offered."

Hearing that Mav talked to Grayson makes sense, but still catches me off guard. Sometimes I forget that all of my brothers have relationships with each other that don't involve me.

"I messed up with Juliette again," I say, my back still turned. "That's all."

"Want me to call Grayson? I think Levi is off for a few hours too. MJ is out of town, but we could call her." My shoulders tense at the thought of anyone else seeing me be raw and open. "I know you hate the idea of opening up, but we could just hang out. You don't have to be alone all the time."

Most of the time I enjoy being alone, but thinking of going home to my quiet cottage with Juliette right next door makes my chest tight. I turn around to face Maverick again.

"Okay, you can call Grayson and Levi, but leave MJ out of it. She likes Juliette and I don't need her ranting at me for messing things up."

"We *all* like Juliette, but if you don't want me to call her, I won't. Now come inside, it's cold out here."

I follow him inside because he's right, it's freezing now that I'm not actively exercising. My skin feels numb from the cold. It's late February and Georgia is still hanging onto winter. Some years we get spring weather early, but apparently not this year.

Thinking of the weather draws me to thoughts of Juliette. Is she cuddling Murphy tonight? Or did she brave the cold to go to the bingo night I saw advertised on the community's Facebook page?

Yes, I got an insipid account to keep up with community events–mainly so that I'd know which ones Juliette would want to go to. My name is fake and I have no profile information but I still feel like I betrayed my morals. I'd do anything to see Juliette smile ... not that it matters now since I screwed everything up.

Grayson and Levi agree to come over when Maverick calls. It's Saturday, so Grayson and Maverick are usually off, while Levi's schedule can vary. It's surprising that he can make it and warms my heart a little that he would come just to talk to me during his free time. While we wait Mav turns on ESPN. He could have left the TV off though because all I can focus on is that moment. When Juliette put her arms around me my first instinct was to hold her tight and never let go, but then doubt wormed its way in and forced me to push her away.

Against all odds, I've started to trust her, even with her mysterious past. But I still don't think I'm right for her. She's like a cup of cinnamon tea, capable of warming the most frigid of hearts. The kind of woman you build a life around. Meanwhile, I'm the guy so emotionally unavailable my own family won't come to me when they're hurting.

I'm jerked out of my thoughts and my chair by Grayson yanking me into a hug. He pats me on the back like he's trying to dislodge something before stepping back and meeting my eyes.

"I'm here for you. Whatever you need, I'll be it."

You're not her. The thought cuts like a switchblade, sharp with an element of surprise. Needing Juliette isn't something I thought I allowed myself to do, but apparently my heart hasn't given me the choice. Because even surrounded by the love of my brothers, my flesh and blood, I still just want her. The desire has created a kind of pain that lives deep in me, tangled up in my muscles and nerve endings so that every step I take *burns* because it's not in her direction.

The toll of this week starts to outweigh my desire to keep my emotions hidden. Maybe if I say something, they'll help me figure out how to fix this.

"I don't know if I deserve Juliette," I blurt out. A hush falls over the room.

"You probably don't," Levi says and Maverick smacks him on the back of the head. "What? We all met her. She's definitely too good for him."

"That's not helpful," Maverick says with a glare.

"Why do you think that?" Grayson asks, ignoring them.

I scrub my hands over my face and fall back into the chair again.

"Because I don't know how to do relationships. I gave up after getting burned too many times in the CIA. I've already messed up with her several times, which only proves that I'm not ready for this."

"After you messed up the first time you talked to us, what did you do?"

I sigh and look at Grayson. "I apologized."

"And what did she do?"

"Accepted my apology." I shake my head. "But that's not the point. I shouldn't *have* to apologize. She deserves someone who won't fail."

"So she's doomed to be alone forever," Grayson states before taking a seat on the couch. He rests his elbows on his knees and waits for me to respond.

"You know what I meant. She needs someone who she doesn't have to teach."

"Do you think that you won't have to teach her things as well? Relationships are about growing and changing. Becoming better together. You both have things to learn, things to give." He looks at Levi, then Maverick, then back at me. "Do you remember three years ago?"

My whole body tenses up. Three years ago Grayson had his first panic attack—well, his first one in front of me. We were in his backyard just us. He was fine one minute and then the next it was like he stopped functioning. His chest was heaving, his eyes were wide with shock and he couldn't speak to me. All he could do was grip the arms of the chair he was in. I ended up calling the paramedics because I couldn't discern what was wrong with him.

But it turns out Grayson had been suffering from high-functioning anxiety for a while, but he kept it to himself. The paramedics stabilized him and then Grayson sat there, in his backyard at sunset, telling me how for the last year he'd dealt with panic attacks in private. I told him he had to get help, and I even went to his first few sessions with him, waiting in the quiet lobby for an hour a week until he was fine to go on his own. I also did some research for grounding techniques to use in case it happened around me again. As far as I know, he didn't tell anyone else.

"I remember." Emotion lodges in my throat, making my words come out rougher than usual.

"You took care of me. That's what you do. Even when you struggle to put things into words, you still show up. You do that for all of us." Levi and Maverick nod in agreement. "So you just have to learn how to verbalize the things you already put into action, that's all."

I suck in a deep breath then let it out. Maybe Grayson is right. He knows me better than anyone else, and he wouldn't lie to me. So if he thinks I have something to offer, then maybe I do.

"You just have to be willing to take the first step," Levi adds.

"Okay, let's say I agree with you." I pause, shaking my head at Grayson's Cheshire grin. "I hurt her deeply. How do I get her to forgive me?"

"You need to do something that shows you're sorry and that you know her," Maverick says and Grayson nods, still wearing a smile.

"A grand gesture!" he exclaims. "Something with fireworks or doves, or if you got the timing right you could do both..." he trails off and I can't help but imagine a situation where there are doves released and fireworks set off. It's not a pretty picture.

"That doesn't sound like something for Juliette," I say.

"Everyone likes fireworks. Does she not like doves?" He sounds completely serious. "I know they're just white pigeons, but they're still beautiful and a symbol of love."

"I thought they were a symbol of peace," Levi says.

"No doves. No fireworks," I say in a tone that hopefully will prevent him from purchasing those very things.

"Then what are you going to do?" Grayson asks.

"I've got an idea"

One that will be simple, but meaningful and require no explosives or birds, thankfully.

"I need to go. Thank you guys." I shoot to my feet and so do my brothers. After a round of hugs and handshakes, I start to leave.

"You aren't going to tell us your idea?" Grayson has the audacity to look put out. But since he helped me work through this, I throw him a bone.

"I'm going to write her a letter," I say as I walk toward the front door. The memory of Juliette looking wistful as she talked about the lost art of letter writing is running through my mind.

"Old school, I like it," Maverick says.

"A letter? There's nothing grand about that at all. Where's the pizzazz?" Grayson shouts as I walk out the door.

"Not needed," I yell back.

As I'm closing the door I hear Levi say, "Please never use the word pizzazz ever again."

I start my car and head to the nearest art supplies store with renewed determination. Juliette *is* too good for me, but maybe this letter revealing how amazing I think she is and how I know I don't deserve her in my life will get her to forgive me. Regardless, I have to try. Because living without Juliette just isn't an option, it's no more possible than surviving without the sun or oxygen. As terrifying as it is to admit, *I need her.* I just have to hope she needs—or at least wants—me too.

CHAPTER TWENTY-FIVE

Adrian Carter

Hot, gold liquid pools on the envelope carrying my letter to Juliette. Streams of glitter catch the dim morning light, winking up at me before I cover the wax with the stamp I bought. After several cups of tea, little sleep, and too many thrown-away drafts, I'm finally done with my apology letter. I likely spent way too long on it, but since I'm not used to sharing my emotions verbally or in written form, it took some time to feel like I got it right. After hurting Juliette the way I did, she deserves more than a half-hearted attempt.

I pull the stamp away from the wax once it's hardened, revealing the floral design pressed into it. Yesterday I bought the best parchment I could find, a seal kit, and a quality pen. Hopefully, she'll appreciate the effort even though the paper isn't from her shop.

My back aches when I stand to stretch. It's fairly early in the morning, but it's Saturday, so maybe if I head to Peaches & Cream I can give Juliette her letter there. If she's not there, I'll know she's likely avoiding me and I'll just stick the letter in her mailbox and hope she doesn't toss it in the trash. I don't think she hates me, but I wouldn't blame her for not wanting to hear from me after I rejected her.

Loud barks puncture the quiet morning, making me frown. Murphy rarely barks like that, and I don't know of any other dogs nearby.

"Murphy, no!" Juliette's voice sounds over the barking.

The distress in Juliette's tone has me rushing out my back door onto my deck. Juliette is standing at the top of her stairs, blanket wrapped around her like a cape. Murphy is in her backyard, but so is another dog. They're growling at each other, the other dog looking worse for wear. The stray has mangy fur and a gaunt figure.

Juliette starts to go down the stairs—which is cause enough for me to go down my own—when she trips over the edge of her blanket and lands at the bottom of the steps. She cries out in pain and I rush across the grass between our houses, the cold ground stinging the soles of my feet.

I step between Murphy and the other dog, shooing it off. Thankfully, it scares pretty easily, whimpering and backing away. Murphy continues to growl at the retreating animal, but I'm more concerned about Juliette.

I kneel in front of where she's slumped over on the last step. "Jules, are you alright?"

"I'm okay–I think."

"What's hurting?" She looks up when I ask the question.

"Would it sound dramatic if I said everything?" Her eyes are watery as she blinks back tears. "My back took the brunt of it I think." She winces and I reach out to brush her hair out of her eyes, wanting to do something to help her. "But I hit the back of my head pretty hard. It's killing me."

She squeezes her eyes shut. If I could take all of her pain I would, no questions asked. The growling stops nearby and I glance over to see Murphy abandoning his stance to come over to us.

"I'm going to take you to the hospital. You need to see a doctor."

"You don't need to do that."

"I do, and I am." I pause, standing up and reaching a hand down to her. "Do you think you can stand?"

She nods, grabbing my hand so I can pull her up. Once standing, she sways a little, falling into my chest. The scent of vanilla washes over me as I hold her close.

"Everything is blurry. I might need to wait a second before trying to walk."

"You might have a concussion. I'm going to carry you inside my house and get my wallet and keys, then we'll go." I shift to prepare to lift her. "Are you ready for me to pick you up?"

"You're not wearing shoes," she mumbles, eyes trained on my bare feet.

A smile tugs at the corner of my mouth. Even with a potential concussion, she's still observant in her unique way.

"No, I'm not. That's on my to-do list as well. Are you ready?"

"Yep."

As gently as possible, I scoop her up in my arms bridal style and walk carefully to my back deck and up the stairs, trying to be aware of any wet or icy patches. Once inside, I lay her down on the couch. Murphy follows after us, sitting on the floor near Juliette's head.

"I'll be right back, don't move."

"I was planning on running a lap or two around the lake, but I guess I'll stay put."

I shake my head at her sassy remark, then walk through my house, gathering what I need–including shoes. Once I'm done, I lean down next to Juliette again.

"It's time to go to the doctor now. I'm going to pick you up," I tell her and she scrunches her face up.

"My head hurts."

"I know, Jules, I know. We're going to get you some help."

"What about Murphy? He's going to be scared if we leave him like this." Her eyes get big with worry.

"I'll ask one of my brothers to come watch him."

"Okay, thank you." She raises her arms to wrap around my neck. I lift her once more and carry her outside.

Once she's settled in the car I send a text into my sibling group chat that I need someone to go by my house to take care of Murphy. Though I don't prefer it, I leave my door unlocked so that they can get in. Then I get in the car and head toward the nearest hospital.

I know she's probably fine, but seeing her hurt is making me tense. I also hate the hospital. After my mom died of cancer, I made it my mission to avoid the terrible place whenever I could. But once again, Juliette has me doing things I usually don't.

"Hey, Jules," I say when I glance over and see her starting to doze off. "I need you to stay awake for me. You hit your head, so you shouldn't go to sleep until we can get you checked out."

"You're mad," she whispers and my brows pull together.

"What? I'm not mad."

"You're all tense and your jaw keeps clenching." She shifts in her seat. I glance over at a red light to find her pressed up against the door, chin wobbling. "I'm sorry you have to take me to the hospital. I-I should have been more careful so I didn't fall. You don't want to be around me."

I wasn't mad before, but now I am. Not at Juliette though, but at whoever made her feel as though she needed to apologize for being hurt. I'd like to use every bit of my training to hunt them down and ensure they won't hurt her or anyone else ever again, however unethical that may be. The sight of Juliette curling up in my car is enough to make me see red.

"I'm not mad at you at all, I'm worried for you. You're hurt and I care about you, Jules."

Using her nickname so much without having apologized or given her the letter might be confusing, but I want to do everything I can to show her I care and I'm not a threat.

"Oh." She fiddles with the sleeves of her sweater, looking down at her lap. "Your worried signs are very similar to your angry ones."

I flip on my blinker and turn left, taking a moment to think of how to phrase a question to her. Maybe I don't deserve to know more about her without apologizing, but my curiosity is mixing with my worry and making me want to ask questions.

"I've noticed you're hyper-observant, is there a reason for that or does it just come naturally to you?" I ask. Silence settles over the car. If I know Juliette, she wants to answer. Over the course of our friendship, I've learned that she wants more than anything to feel safe with someone. Hopefully she still trusts me enough to let me be that someone.

"My parents were abusive growing up–mostly emotionally, but also physically–and so I had to learn their triggers and adjust to not step on them." Her voice is quiet and tinged with a deep pain. I open my mouth to tell her she doesn't have to talk about it, but she continues.

"Every day in that house was torture. I spent so long holding my breath it felt like I lived underwater. I made sure to be a quiet, good child. No matter what I did, they found something wrong with me. Each time they pointed something out they didn't like, I got rid of that thing. I made myself smaller and smaller, desperately trying to not be seen or heard ... until one day I looked in the mirror and realized I was withering away.

"I decided that day I would get out no matter what it took. I hid money from my waitressing job and bided my time. Then I ran away in the middle of the night. I left a letter on my bed saying not to try to find me and I never looked back. The only person who knows where I live is Caroline."

She stops speaking when we pull up to the hospital. I know I need to say something, but I can't for the life of me figure out how to respond to something so awful, so terrible. Especially since I know she's in physical pain right now too and needs to get to a doctor.

"We need to get you inside," I say, my throat tight with emotion, making my voice rough.

I get out of the car and open her door, leaning in to unbuckle her seatbelt and gently lift her. Once she's settled in my arms I meet her gaze. Her green eyes are shining with emotion, like dew on evergreen leaves. The emotion swirling in them steals my breath, so much so that it takes me a moment to speak.

"Please don't ever hold back or change yourself around me. You're *incredible*, Jules. You're like a sunflower, always growing toward the light. You make everyone around you want to be better, including me—*especially* me. I'm sorry your parents didn't love you the way they should have. You deserve better. If someone isn't giving you what you deserve–even me–you don't have to settle for less, okay?"

Tears stream down her face as she nods.

"Okay." Her voice is hoarse and cracks on the word.

Before I can overthink it, I press a soft kiss to her forehead and whisper, "Good girl."

I feel a shiver go through her and take satisfaction in the reaction. Then, with renewed purpose, I kick the passenger door shut and start walking toward the emergency room doors. Cool air scented with antiseptic hits me in the face upon entering. Juliette leans her head against me and trembles.

"Is now a bad time to mention I hate hospitals?" she murmurs.

I look down at her, taking in her fragile state. There's no chance I'm leaving her side. And there's only one way I can think of in the moment to push my way past those hospital doors.

"If anyone asks, we're married."

I only have a second to enjoy the surprised raise of her brows before someone asks us what's wrong.

Chapter Twenty-Six

Juliette Monroe

"Hello, I'm Dr. Phillips, you must be Juliette," the doctor says upon entering, shooting me a warm smile. He's older, with receding white hair and kind blue eyes.

"I am, and this is my husband, Adrian." I gesture to the scowling man at my bedside.

Adrian has been quite firm with every hospital personnel we've come into contact with so far. It's clear he's experienced typical hospital protocol and is not a fan of it at all. When the nurse tried to get him to wait in a separate room, he looked her straight in the eye and said *no* in a voice laced with the kind of authority she didn't seem to have the energy to question.

Then, when a different nurse tried to put me in a bed in the hall because there weren't any clean rooms, he glared at him until the guy scurried off to prep a room for me even though I'm pretty sure that's not his job.

"I know you're probably tired of talking about what happened–"

Adrian cuts him off with a growl, "Yes." I try to give him a look that conveys *calm down*, but I don't know if it registers.

"*But* it's important for us to gather as many details as we can. So if you could repeat it once more, that would be helpful."

I go through the story of sliding down the steps again, describing my pain and letting the doctor examine my head and back. The entire time, Adrian watches Dr. Phillips like he's a murder suspect. The only time he looks away is when it's time to look at my back. Hospital gowns are rather exposing, so I'm grateful for his discretion.

"You seem like you're doing well, all things considered, but we'll do an MRI to be sure. You definitely have a minor concussion and some bruising along your spine. If your scans come back clear, you'll be free to go home as long as you have someone to wake you up every two hours to ask you a few questions and monitor your concussion."

My heart sinks. I can't ask the doctor what I should do if I don't have someone to watch over me, because he thinks Adrian and I are married. But unless Adrian comes to stay with me–which I don't want to ask of him–I might not have anyone to check on me. Poppy could help, but there's no way of knowing for sure until I can call her.

"When will they come get her for the scan?" Adrian asks.

"Within the hour."

"How long will it take for the results to come back?"

"It depends on how busy radiology is, but it shouldn't take too long."

"That's not an answer."

I grab Adrian's hand and squeeze it.

"Hey, Sunshine, why don't we try being nicer to the people taking care of me?" I whisper under my breath to him.

"I don't like vague non-answers," he grumbles. When I give him a pleading look he huffs and shifts in his seat, not letting go of my hand.

I turn my attention back to the doctor. "Thank you, Dr. Phillips. I appreciate your help."

"You're welcome." He nods. "I'll have a nurse bring you some prescription-strength Tylenol to help with the pain." He leaves and when the door closes behind him, I roll my head toward Adrian.

"I hate hospitals," he says, knowing my thoughts before I speak them.

"I do too, but that doesn't mean I start growling at all the nurses and doctors."

He sighs, raking a hand through his hair. Butterflies flutter to life in my stomach the longer he keeps hold of my hand. No one is around right now, he could let go, but he's not.

"I'm sorry, I watched my mom get jerked around by this system for years while she was fighting cancer. I just don't want them to take advantage of your kindness."

For the first time since getting to the hospital, I study Adrian. His mouth is downturned, his jaw tight, and he's sitting on the edge of the chair like he can't quite make himself settle in. Every part of him seems tense and he's got these two lines between his brows that I have an urge to smooth out ... so I do. My thumb brushes over his warm skin and I feel his eyes on me, but I don't meet them. He relaxes at my touch, and I have to bite the inside of my cheek to keep from smiling. *I have an effect on him.*

"I'm sorry this is hard for you," I say, daring to meet his gaze. His eyes are like a roaring waterfall, blue and wild. There's so much emotion trapped within him. I feel as though I've been standing at a door with a ring of keys, trying to see which one will let me in–which one will let me see beyond the surface.

"You don't have to stay here," I tell him.

His mouth quirks up into a faint half-smile.

"Now, what kind of husband would I be if I left you here?" A delicious tingle shoots through my body, making me forget my headache and injuries for a moment.

His thumb runs over the back of my hand, electrifying the air between us. It could be my concussion, but I swear he wants to kiss me as badly as I want to kiss him.

"I'm going to stay until they release you, and then I'm going to bring you back home and you can stay the night at my place or I can stay at yours."

"W-what?" I sputter, not expecting him to offer that. "No, you don't need to do that. You've already done enough for me."

"Jules." His voice is deep yet gentle. My heart skips at the sound of my nickname. I still can't believe he started calling me that. "I saw your face when the doctor mentioned needing someone to stay with you."

"I can ask Poppy—"

"She's going to spend a few days with her grandkids. She's out of town."

I hate that he's right. I remember Poppy mentioning the trip the last time I was at Peaches and Cream. So I truly have no one to take care of me.

I look down at our interlocked hands, watching his thumb trace circles on my skin. The soothing gesture eases the sting of loneliness.

"I don't have anyone." I feel like someone else is speaking. I've never admitted my loneliness out loud, even to Caroline. My tendency is to make everyone think I'm doing great even when I'm not.

"You have me."

His words are a flickering candle in the darkness of my thoughts. I may not know exactly where we stand after the incident on my porch, but him being here and touching me and offering to stay with me means something. He wouldn't do this for just anyone.

I look up again, tears filling my eyes. His own eyes are shining and I feel as though I might have cracked the door to his heart just a little, and that pent-up emotion is starting to leak out.

"Adrian—"

The door flings open and a nurse rolls in a wheelchair with one hand, carrying a medicine cup in the other.

"I'm here to take you to your scan, sweetheart," she says in a syrupy southern accent. "And I've got some pain meds for you too."

"Okay, thank you."

Adrian assists the nurse in getting me to the wheelchair, even though I'm capable on my own. One of his hands holds my bicep while the other presses gently against my upper back. When I step out of the bed the gown shifts and his hand slips beneath the fabric, brushing between my shoulder blades and sending a cascading warmth down to my toes. His hands on my skin are strong and sure in a way I've never known. What would it be like to be held by those hands every day? To wake up encircled in his arms?

As the nurse rolls me down the hall away from Adrian, my mind races with fantasies fueled by the knowledge I now have of how it feels to be touched and carried by him. He's ruined me, I realize. Unless I meet someone new and better–if that's even possible–I'm going to forever be branded by today. The memories of him rescuing me and caring for me will cling to my mind like bonfire smoke to clothes.

But maybe I won't have to scrub the memories out years from now. Maybe they'll be ones we look back on fondly as we drink tea together snuggled up in our home. A girl can hope.

"Grayson is here watching Murphy, but he knows you're not feeling well so he should be less ... exuberant." I laugh at Adrian's word choice as we pull into his driveway.

After my scans came back clear and the medicine kicked in, I felt a lot better. The doctor sent me home with some meds and instructions on watching my concussion for the next twenty-four hours. Now that my pain has dulled, I'm free to dwell on the anxiety building within me about a night with Adrian.

Where will I sleep? Where will *he* sleep? Our cottages have two bedrooms, but I don't know what he keeps in his second bedroom. Mine is an office, but his could be a guest bedroom. Though he doesn't seem like a man fond of guests. There's always the couch, but neither of our couches are big enough for Adrian and I can't sleep on one with my back in this condition.

The passenger door opens and Adrian helps me out of his car. He keeps a hand on my arm to guide me to his cottage.

"I can walk, you know," I say, looking up at him.

"I know." The slight smirk on his lips makes my face heat.

I don't know if I can handle this after the day I've had. If he doesn't stop with these subtle hints and gentle touches I might try to kiss him again. Which is inconvenient because after he rejected me I made a vow to never make the first move *ever* again.

Adrian opens the door to reveal a host of balloons, a bouquet of flowers, three gift baskets and one giant teddy bear. In the midst of the living room turned gift shop is Grayson, who is attempting to balance a tennis ball on Murphy's nose. As soon as he lets go, it rolls off and skates across the floor. Murphy bounds to get it, tail and tongue wagging.

"Oh, hey guys!" Grayson grins at us, taking the slobbery ball from Murphy. "How are you feeling?" he asks me.

"I'm okay." I draw out the last word, taking in the room. "What's all this?"

I step out of Adrian's grasp and study one of the baskets on his coffee table. There's several boxes of tea, a fuzzy blanket, and a photo frame with one of those photos Maddie took of Adrian and I at his dad's house. We're looking at each other starstruck, like if we looked away we'd stop breathing. I trace the wooden frame, a smile tugging at my lips.

"When Adrian texted our group chat that you were hurt, everyone wanted to send something over to help. MJ and Maddie sent that basket," he gestures to the one I'm looking at. "Mav sent over some baked goods and Levi–ever the practical one–sent a basket of first aid supplies for future injuries."

"I'm guessing the balloons and bear are from you then?" Adrian asks drily.

"Of course," Grayson answers with a cheeky grin.

I lift a shaking hand to my mouth. The boys grow silent as my eyes fill with tears.

"Jules?" Adrian wraps an arm around my shoulders.

"I'm sorry," I choke out, swiping tears away. "I-I'm just a little overwhelmed that they would do all this for me."

"Why wouldn't we? You're a part of the family," Grayson says and I have to bite back a sob.

I've met them a handful of times, but they consider me *family*? I've never experienced anything like this before. My parents made me believe I was too difficult to love. If the people who were supposed to love me didn't, how could anyone else? But Adrian and his family have dropped everything to help me. This room attests to how much they care for me.

"It's too much," I whisper, not sure if anyone can hear me.

"I think she's tired after everything today," Adrian says to Grayson. "She should probably rest. Thanks for staying with Murphy, I'll keep everyone updated in the group chat."

"Okay, let me know if y'all need anything."

"I will."

I look up to see Grayson give Murphy a pat on the head before leaving.

"Come on, let's get you to bed."

The weight of the day settles onto my shoulders as he leads me to the master bedroom. My eyelids start to feel heavy, but all the while my mind is racing. I'm staying in *his* bedroom.

"You don't have a guest bedroom?" I ask as I sit down on his large bed.

The bed frame is a dark wood that reminds me of a whiskey barrel, strong and masculine yet not modern. All of his pillows and blankets are a crisp white, but the kind that reminds you more of a cloud than a hotel bed. I instantly fall in love with the space and its cozy essence.

"No, I converted my spare bedroom into a home gym. Are you okay to stay here or do you want to go back to your house?"

"Here is okay."

I'm suddenly too tired to consider going anywhere else. I slide my shoes off and burrow into the covers. The large, downy comforter smells like him–fresh and clean with a touch of spice. There's a chance I hum after taking a deep breath in. If I do, it's because of the concussion, not because I'm trying to commit this feeling to memory.

"I'll wake you in two hours," Adrian murmurs. As I'm drifting off, I think I feel a brush of lips against my forehead, but I can't be sure.

CHAPTER TWENTY-SEVEN

Adrian Carter

Juliette is sleeping in my bed. I rake a hand through my hair before checking the time on my watch again. It's almost ten at night now. She's been in and out of sleep since we got back from the hospital. I've been waking her up every two hours to ask her questions, but a while ago she padded into my living room with bedhead and a sleepy smile that had my stomach in knots.

I made her a grilled cheese sandwich while she sat on my couch. When I sat down beside her to eat it was as if my world stopped and began to rearrange itself. The images of my future shifted to fit her. At first, it was just picturing us eating together like this often. But suddenly, when I thought of Christmas, she was there, twinkling lights shining in her green eyes. When I thought of one of my brothers getting married, she was the one I spun around the dance floor at their reception.

For the first time, I had hope for a future that wouldn't be spent by myself. It made panic claw at my chest for a moment, but after hearing Juliette giggle when Murphy nudged my plate—all my fear dissipated. It made me want to grab the letter off my dining room table and drop it in her hands. But it didn't seem fair to give it to her after all she went through today. I don't want her to feel like I'm taking advantage of the state she's in.

Which brings me to my current predicament. Standing outside of my bedroom door. I'm exhausted, and my couch is far from long enough for me to comfortably sleep on. So that leaves me with the floor ... or the other side of my king bed. I'm being idiotic. We're both adults. We can sleep on opposite sides of the bed without it being awkward. I'll be more comfortable and it'll be easier to check on her when my alarm goes off.

I take a deep breath and push open my bedroom door. Juliette is sleeping soundly in a puddle of moonlight, her head peeking out of the top of my comforter. I kneel beside the bed, gazing at her peaceful expression. Each time I've had to wake her today I've been struck by her beauty as if I'm seeing it for the first time.

My fingertips brush back her hair as I whisper, "Jules." Her lips part and a wave of desire rises deep in my abdomen. "Jules, wake up." I nudge her shoulder gently and she stirs, her face scrunching up before she blinks her eyes open. Her irises are dark in the shadows of my room, the green turning inky black in the low light.

"I'm awake," she croaks.

"How are you feeling?" I push up off the floor to stand and help her sit up in the bed. This has been our routine since we got back. Wake her, sit up, check in, then let her go back to sleep if she wants.

"I'm okay, my throat is dry," she rasps and I reach for the water on my nightstand. Her fingers brush mine as she takes it from me. The darkness of the room adds to every touch and sends tingles rushing from my fingertips up my arm.

"Thank you," she says after she takes a sip.

"Do you have a headache? Are you nauseous?"

"No, I'm alright, besides being annoyed at this whole every two hours stuff." She rolls her eyes, then cringes. "I'm sorry, I shouldn't complain. You're waking up too."

"Well, I haven't gone to sleep yet." I clear my throat. "The couch is too small for me to sleep on, so I was thinking I'd sleep in here. If that makes you uncomfortable though, I can make a pallet on the floor."

"Oh." She bites her lip and looks down at the comforter bunched around her legs. "Of course that's okay. There's plenty of space for ..." she trails off, swallowing before speaking again. "Both of us."

"Are you sure?"

"Yes?" Her answer comes out like a question. She tries again. "Yes. I'm sure."

"Okay, good."

I walk around the bed and slide under the covers. There's ample space between us, but when I turn on my side to face Juliette it feels as though we're centimeters apart. Her eyes shine in the low light and when I focus on her I can make out the curve of her lips and line of her neck. An urge to trace that line with more than my eyes burns hot and fast through me.

This was a mistake. I should sleep on the floor. Maybe take a cold shower too.

"Hey, Sunshine?" she whispers into the dark.

"Hm?"

"Do you think Grayson will be offended if I deflate all of those balloons? They take up *a lot* of space."

I chuckle at the random question. Only Juliette would be thinking of balloons right now.

"I don't think so, but you can tell him I popped them. I don't care if he gets mad at me."

"Okay, I might do that."

Quiet fills the room. I close my eyes to try and block out the knowledge that Juliette is in my bed, but that only heightens my other senses. Her sweet and spicy scent seems to permeate the air between us and every little move she makes has the impact of an earthquake.

"Sunshine?" she whispers again and I smile.

"Yeah, Jules?" I can't hide the amusement in my voice.

"Thank you, for … everything."

I open my eyes again to look at her.

"You're welcome." I pause, not sure I'll be able to hold back all my thoughts if we keep talking. "You should get some more rest."

"Yeah, probably should." She shifts again, tugging on the covers some. I briefly wonder if she's the type to steal blankets. I suppose I'll find out by morning. "Goodnight, Adrian."

"Goodnight, Juliette."

I wake up to bells chiming–the least obnoxious alarm I could find for these wakeups. As I come out of sleep, my whole body tenses.

Because nestled into my chest is a head of soft blonde hair. Juliette must have rolled closer in her sleep. She's tucked into my arms and all I want is to keep her there, but I do have to wake her up.

I reach behind me and turn the alarm off, then run a hand down Juliette's arm.

"Jules, it's time to wake up again," I say in a low voice.

When she stirs awake I expect her to move, but she only snuggles closer, humming happily. I stifle a chuckle and let my arm settle around her, rubbing her back. In the morning I'll put distance between us again—at least until she reads the letter or we talk through everything, whichever comes first. For now, I'll enjoy this moment.

"How are you feeling?"

"Amazing," she says into my chest.

I smile down at her as affection swells in my heart. She's so easy to adore. I could see myself falling in love with her. When her hands clench the fabric of my shirt, I realize I already am. It's as if there's been a pile of embers in my heart and she came along and stoked them back to life. I'm not worried about it going wrong though. No, as I gaze down at her figure cast in the shadows of midnight, I know that she's worth the potential heartbreak. I'll give her the heart straight out of my chest if it means I get to soak up the sweetness of her presence for even the shortest length of time.

"Your head isn't hurting?"

"Nope," she says, then suddenly her face is pressed into my neck. Her breath on my skin makes my stomach dip.

She takes a deep breath in. "You smell so good."

I'm unable to constrain my chuckles after that.

"I'm happy you think so."

Her feet tangle with my own as she presses even closer. We're in a cocoon of warmth and softness that I never want to leave.

"I saw your cologne in your bathroom. I'm going to buy it."

"Yeah?" I trace circles on her back, making her shiver. "What are you going to do with it?"

"Spray it on my pillowcases."

I snort. It sounds like she's thought this through.

"I like your bed," she mumbles before I can respond to her previous statement.

Will she remember any of this in the morning? I press a kiss to the crown of her head.

"I like you in my bed."

My confession hangs in the air and I wonder if she's fully awake now. A beat of silence passes before I hear soft snores once more. She must not have been entirely conscious then. I'm not sure if it would be good for her to remember this exchange in the morning, she might melt into a puddle of embarrassment.

I, however, am going to hold onto this for years to come. As I fall back asleep I do the grounding technique I taught Juliette for her anxiety, except instead of using it to calm down, I'm using it to catalog every detail of this period in time. I can hear the wind in the trees, Juliette's soft snores, and Murphy's loud ones down the hall. I feel the brush of her blonde hair over my skin and the way my heart is beating to a new rhythm just for her. I commit it all to memory, because I don't want to miss a thing.

CHAPTER TWENTY-EIGHT

Juliette Monroe

I squint into a ray of morning light as I wake up. My eyes feel dry, but when I go to rub them I'm frozen in place. Because my hands are tucked between my chest and a warm *man's* chest covered in a white t-shirt. Slowly, I tilt my head back to look at Adrian's face. His usual stoic features are softened by the peace of sleep. *He's beautiful.* Dark lashes fan out against his cheekbones, his jawline is strong and sharp, and his slightly parted lips are full and devastatingly tempting.

And I'm in his arms right now. In his bed. Nerves bubble up my stomach and into my throat, but they go from a roiling boil to a simmer when Adrian stirs and pulls me closer, burying his face in my hair. I melt into him, closing my eyes again to bask in the hazy glow of this sweet moment. He wants me here.

It's only when I take a deep breath in that the memories of what I said the night before come rushing back. It feels like someone threw me into the frigid lake outside. A horrified gasp catches in my throat.

I told him I was going to *buy his cologne* and *spray it on my pillow-cases*. What is *wrong* with me? If I blame it on my concussion, will he believe me? Suddenly, I'm too hot. I need air, space, *something* to help me calm down. With all the care I can manage in my frazzled state, I slip out of his arms and roll out of the bed.

I snag my phone off the nightstand and tiptoe out of the room, praying that the alarm to tell him to wake me up isn't for a little while. My poor nerves need a second before seeing him again. I shake my hands out like there's water on them as I walk down the hall.

Murphy doesn't stir from his spot on the couch when I slowly slide the back door open and step out onto the porch. I suck in the crisp air, thankful that it's still cool in February and hasn't shifted to spring just yet. The urge to actually jump into the lake is overwhelming. If I didn't think I'd get hypothermia, I just might.

Eventually, my body cools and my heart rate slows. *It's not so bad,* I tell myself while pacing the length of the deck. If he thought I was a creepy stalker girl he wouldn't have been holding me in his arms like that. The hairs on my arms stand up as I recall the feeling. With as many details I've collected about him and the conclusions I've made, I wouldn't have expected him to be so affectionate.

This new little fact about him has my mind whirring, turning my thoughts into a projector screen that flashes through images of him being the kind of man who's attached. The kind of man who doesn't believe in *personal space* when it comes to his girl. He'd wrap his arms around me while I was making tea and pull my legs over his lap on the couch because sitting next to each other wasn't close enough. Our kisses would be the kind where we'd only break apart once we were gasping for air...

A scalding blush heats my face and neck. Coming outside in the cold was smart because I'm burning up. I shake my head and try to think of the night before and what all was said. My memories of our conversation are fuzzy. It feels like trying to do a puzzle while missing half the pieces.

I like you in my bed.

The words curl around me like the sweet smoke of a blown-out candle. Did he really say that? Am I misremembering? I bite my lip. All I seem to have are questions, with no answers to accompany them.

The cold starts to set in and I return inside, shivering. Adrian's apothecary cabinet catches my eye, so I walk over to it with the intention of snooping until he wakes up. His tea collection is a sight to behold. Each drawer I open reveals several different teas, and above the apothecary is a series of floating shelves with lines of tea tins. It's possible that he has more tea than me.

I'm studying the packaging of a pumpkin chai blend when I hear the sound of a car pulling up. But for the first time maybe ever, my stomach doesn't clench at the sound. It could be the growth I've experienced lately, but I have a distinct feeling that it has to do with the man sleeping down the hall. He makes me feel safe.

I set the tea down on top of the cabinet and walk over to peek out the window. Maybe one of Adrian's siblings came to check on me. It wouldn't shock me if Grayson made an impromptu visit. He seems like the type to love surprises.

When I pull the blinds down it's not Adrian's driveway that has a new occupant, but mine. Parked behind my car is a silver sedan with a rideshare company logo on the windshield. Though I know I'm safe, I can't help but be a little nervous at a random car appearing in front of my home.

The back door opens and a familiar head of cinnamon-colored hair pokes out of the sedan. I gasp and drop the blinds, rushing to fling open the door.

"Caroline!" I shout and her head whips toward me. She pushes her sunglasses onto her head and grins at me.

We meet in the middle and slam into a hug. She smells like peppermint and the best parts of my childhood.

"I missed you," I say as I pull back. "What are you doing here?"

"I was worried about you when you said you got a concussion so I hopped on a red eye flight to get here." She looks me over. "But judging by the lovestruck glow all over your face and the fact that you walked out of your hot neighbor's cottage ... I didn't need to worry at all."

"I slept at Adrian's because the doctor recommended someone watch my concussion symptoms overnight."

"Mhmm." I roll my eyes at her skeptical eyebrow raise.

"Don't look at me like that," I say and hit her arm. "I'm not lying."

"You might not be lying but you're withholding," she challenges.

I bite my lip, failing to conceal a smile. "Fine, I might have woken up in his arms this morning" –her squeals interrupt my sentence– "*but* nothing official has happened yet."

"Tell me *everything*. Is he in there waiting on you? I can wait in your house if you need to give him a morning kiss or two." She wags her eyebrows, making me giggle.

"He was asleep when I spotted you through the blinds."

"Jules?" Adrian's voice calls out and I turn around. He's standing in his doorway looking way too gorgeous in a pair of gray sweatpants and a white t-shirt. His hair is mussed in a way that makes me long to run my fingers through it.

"He's got a nickname for you?" Caroline murmurs behind me.

"Hey, sorry if I worried you," I tell him as he crosses the yard toward us. "Caroline flew in from California to check on me."

I can feel Caroline's eyes on me. She knows how rare it is for me to give details about where I used to live and my childhood. She's likely surprised that I told him about her in the first place.

"Caroline, this is Adrian," I say, ignoring her inquisitive stare.

"Nice to meet you. I've heard *a lot* about you," she says. I shoot her a glare but she just smirks.

"It's nice to meet you as well." Amusement dances in his eyes when he looks at me.

"Thanks for taking care of her. I'm still trying to convince my husband that we should quit our stable jobs, leave our immediate family behind and move here, but until then it's nice to know that she has someone."

"Anything for Jules," he says, directing a heart-stopping grin my way.

This is too good to be true, maybe I hit my head harder than I thought yesterday and in a little while I'll wake up in the hospital bed because this has all been a dream. *Don't get overexcite*d, I scold myself. This could just be him being a good friend. The way he held me this morning was more than *friendly*, but he was asleep. I told him I wanted to douse my bed in his cologne while half-asleep, so I can't hold him to his actions.

"Mind if I steal her from you for a little while?" Caroline asks as if I'm not standing right here. "I'm only here for the next day before I have to fly back to work."

That detail makes this moment bittersweet. The worst part of being best friends with someone who lives far away is knowing that you have to say goodbye at some point.

"Steal away," he says. "I'll watch Murphy for the rest of the day so y'all can have fun."

"Are you sure?" I look up at him. "You've done so much for me already."

"Murphy is an easy dog to take care of, and Sundays aren't busy for me. Go enjoy the day. Just don't overexert yourself."

A grin stretches across my lips. "Thanks, Sunshine, you're the best."

"Like I said before, anything for you."

His words don't just sink beneath my skin, they burrow down into my heart and make a cozy little home there. I feel as though I might float away, I'm so happy. There's still unanswered questions bouncing around my brain, but right now I'm choosing to live in the moment and enjoy this with him.

"I can't believe you have to leave tomorrow," I whine, leaning my head on Caroline's shoulder. "Do you think if you just stayed here Josh would give in and move?"

We're settling in for a movie night with my laptop on my bed. I've never been much of a TV person, so I didn't bother buying one when I moved in here.

"He'd probably come and throw me over his shoulder to take me back home…" she trails off. "Maybe I should do that. It would be so hot."

I lift my head off her shoulder and laugh. "You'd make him come all the way here for that?"

"To see him go all caveman protective?" She fans herself. "Yes, yes I would. Why do you think I cause so much trouble?"

We collapse into a fit of giggles.

"I hope I have that kind of marriage one day."

"I think you're well on your way," she says, a mischievous glint in her eye. "Adrian looks like the kind of man who'd throw you over his shoulder."

I blush at the thought. "I still don't know where we stand." Caroline opens her mouth to say something. "*And* I made a vow not to make the first move again." She closes it.

"Okay, that's fair." She leans her head back against the headboard and shrugs a little. "Well, you can just wait it out and see what happens. For now, let's watch Emma and Mr. Knightley fall in love."

"Sounds like a plan."

I smile and press play on one of my favorite movies. Even though Caroline prefers to watch true crime shows and thrillers, she's a sucker for this movie as well. We always end up laughing and swooning the whole way through.

I'm pulling a handful of popcorn out of the bowl between us when my phone buzzes in my lap. I wipe my hands on a napkin and grab it.

Sunshine: How are you feeling?

I smile down at the screen. He's checking on me.

Juliette: I'm good! My back is sore, but that's it.

Sunshine: Good. I hope you sleep well tonight.

Juliette: Unlikely, since I'm sharing a bed with Caroline. She sleeps like a starfish.

Sunshine: Would it help if I came and sprayed my cologne on your pillowcase?

I bite my lip to stifle a giggle and shake my head

Juliette: You weren't supposed to remember that.

Sunshine: You're hard to forget.

Someone pinch me because I have to be dreaming. Adrian Carter is *flirting* with me.

Sunshine: Can I see you tomorrow morning? I have something I want to give you.

My eyes widen. What does that mean?

Juliette: Sure, same time as usual?

Sunshine: See you then. Goodnight, Jules.

Juliette: Goodnight, Sunshine.

CHAPTER TWENTY-NINE

Juliette Monroe

I haven't had an ounce of caffeine this morning, but I am *wired*. It's approaching five in the morning and I've been up for an hour. Sleep? I don't know her. All I know is I'm beyond nervous for what Adrian is going to give me.

When I peek out my window I don't see Adrian on his usual run, so he must have decided to forgo it and just wait on me. My stomach flip-flops uncomfortably. After everything the past two days has brought, I'm bursting with questions. I have a feeling this gift–if it's even a gift–from him will answer at least a few of them.

Which is why I'm trembling with my hand on my back door, asking God for the courage to take one step. I can put myself out there one more time. I've been through *much* worse than a man rejecting me. Though one could argue that my past trauma just made everything harder for me to deal with rather than easier.

I shake my head, trying to dislodge the seeds of doubt in my brain.

You can do this, Juliette. Just go out there and see what's waiting for you. No more being careful. One deep breath in and I'm ready to go. Or as ready as I'll ever be.

The cool morning air blows my hair back, making me shiver. My eyes zero in on Adrian immediately. He's lounging on one of his deck chairs. He looks effortlessly gorgeous in his black joggers and matching hoodie.

His head raises when I step out onto my deck and the smile he gives me threatens to take my feet out from under me. He's looking at me like he's never seen a star before and I'm a whole galaxy. I'm not sure I'm worthy of such unabashed affection and wonder.

He crosses over to my deck and up the stairs, still smiling when he reaches me.

"How did you sleep?" he asks and my abdomen tightens at the raspy quality of his morning voice.

"Terrible. You?"

He chuckles. "The same."

Our eyes lock and there's a boyish vulnerability there that makes my heart pick up speed. Whatever he's about to give me means a lot to him. It was enough to lose sleep over. I start to toy with the sleeves of my oversized sweater, but he catches my fidgeting hands in his strong ones.

"Are you okay?" he asks, his brow furrowed in concern.

"Just nervous," I say on a breathy laugh.

He gives me an encouraging look before dropping my hands and pulling something out of his hoodie pocket. He takes a second to smooth it out, then places it in my awaiting hands.

It's a folded piece of high-quality parchment, with my name scrawled in beautiful cursive on one side. I flip it over in my hand, letting out a little gasp when I see the beautiful gold floral wax seal.

"I wrote this a few days ago," he explains. "I had planned on giving it to you the day you fell, but then it didn't seem like a good time. It's an apology, but there's some other things in there too." He takes in a long breath and lets it out. "I know you have to take Caroline to the airport, so just read it once you're back home alone."

I run my fingertip over the wax seal. *He wrote me a letter.* Our conversation about the lost art of letter writing comes back to me and I have to bite the inside of my cheek to keep myself from tearing up.

"Or if you want to wait until tomorrow to read it, or never read it at all. I understand." He clears his throat, drawing my eyes back up to him.

"You're cute when you're nervous," I tease him. The muscles around his eyes and mouth relax at my words.

"I'm not sure how I feel about being called cute." He attempts a scowl, but his mouth is tugging up at the edges.

"You love it."

"I've heard people say the line between love and hate is thin."

I laugh and shake my head at him. His phone beeps and he pulls it out of his pocket to silence it.

"Forgot to turn off my usual alarms, but I should probably go get ready for work anyway. Do you want me to drop Murphy off or let him stay in my house while you go to the airport?"

"You can let him run back over here. I'm sure you're tired of him hogging your couch."

"It's not so bad." He pauses and gives me a meaningful look. "Drive safe, airport traffic is terrible."

I don't think this feeling of utter safety when I'm with him will ever get old. Growing up in a house where no one cared about me except when they were angry with me has made his simple words mean so much more. He said *drive safe*, but my heart heard: *you matter*.

"I will." I hold up the letter. "And I'll read this once I'm back home."

His eyes flick to the letter and back to my face. It's sweet that he cares enough to be nervous, especially since he's the kind of man who doesn't seem to ever be anxious.

"Sounds good. I'll send Murphy over." He smiles and then walks back over to his house.

"Hey, Sunshine?" I call out as he opens the door for Murphy. "Thank you for the letter."

"You don't know what's in it. You might hate it."

"I won't hate it."

"I hope you're right."

"Josh, can I keep her, *please*?" I ask the burly, bearded man on Caroline's phone screen. We're waiting for her plane to board at the airport, so Caroline decided to check in with her husband while he was on his break at the hospital.

"I like her a little too much to let her go," he says, his brown eyes soft.

"She's basically a racoon. She stays up late, eats junk food, and causes trouble. You *sure* you want her?"

Caroline hits my shoulder, laughing.

"On second thought..." he trails off.

"I'm going to leave *both* of you," Caroline says with an eyeroll, taking the phone out of my hand.

"My plane should be boarding in a little while. I'll see you soon, handsome."

"Text me when you land. I love you, beautiful."

"I love you too." She blows him a kiss, then hits end on the call.

"You two are adorable," I tell her and she grins.

"I know. But you and your *Sunshine* might have us beat. I can't believe he wrote you a letter."

My heart jumps to my throat at the mention of his letter. I left it at home so I wouldn't be tempted to read it in the car. Knowing me, I'd open it in the parking lot and then have at least an hour long drive to Adrian. And having to wait that long to see him would be even more agonizing than this wait to read it.

"I know, right? I've never had a man do something like this for me."

A letter might seem like a small gesture, but it's the thoughtfulness of it that keeps stealing my breath. He remembered our conversation and the wax seal and beautiful calligraphy attest to his efforts beyond just putting pen to paper.

"You don't have to tell me what's in it–"

I cut her off. "But you want me to call and tell you what's in it?"

We both laugh together, earning looks from those waiting around us.

"You don't have to read it word for word ... just give me the Sparknotes."

"I'll call you tomorrow and tell you all about it. I'm sure Josh isn't going to want me calling tonight."

"No, he definitely won't want that." She shoots me a wicked grin that implies a double meaning. I shake my head at her insinuation.

Caroline and Josh are usually inseparable. If it wasn't for me, Josh would have had her wait for him to take off work and come with. His job as an ER doctor doesn't make it easy to travel last minute. So I'm sure her being gone–even during work hours–is making him anxious. I think their attachment is cute. I hope one day I have a man who's that obsessed with me.

"Flight 227 is now boarding." The announcement dampens our moods in an instant. As excited as I am to get home and read Adrian's letter, seeing Caroline go after such a short visit is hard on my heart. That's why I didn't mind buying a ticket just to be able to spend more time with her before she has to board the flight. She told me I was crazy, but she looked grateful when she said it.

"I guess I need to get going." She stands, tugging up the handle of her carry-on bag.

"Text me when you land so I know you're safe. I'll miss you."

We hug so tight it hurts the bruises on my back, but I don't say a word. I'm barely holding in tears when we break apart.

"Do you–" Caroline cuts herself off, looking conflicted.

"What is it?"

She shakes her head.

"Come on, Care. You can ask me anything."

"Do you think you'll ever come back to California? Not to live, but to visit. It's just I miss you so much and it's easier for you to travel since you're your own boss. And I live hours away from where we grew up."

Anxiety flickers to life in my chest. I take a second to go through a round of the grounding technique Adrian taught me. It doesn't take much since I'm not in a major panic attack. Once I'm settled from the initial onslaught of emotions, I consider the idea.

Maybe I could go and visit. It's been years, and it's unlikely I'd run into my parents. I can't live in fear forever, well I can, but I don't want to.

"I'll think about it. I know that's not a real answer–"

Caroline cuts me off with a wave of her hand. "No, the fact that you'd think about it after all you've been through says something." She glances back at the gate. "I should go. I'll talk to you soon. Love you, J."

"Love you, Care."

We hug once more, and then I watch her disappear into the throng of people boarding. I wipe tears away with the sleeve of my sweatshirt as I walk back to my car.

The only thing lifting my spirits right now is the thought of that folded up piece of parchment on my table back home.

The whole drive home I listened to the Pride and Prejudice 2005 soundtrack and tried to guess what Adrian's letter might say.

Now that I'm back, it takes all my self-control not to yank the seal off. I want to be sure to preserve it in case this is the kind of letter I look back on fondly years from now. So, after carefully removing the

seal in a way that won't damage the paper, I smooth out the letter
and begin to read.

Dear Jules,

*I'm writing you this letter because I made a mistake. I
should have kissed you on your porch. Actually, I should
have kissed you long before that. I'm known to be a man
of action and not of words, but since I failed you in the
area of action, I'm hoping words will help aid me in
winning back your affection.*

*It's not easy for me to trust others. In the past, I was
betrayed by people I worked closely with in order for
them to climb the ladder. After experiencing that, I
thought it was better to live life on my own. But you
came along and changed everything.*

*The first time I saw you, something shifted within me.
You were this ethereal being made of softness and light.
I was immediately mesmerized and hated it, so I at-
tempted to push you away. Now I know better than to
think you'd be so easily deterred.*

I didn't deserve your efforts–I still don't. Your kindness and gracefulness are boundless. But I've come to accept the fact that while I can't be who you deserve, neither can any other man. So, I'm asking for permission to fail you.

Over the course of our friendship, I've failed you many times, and you've still remained by my side. I'm hoping and praying that you will do the same if we become something more. Because I'd like to be so much more.

I need you, Jules. Watching you walk away was a pain I've never known. I'm determined not to experience it ever again. Please forgive me. If you do, come find me when you finish this letter. If not, I'll understand and leave you alone.

Yours,

Sunshine

Tears flow down my face for the second time today. I push the letter away so that my tears don't blur the ink. I want to keep this letter for the rest of my life. No one has ever written me something so heartfelt before. I feel as though I read his heart on the page and it was *beautiful*.

He didn't try to be someone else, either. Everything about the letter is so very *him*, down to the slant of his handwriting. I loved it. *I think I love him.* The thought of loving him is warm and comforting like the first sip of hot apple cider on Christmas morning. There's no fear, just a sweet bubbly happiness filling my chest.

It might be too soon, I don't know. All I know is I have to find him.

CHAPTER THIRTY

Adrian Carter

EARLIER THAT DAY...

"I gave her the letter," I announce upon walking into Grayson's office.

I tried to keep myself occupied with work today, we even had a big client come in requesting our services, but I haven't been busy enough to get my mind off of what Juliette thinks. I'm not sure it's even possible to reach that level of busyness.

I know she likely won't read the letter until I'm home for the day since Caroline's flight leaves in the afternoon. Knowing this only makes the nervous energy inside me grow.

Grayson looks up from his laptop.

"And? Are you married yet?"

I give him a flat look before falling down on his couch. Something jabs me in the back, so I reach beneath me. A mini football. Of course. Shrugging, I start to toss it in the air above me.

"No, she hasn't read it yet." *That I know of.* At least, I hope she hasn't. Because she hasn't tried to get in touch with me all day.

"You're nervous," Grayson states.

I glare at him and chuck the football at his head. But because we have the same genes and a penchant for athletics, he catches it easily.

"It's nice to see you sweat for once," he says and throws the ball back to me.

"I'm not sweating."

I stand up to throw the ball easier and we start tossing it back and forth as we talk. It reminds me of when we were teenagers and we used to throw a football or baseball across the living room. Mom would yell at us half-heartedly to take it outside, but she never forced us to leave. I pull my pendant out from under my sweater and squeeze it, almost missing the ball when Grayson throws it.

"Mom would have loved her," Grayson says. I can't help but smile knowing he's right.

Juliette's sweet demeanor mixed with the little doses of sass would have meshed well with our mom's personality. The thought that Mom won't ever get to meet Juliette makes my chest tight and my eyes sting.

I clear my throat. "Did you ever cry after Mom died?"

It's Grayson's turn to fumble the ball now, no doubt surprised that I brought up emotions without being prodded.

"Not for a while." He rolls the ball from one hand to another, looking thoughtful. "When I went to therapy we talked about her and I finally let it out. I realized I didn't let myself grieve her and that contributed to my anxiety."

Even though I encouraged Grayson to go to therapy after his panic attack, we didn't talk about it much after that. I gave him the grounding techniques I learned and told him I'd be there for him, but that was it. We certainly never talked about *my* emotions or issues.

"Did crying help anything?"

Growing up, our mom tried to encourage us to be open about emotions, but our dad's strict upbringing and military background made him less accepting. If I had a nickel for every time I heard 'crying won't solve anything' come out of his mouth I'd be a very rich man. But even he shed a few tears when Mom died. Somehow, I still felt like I couldn't.

"Yes and no." Another toss of the ball. "It didn't make me miss her less, but it did help me process some of the stuff I had pushed down."

I nod. "That makes sense."

"Do you love her?" He changes the subject. I'm thankful he didn't ask me if I've cried over Mom, but I could do without him questioning me on my feelings for Juliette.

"Yeah. I haven't known her long, but I do."

"Time doesn't matter. What's that cliché? When you know, you know?"

"Have you been watching Hallmark with Maddie?"

He laughs and shakes his head. "No, but did you know that MJ watches them now?"

"Maddie told me a while back. Who would have thought MJ would go soft?"

"It's almost like falling in love changes people." A teasing smirk stretches across his face. "Makes them write letters and talk about their feelings."

I throw the football extra hard on my turn and it slips through his hands, hitting him in the chest. He just laughs, not phased at all.

"Okay, we're done talking now."

"Aw, come on, Sunshine! Don't shut down now."

I turn on my heel and walk out of his office. His laughter echoes down the hall. And even though I act annoyed, I'm smiling as I walk away. Because I am a changed man–or at least a *changing* one–and I don't mind it at all since it's because of Juliette.

My lungs burn in my chest as I make my fourth lap around the lake. Juliette wasn't home when I pulled into my driveway. So, I decided to make the most of my restlessness and go for a run. I've forced myself not to run back up after each lap to check if her car is in her driveway. Though that won't stop me once I walk up to my door after this last one.

I cut off the path and try to keep my head down on the way back up to my cottage. I'm waiting until the very last second to check for her car, to prolong my nerves a bit longer.

"Adrian!" Juliette's voice floats on the wind and I stumble to a halt, almost tripping over my own feet.

She's standing on her back deck, leaning against the railing. My feet pick up speed, eagerly closing the distance between us. The closer I get, the lighter I feel.

Her blonde hair is down around her face in messy waves and she's wearing what I've come to realize is her favorite sweater–the one that always falls off her shoulder. She's smiling in a way that lets me know she's forgiven me before she even says a word. Relief pours over me like a warm shower after a long workout.

"Jules," I breathe out after I've climbed the steps to stand in front of her.

She looks up at me, her green eyes rimmed in red, but crinkled at the edges. I want to touch her, to pull her in, but I wait to hear what she has to say.

"I was coming to find you. Your letter." She pauses. "I don't have the words to convey how much it means to me. Adrian, I forgive you and I want more with you too. So much more," she whispers the last three words. Happiness like I've never known washes over me.

I slide one hand under her jaw, holding the side of her face. She leans into the touch, igniting the burning desire within me that I've sought to keep at bay. My other hand settles onto the curve of her waist, pulling her against me. Her pupils are dilated and when my thumb strokes her cheek, her lips part.

"Are you sure?" I ask her, though her body is telling me everything I need to know.

"I'm sure." Her voice is quiet and breathy, a tinge of nerves in her tone.

I lean down, hovering my mouth above hers, relishing in the way she tilts her head in expectation. Our hearts beat in tandem like a drum roll anticipating what's to come.

The first brush of my lips against hers is a burst of light into the darkness, like the first rays of morning light breaking through the trees that line our shared lakeshore. Her hands– resting on my chest–fist the fabric of my running shirt as if her legs might give way beneath her. The desperate gesture sets something off within me and the reins on my desire drop.

My hand sinks into her hair as we melt together and I back her against the glass door of her cottage. She gasps against my lips and I steal the sound with another kiss. Her tight grip on my shirt is the only harsh thing about Juliette in this moment. Everything about her is soft and giving. Her mouth parts further, deepening the kiss. She tastes even sweeter than I imagined, like warm cinnamon tea.

There's nothing but us. Nothing but my fingertips sifting through her silky hair and the warmth of our mouths colliding. Nothing but the way my hand splays her hip like it was made to. Nothing but giving and taking freely, no holding back. *Nothing but us.*

The need for air wrenches us apart. We're left gasping in the cool breeze. Her eyes meet mine and her pink lips tilt into a secret smile reminiscent of the one she gave me on my doorstep weeks ago.

"What are you thinking?" I rasp.

She gives me a little shake of her head, still wearing that smile. "Just a theory I had about you. I was right."

I trail my lips up her jaw to her ear.

"What were you right about?" I whisper against her ear, making her shiver.

"The way you kiss," she breathes out. I brush my lips down her neck, heading toward the exposed shoulder that's teased me since the first time she wore her favorite sweater.

"Care to elaborate?" My teeth graze the dip where her neck meets her shoulder. I'm rewarded with a gasp that has me smirking against her skin.

"I-I thought we wouldn't break apart until we were gasping for air. That you'd be the type to not let go once you decided to hold on."

"Mmm," I hum against her shoulder, pressing one last, lingering kiss there before drawing my gaze back up to her. "You're right, but it's not because that's the way I am." I brush her hair out of her face. "It's because of you, Jules. You're worth holding onto."

A tear escapes the corner of one of her jade eyes. I gently swipe it away with my thumb then tip her chin up to press my lips against hers. I'm quickly becoming addicted to the feeling. More tears begin to fall. I pull her against my chest and kiss the crown of her head. Her arms wrap around my waist and squeeze.

"Are you okay?" I whisper and she sniffles.

"I've never felt worthy before, I'm not sure I believe I am."

I'm gutted by her words, heartbroken that anyone could look at this angelic woman and think of her as anything less than priceless. "Then take your time. I'll be here showing you your worth every day, until you see it too."

Her tears wet my shirt as we stand in the fading afternoon sun. After what seems like both forever and a breath, Juliette speaks.

"Sunshine?" she murmurs into my chest.

"Yeah, Jules?"

"Thank you."

"Anything for you, Jules."

CHAPTER THIRTY-ONE

Juliette Monroe

"Good morning, Sunshine," I greet Adrian as I step onto my front porch.

"Good morning, you look beautiful." His deep voice and the sweet compliment send warmth to my face. I spent an hour this morning deciding on my outfit, finally settling on a beige plaid skirt and a cream long-sleeve shirt.

"Thank you," I say, dropping my head to hide my blush.

His fingertips lift my chin up, coaxing me to meet his gaze. I remember once thinking his eyes were cold and icy, but now I see the striking color in a new light. Perhaps they were cold at one point, but now staring into them feels like swimming in an ocean of adoration.

"Don't hide from me, Jules," he murmurs, leaning down to brush his lips against mine. "You're much too pretty when you blush."

My head spins as if I've had one too many glasses of champagne. Adrian has always been very intense in nature, and being under the full force of his affection is disconcerting. My dating experience is limited, but I have a distinct feeling that even if I had dated more, nothing would compare to this, to him. I'm floating when he takes my hand to lead me down the driveway to the sidewalk.

I lean into Adrian's arm as we walk toward Peaches and Cream. This is the first Saturday since we've started dating and I thought Adrian would suggest doing something different, but he said he wanted to keep my Saturday tradition of tea and an almond croissant.

"Poppy is going to be incorrigible," I tell him as we get closer.

He chuckles. "Do you want to go somewhere different?"

"No use in putting off the inevitable," I say with an exaggerated sigh.

The truth is, I'm kind of excited to see Poppy. I'm sure she'll gloat that she was right about us, but she's become something of a maternal figure in my life and I'll be happy to have her approval.

We're coming up on the door to the café when I hear Mr. Kipton's weathered voice call out, "Julie!"

My usual knee-jerk reaction is lessened thanks to Adrian holding my hand, but I still flinch a little. Mr. Kipton hobbles to us, his bushy brows turned downward.

"Good morning, Mr. Kipton," I say and he grumbles something about his knees making every morning terrible before clearing his throat and pointing a knobby finger at me.

"I need you to vote against the ducks this week. They are an invasive species that are constantly multiplying. Those baby ducks are going to terrorize the neighborhood!"

I sigh. Yes, the adorable baby ducks waddling behind their mother are absolute *terrors*.

Adrian squeezes my hand, getting my attention. When I look up at him, he tilts his head toward Mr. Kipton with an encouraging look. As if he wants me to stand up to the old man. It's not as though Mr. Kipton is a particularly scary man, but my polite ways have stopped me from ever going against him. With Adrian beside me though, I feel strong enough to take this small step.

"Mr. Kipton," I say, straightening my back to appear confident. "I like the ducks. They are cute and give the neighborhood character. I think you should stop bothering the community about it, too. It's a waste of time."

He opens and closes his mouth like a trout. "Well, I've never–"

"And another thing, please stop calling me Julie. My name is Juliette."

He blinks at me, clearly in shock at my speaking up. "Oh. Alright." His words are stilted. He looks like he might try to say more, but Adrian tugs me around him.

"Have a nice day," I say, trying to end on a positive note. If he responds, I don't hear it. Adrian opens the door to Peaches and Cream, smiling down at me as I walk past.

"I'm so proud of you," he says before tugging me into his arms and kissing the top of my head.

The elation I feel is indescribable. My parents never told me they were proud of me unless they were trying to look good in front of their friends or coworkers. Any accomplishments of mine meant nothing to them unless they could use it for their own gain. So to hear Adrian say that over something as simple as speaking up for myself makes tears burn the back of my eyes. I blink them away, feeling foolish for getting so emotional over a small thing.

"I knew it!" Poppy shouts, helping ease my emotional state. I laugh at her and roll my eyes when I step out of Adrian's arms.

"Go ahead." I gesture toward her. "Get it out of your system."

"Oh if you think I'm not going to be telling your kids and–if I'm around long enough–*their* kids all about how I called this match, you don't know me very well."

I shake my head at her and look up at Adrian. A smile tugs up the corners of his mouth, which makes me grin.

"Gerty owes me five bucks now. Y'all need to come to bingo night so I can rub it in her face."

My mouth drops. "Poppy, you did not bet on us!"

"Every smart woman knows to always bet on a sure thing."

"I thought there was no such thing as a sure thing?" Adrian asks with a raised brow.

"If you have a woman's intuition, there is." She winks at him and he chuckles.

"Fair enough."

"Now, what can I get for you two love birds?"

I look up at the beautiful chalkboard menu, tilting my head to the side as I try to decide.

"I think I'll have a white chocolate peppermint tea latte," I say and Poppy nods, tapping on the screen of her check-out system.

"I'd like a hot cinnamon plum herbal tea," Adrian says, getting the tea that I almost chose.

"Okay, I'll get those for you. Juliette, I know you want an almond croissant," Poppy says with a warm smile. "Adrian, would you like something? I have a vanilla scone that would pair well with your tea."

Adrian nods. "Sounds perfect, thank you, Poppy."

We settle into our favorite booth and I look out the window at the community square. It's a beautiful, clear day. There's not a cloud in sight and even though it's still brisk in the morning air, you can tell Spring is on its way. The trees are regaining their leaves and the grass is becoming green once more. I smile as I see an older couple, Mr. and Mrs. Harrington, walking hand in hand toward the market.

I turn back toward Adrian and catch him staring at me. He's wearing a soft smile that turns my insides to mush.

"What?" I ask.

"I love seeing you happy."

If there was ever any question as to if I'd fallen for Adrian yet, there isn't any longer. I feel as though I'm becoming new again along with the grass and trees I was just gazing at. I don't believe that a man is capable of saving me from my struggles, not even one as wonderful as Adrian. But I do believe that he's helping nurse my bruised and battered heart back to health.

And though it's probably too fast, too soon, my love confession sits on the tip of my tongue, begging to be declared. I hold it in, not sure that here and now is the right time.

Unable to respond due to my emotions, I reach out and grab his hand on top of the table. He flips his hand over, grasping mine tenderly. Our eyes meet and I know that I won't be able to hold in my feelings for long.

"Come on, Sunshine, I don't want to be late," I say, dragging–or rather, attempting to drag–Adrian up the church steps.

It's bingo night, and after Poppy gave us our lunch for free on Saturday morning, I thought it would only be appropriate to come to help her win her bet.

"They're going to take forever to get started anyway," he grumbles, wearing a scowl.

Adrian's vote was to stay in tonight. He almost convinced me with a few low-spoken words in my ear, but I promised Poppy we would come.

"You know you'll have fun once we're in here," I tell him as we climb the final step.

"No, I will not. *You'll* have fun."

I stop and turn to him before we open the door. Muffled talking flows through the walls and light spills out of the stained glass windows into the night.

"Are you really against going? I don't want to force you if you'll be miserable."

He sighs, the corner of his mouth hitching up in a half-smile before he presses a kiss to my forehead. "I wouldn't go if it wasn't for you, but I will have fun because I'm with you."

I press onto my tiptoes and wrap my arms around him, kissing him softly. "Thanks, Sunshine."

His arms wrap around my waist, drawing me close for a deeper kiss that sends tingles from the top of my head to the soles of my feet. I play with the hair on the nape of his neck, eliciting a low sound in the back of his throat.

A loud gasp punctures our bubble of happiness.

"*Juliette Monroe!*" Georgiana shouts as she stomps up the stairs in her nude kitten heels. I cringe and step out of Adrian's arms, face burning. The very last person I'd want to catch us is her.

"Hi, Georgiana," I say quietly, clasping my hands together in front of me, attempting to look as innocent as possible. Judging by the pinched look on her face, I am unsuccessful.

"I cannot believe you are canoodling on the church steps," she scolds. When she opens her purse to dig through it, my heart sinks. *Oh no.*

"We're adults, not children in need of reprimanding," Adrian informs her, but he doesn't know Georgiana.

Georgiana doesn't care how old you are, or how important you are, she will say her piece. I truly believe she'd walk up and shout at a member of the royal family if they weren't doing what they were supposed to in her eyes.

Georgiana slaps a pamphlet to Adrian's chest, then shoves a different one in my hands.

"You two read these and educate yourselves on the dangers of your *promiscuous* behavior," she spits, then pushes past us and into the church.

"I wouldn't read that if I were you," I tell Adrian once she's gone.

He raises an eyebrow and opens it anyway. I try to snatch it from him, but it's no use. He's much taller and stronger than me. He traps me with one arm around my waist, holding the pamphlet up to his face with the other.

A sound of amusement escapes him and I feel my face getting hot. I know what's in there. It's not terrible—mostly just cartoon diagrams of how fast kissing can lead to *more*—but it's enough to have my heart rate kick up.

"I don't think Georgiana would have approved of our first kiss," he says and I laugh.

"Probably not. What page are you on?"

"Seven. It's ... enlightening."

I choke on nothing but air and he lowers the pamphlet, patting my back. Page seven involves some odd descriptions of the sensuality of breathing too close to someone. The diagrams are ... *intense.*

"Please stop reading," I beg and he chuckles, the deep sound making me shiver.

"Fine, I'll read it later."

I snatch it out of his hands when it's in reach. His laughter increases in volume when I rip it and throw it away in the trash can by the door.

"Just when I was starting to learn something," he teases and I shove his shoulder.

"We should have stayed home."

"There's still time," Adrian says, taking a step toward the stairs.

"Nope, too late. Now you're going to be punished for teasing me. We're sitting through every round of bingo tonight."

"Including the blackout round?"

"Yep!" I chirp and pull on the heavy door. He groans but helps me open it.

"Has anyone ever told you you're beautiful but evil?"

I grin up at him as we walk into the church. "You're the first."

"That's hard to believe."

I stick my tongue out at him–immature, but effective–and he chuckles. The sparkling light in his eyes warms my heart. I could look at him smiling forever. With any luck, I'll get to.

CHAPTER THIRTY-TWO

Adrian Carter

I am not–and never have been–*soft*. To prove that I'm not, I am out running this morning instead of going straight over to Juliette's deck for tea. Because I won't be a man who shirks all of his responsibilities and habits for a woman. Even if that woman looks cozy and adorable in the sweatshirt she stole from me over the weekend.

However, I *might* be the kind of man who cuts his run short in order to have more time with said woman before work. I'm blaming it on seeing her in my clothes. She usually comes out once I'm already running, but it's like she was tempting me on purpose this morning, walking out early to wave to me before I went down to the lake.

I jog up the slight hill toward her house after only two laps instead of my usual four. Her messy bun pokes out of the large comforter she's under and the sleepy little smile she's wearing does something to my heart I wouldn't admit out loud in front of my brothers.

"Good morning, beautiful," I say and dip down to press a kiss to her pink lips.

When I go to pull back, she surprises me by grabbing the front of my shirt and holding me in place for a longer kiss.

"I missed you," she says against my lips.

A small, logical part of me says I saw her yesterday at lunch. A much bigger part of me doesn't care because...

"I missed you too."

I sit next to her on the patio couch and she snuggles into my side, fanning her blanket out so it's over me too.

"We can go inside, you know," I tell her as I wrap an arm around her.

"I want to watch the sunrise," she murmurs with closed eyes.

I press a kiss to her temple and settle in. It's not long before her breathing deepens and it's clear she's asleep. There's a carafe on the table in front of me and two floral teacups beside it, but I don't dare move to pour myself a cup.

Warm pinks and pale yellows paint the sky as the sun's rays peek over the tree line. The glittering lake ripples as a family of ducks paddles across it. It's serene, something MJ would love to paint. But none of it compares to the woman next to me.

Her mouth is slightly parted, the sweet pink color rivaling the cotton candy clouds dotting the sky above. I brush wisps of her blonde hair away from her face, the golden color of the strands making the sun itself pale in comparison.

My phone alarm begins to go off in my pocket, and I quickly silence it so it doesn't wake her. She stirs, burrowing further into my side but not waking. I slowly shift so that I can lift her. I'll lay her on her bed so she can rest, then write her a note and slip out the door for work.

Her head rests on my shoulder as I carry her inside and down the hall to her room. It takes a little effort to open the door, but thankfully her bed is unmade so I don't have to deal with the covers too. I'm tucking her in when her eyes blink open.

"You fell asleep," I tell her in a low voice, brushing my thumb over her cheekbone. "I thought you'd be more comfortable here."

"You're leaving?"

"I have to get ready for work."

"You can't stay? Just for a little while?"

I rake a hand through my hair. I'm not sure I've ever willingly taken a day off since starting this company with Grayson. And I know that if I lay down with Juliette right now, there's no way I'm going to have the willpower to go to work.

"What about you? Don't you have to work today?"

"I can take off. Perks of owning your own business," she says and I chuckle.

I've never been one to take advantage of that aspect of my title at Carter Security, but maybe just this once wouldn't be so bad...

"And you don't care that I'm sweaty from my run?"

I'm not sweaty at all. Not only was the morning chilly, but I didn't run long enough to break a sweat. Trying to come up with reasons not to do this is becoming more and more difficult though.

"I'm too tired to take any more questions," she says with her eyes closed as if she's famous and I'm some paparazzi trying to interview her.

I slide off my shoes and climb into her bed next to her. It smells like fresh laundry with a hint of baked goods. I send a text to Grayson telling him I won't be in today, then turn my phone off because he's bound to call upon seeing my vague message. Once my phone is on the nightstand, I wrap an arm around Juliette's waist and pull her back against my chest. She lets out a happy sigh and silence settles over the room.

I breathe in Juliette's cinnamon sugar scent as my eyelids begin to feel heavy. Everything is warm and peaceful. The last time I was this comfortable was when Juliette was in *my* bed. I fall asleep thinking of a life where I spend every morning this way.

"I'm capable of cooking much more than this, just so you know," I say to Juliette as I place another sandwich on the pan.

We slept most of the morning–I don't think I've done that since I was a teenager–and then had tea and croissants from Peaches and Cream. Now, I'm making grilled cheese at my house, per Juliette's request.

"The heart wants what it wants," she replies with a grin, swinging her legs from her spot on my counter. "Who taught you to cook?" She grabs a grape out of the bowl beside her and pops it in her mouth.

"My mom. She said she didn't want any of her kids unable to take care of themselves. All of us learned to cook from a young age."

"That's smart. When I first moved out I had to teach myself."

"I was annoyed with it at the time, but now I'm grateful for it." I flip the sandwich, revealing a buttery brown top. "She was the best."

"I wish I could have met her."

Emotion lodges in my throat. "I wish you could have too," I say, my voice coming out more gravelly than intended.

I take the sandwich off the pan and turn the stove off. Then I tug my necklace out from under my t-shirt and turn toward Juliette. "I got this a few years ago on the anniversary of her death." I lift the sunflower pendant and step in between Juliette's legs.

Her fingertips brush over the gold, a soft smile on her lips. "That's a beautiful way to honor her."

I take a deep breath, preparing to be vulnerable in a way that I haven't been with anyone in a long time. "Tomorrow's her birthday." Juliette looks up from the pendant, surprise evident on her face. "My family likes to get together, but the last few years I've made myself busy. It's uncomfortable to talk about her with all of them."

Maybe it's because I haven't grieved much on my own, but talking about my mom in front of my siblings makes my chest tight. I feel like they expect me to act a certain way, but on those difficult anniversaries and holidays I never have the energy to pretend.

"Do you want me to go with you? Or we can be alone, or I'll even let you be if you want to be by yourself."

I smile down at her. She's the kindest person I've ever met. And she doesn't expect me to be someone I'm not.

"Maybe if you came it wouldn't be so bad. I'm more comfortable with you than anyone else." I tuck her hair behind her ear and she wraps her dangling legs around my waist to draw me closer.

"Thank you for being vulnerable. I love being the one you talk to."

I love you, I think to myself. Perhaps it wouldn't be so bad to admit it out loud, though. I gaze into her forest-green eyes before leaning in and softly kissing her. She wraps her arms around my neck and tilts her head to deepen the kiss.

I'm quickly lost in her. My hands settle on her hips as she toys with the hair on the nape of my neck. The world around us disappears and my senses are dulled to everything but Juliette. I can only hear her breathing, taste the honeyed sweetness of her lips, feel her hands in my hair, breathe in the vanilla scent she wears. All I want and need is more of her. Everything else is muffled like hearing a song playing in another room.

I break our kiss, resting my forehead against hers.

"Jules," I breathe out, overwhelmed by the heady feeling of her mouth on mine. "I–"

A loud series of knocks cuts off my confession. I stiffen for a moment, preparing to protect Juliette from whatever could be outside.

"Adrian, if you don't answer this door I'm going to assume you've been murdered," Grayson announces.

I growl in frustration, but Juliette just giggles and drops her arms from around my neck so I can step back. "Go away," I yell to him.

"So you are alive. That's good to know, especially since you've had the entire family worried about you."

I sigh and stalk over to the door, ripping it open to reveal my brother leaning against the support beam. "What are you talking about? Why are you here in the middle of the day?

"Well, when you sent that vague text this morning and then ignored my returning texts and calls, I was concerned that you were in the hospital and not telling anyone."

I roll my eyes at him. "I did that *one* time. It was just my appendix bursting, not even a big deal."

Grayson narrows his eyes and crosses his arms. "So, once I could get away from work I came to check on you." He tilts his head to the side to look past me and smirks. "Oh, that explains things. Hi, Juliette."

"Hey Grayson, nice seeing you again!" Juliette says, sliding up beside me. "Did you really go to the hospital and not tell anyone?" She looks up at me with wide eyes.

"Yes, he did. This is the man you've chosen. If you get cold feet, I look just like him and I actually talk to my family." Grayson winks.

"I think I'm okay," Juliette laughs. "I prefer a brooding Mr. Darcy over the amiable Mr. Bingleys of the world." She grabs my hand and gives me a sly grin.

"Who and who?" Grayson's brows furrow.

"Characters from a Jane Austen novel, which you would know, if you ever sat still long enough to read," I answer.

"I read! I listen to audiobooks all the time."

"Audiobooks don't count."

"I'm not getting into this argument with you again," Grayson says, looking as close as he can to frustrated. It's hard for Grayson to ever look truly mad. I've seen it only a handful of times in my *life*.

"Well, now that you've confirmed I'm alive and not in a hospital, your conscience is clear and you can leave."

"Have you seen any of the messages from the sibling group chat?"

"My phone is off."

"Of course it is," he groans and then looks pleadingly at Juliette. "Please, I'm *begging* you, marry my brother so that we maintain contact with him. I'm worried he's going to hide away from the world in a cave somewhere."

"I enjoyed our quiet morning actually, so I can't complain about him being off the grid." The little smirk playing on her lips makes me all the more eager to be rid of Grayson. When she meets my eyes, desire courses through me like a swift river.

Grayson tilts his head back, looking toward the sky. "Am I to never know peace in this life?"

"Are you going to quit being dramatic anytime soon?" I ask and he lets out an exasperated sigh.

"If you'd just *check your phone*, I wouldn't even be here." His expression sobers. "I'm sure you know, tomorrow is Mom's birthday. MJ and Bash invited everyone over to their house for dinner. We all want you there. Juliette is welcome, of course."

I look down at Juliette, who squeezes my hand and gives me an encouraging nod. "I'll be there."

Grayson's face softens into a smile once more. "Good."

"Now go before I drag you off my property."

"As much as I'd love to take you down, I'll leave. Wouldn't want Juliette to see how strong I am and get tempted to leave you."

I shake my head at him, laughing as he saunters away.

"Enjoy your day off!" he calls out as he opens his car door. "I'll be slaving away keeping our business afloat while you make out with your girlfriend."

"He's hilarious," Juliette says, waving to Grayson's retreating car.

"He's something alright."

"I'm glad you're going to go tomorrow. I'm proud of you."

I smile down at her and draw her in for a hug. "You might turn me into a Bingley if you keep this up."

She presses a kiss to my chest over my shirt. "Darcy had a soft heart all along, if you recall. So I'm not changing you, just exposing what's already here."

"Whatever you want to call it, it's all for you."

She tilts her head back and smiles up at me. "I'll take it."

I resume the kiss from before Grayson interrupted us, not sure when to tell her I love her, but all the more sure that I do.

CHAPTER THIRTY-THREE

Juliette Monroe

Trees blur outside the window as we drive toward Adrian's sister's house. The car is silent, the low sound of the radio and the hum of the air conditioning are the only things breaking the hush. Adrian has been—understandably—more quiet and introspective today.

This morning, we walked around the lake together then had tea. He went to work but responded to my check-in texts throughout the day. Our relationship is still new, so I didn't want to push him too much, but I did want to be sure that he was okay. He picked me up right after he got off work and now we're on our way to see his family. I'm not sure what to expect, but I'll be here for Adrian no matter what.

He's taken care of me both physically and emotionally, so being here for him while he's grieving is the least I can do.

"You can talk, you know," Adrian says, startling me with the sudden break in silence.

"I didn't want to bother you. I figured you wanted the silence."

His grip tightens on the steering wheel, then loosens again. I take in his tense shoulders and jaw, wishing I could help him relax. He's not been very open about how he grieves, so I'm not sure what to do.

"I'm not sure what I want, if I'm honest." He sighs and pushes a hand through his hair. "I haven't let myself grieve much."

The admission hangs in the air between us. It makes sense now why he's not voiced what he wants today. He doesn't actually know.

"That's okay. We can just be. And if you decide you want to talk or cry or turn the car around and go home, I'll be with you."

A small smile stretches across his lips. He reaches a hand out and rests it above my knee, drawing slow circles with his thumb.

"Thanks, Jules." His shoulders seem to relax a little. "Could you tell me about your day?"

"Sure," I say with a smile and then begin to tell him about my mundane work day. I don't leave any details out, telling him about every order I fulfilled and the new digital products I'm working on.

Soon enough, we're pulling through a gate armed with security, up to a house made entirely of glass. I knew MJ and Sebastian had to be well off since Sebastian is the coach of the Georgia Thrashers, the wealthiest football program in the state—yes, I googled him—but their house shows just how rich they really are.

We pull up behind a collection of beautiful vehicles and I try not to gape as I walk hand-in-hand with Adrian to the front door. Adrian doesn't knock, instead, he walks right in and I'm entranced once more by the sheer beauty and size of the home. The ceilings are high and every window seems to have an indoor garden in front of it.

It feels as though we've been transported to a jungle, if the jungle was decorated with hand-knit quilts and paintings galore. I don't know if I've ever been in a building that has felt so *alive*.

"Wow," I whisper, incapable of playing it cool.

"It's something else, isn't it?" Adrian leads me through the large family room, my eyes catching on a gorgeous sunrise painting above the fireplace. If MJ did all of these, she's insanely talented. I bet she'd make millions in a gallery.

"MJ has more talent in her pinky finger than I have in my whole body," I say in awe and he chuckles.

"Don't say that too loud," Sebastian says as he walks in from the backyard. "She'll figure out she's too good for me."

I laugh and even Adrian cracks a smile. Sebastian isn't as vivacious as Grayson, but he has a similar talent of pulling smiles out of people. It's good that they're both here today. I'm sure people will need those smiles.

"Everyone is outside. Sophie catered all of the food and it's out back on a table."

"Thanks, Bash," Adrian says and Sebastian nods then walks into the kitchen, likely knowing that Adrian won't say much more than that. "Sophie is one of MJ's best friends, she's a chef," Adrian explains to me and I nod.

Through the wall of windows I spy a crowd of people chatting and eating at plastic tables. There are more people than I expected here, and I'm not sure how Adrian feels about the larger group.

"You ready?" I ask him in a low voice.

He leans down and steals a quick kiss.

"I'm ready."

We walk out together and, thankfully, Grayson doesn't dramatically announce our arrival. It seems like everyone is trying to talk like normal, but you can instantly feel the grief that hovers over the yard like a storm cloud. I suddenly feel as though I don't belong. I didn't know Adrian's mom, and even though we're dating, most of these people don't know me.

"Hey." Adrian tugs me closer to him and lets go of my hand to drape his arm over my shoulders. "Thank you for coming with me. I don't know if I could handle all this without you."

His words soothe my outsider anxiety. It doesn't matter what anyone else thinks. I'm here for Adrian like I promised him I would be.

People nod to us as we pass by and I notice that they seem to not know how to act around Adrian. It breaks my heart that he doesn't have a true support system, even more that he could have had one if he would have felt capable of trusting someone. Maybe tonight can be a step in the right direction for him. I don't expect him to become a fountain of emotions, but I know it would do him good to feel safe enough around his family to be able to grieve his own mother.

We make our plates and sit at a table with Maverick and a couple I don't recognize. The woman has a toddler on her knee, feeding him tiny spoonfuls of mashed potatoes. My heart warms just looking at them. Maybe one day I could have that. When I chance a glance at Adrian, I find him already looking at me, affection in his gaze.

"This is my best friend Drew and his wife Kayla, plus their son Archie," Maverick introduces the couple with a smile. "Drew practically lived at our house growing up."

"It's nice to meet you, I'm Juliette, Adrian's girlfriend." It feels weird to say it out loud, but also right. Adrian finds my knee and squeezes it under the table, a small smile on his lips.

"Where's Evie?" Adrian asks, looking around the backyard. Sensing my confusion, he clarifies, "Drew's sister."

"She's up in New York, working. She keeps busy," Kayla answers.

"Too busy if you ask me," Drew grumbles, earning a look from his wife. "What? I just think she works too much."

"Maybe she'll find someone. Adrian started dating Juliette and took his first ever day off," Maverick says.

I blush under the attention, but it's not on me for long, because Drew continues his thoughts on his sister's life.

"She is dating someone the last I heard. He's a jerk, some male model so full of himself it's unbelievable. He treats her like crap too."

Adrian tenses slightly and so does Maverick. I look to Maverick and see more than a friendly protectiveness though, there's a deep concern in his expression that doesn't match Adrian's. If they all grew up together, I wonder why Evie means more to Maverick? Is it a friendship thing or something more? I file the information away to bring up to Adrian later. It's likely he noticed it too. That's a perk of dating someone as observant as me: we can talk about everything we caught later.

"I'm sure the table doesn't want to hear about Evie's dating life," Kayla says through gritted teeth. "And if she found out you were talking about it, she'd be upset."

Drew sighs. "Fine, I'll drop it. I just wish she was here."

"She wanted to be," Kayla assures Adrian and Maverick by addressing them directly. "But her boss threatened to fire her if she left. She said she would call you tonight, Mav."

Maverick nods, then pushes back from the table. "I'm going to get some dessert."

Once he's out of earshot Drew sighs again. "I thought for sure he'd say something about Evie. I guess he's still messed up over Alexis leaving."

"Did you think talking about her was going to make him up and go to New York?" Kayla scrunches her nose up. I watch their conversation with unabashed curiosity.

"The man has *savior complex* tattooed on his forehead. I thought mentioning that jerk boyfriend of hers would trigger something in him."

"Now is not the time to be matchmaking your sister and best friend," Kayla scolds him, then shoots an apologetic look to us.

"You're right, I'm sorry man."

Adrian shrugs, a ghost of a smile on his lips. "Mom would be helping you if she were here. She loved Evie like her own."

Drew and Kayla both smile at his words. I do too, but not because I know what they're talking about. I'm smiling because Adrian brought up his mom on his own and I know that's not easy for him.

"She did. I don't think either of us would have made it through our parents' divorce without her and your dad letting us stay over so much."

"She always said everyone was welcome. That was her way."

"She was the best," Drew says, his eyes wet with unshed tears.

"Yeah, she was."

The crackle of the bonfire in front of us is enough to lull me to sleep if I let it after such a long evening. Most everyone has gone home except the family. I'm nestled in between Adrian's legs, leaning back on his chest. He gave me his hoodie out of his car earlier and I've been ready for bed ever since. But I won't even consider leaving until Adrian wants to go.

He's been more open tonight than I've ever seen him–barring when we're alone. So even though my eyelids feel like tiny weights are attached to them, I'm going to hang out just for him.

"What if we went around saying some of our favorite memories of Mom?" Grayson suggests and everyone gives some form of agreement. "I'll go first. One time, when I was ten, I ran my bike into a bunch of briars. Mom didn't call me dumb or even scold me much, just got me cleaned and bandaged then gave me a Kool-aid pouch and let me watch my favorite movie."

I smile at the sweet memory, ignoring the pangs of jealousy stinging my heart. I shouldn't be jealous. They don't have their mother. But at least when they did, she loved them. Anytime I made a mistake, even if I got hurt doing it, I was yelled at. My parents never forgot anything either, so they'd bring up the mistake years later just to hurt me all over again.

"When I broke my arm skateboarding, she did something similar," Levi says from his place across the fire. "She got me stickers for my cast and let me get ice cream on the way home."

"She let us be kids," MJ adds, brushing Maddie's hair back from her forehead as the young girl rests in her lap. "Raising Maddie has shown me even more how great Mom was at that. We didn't grow up any faster than we needed to, even with her diagnosis."

It's hard not to tense up as they talk about their beautiful childhood. Adrian's arms tighten around me and his lips find my ear. "You okay, Jules?"

I nod, unwilling to be selfish on a day like today. I can manage for him. Even if my chest is starting to feel tight. Maybe I can sneak away and do some deep breathing while everyone talks.

"I think we're going to go home," Adrian says and I glance up at him. He gives me a look that says there's no room for argument.

"Are you sure?" I try to keep my voice low, but it's impossible to have privacy around a quiet fire.

"I'm sure, let's go." He stands and helps me up.

Everyone starts to say their goodbyes, but before we walk away, Adrian pauses. "When I was fifteen, I caught my first girlfriend kissing another guy under the bleachers after football practice. I came home angry out of my mind. Mom got me to talk like only she could. She told me that one day I'd find someone who would love me and wouldn't betray me. And then she gave me a cookie and told me I could play video games past curfew."

Everyone is quiet, soaking up the fact that Adrian just shared a memory.

"I can't believe I'm just now finding out your girlfriend cheated on you. We're *twins*, does that mean nothing?" Grayson asks and everyone laughs.

"Well, now you know." Adrian wraps an arm around me. "We'll see y'all later. It's a long drive back to Peach Hollow."

We walk back to his car, the echoes of *love you's* and *drive safe's* following us.

He stops before opening the car door for me, taking my hands in his. In the dim light, his eyes are like pools of navy ink.

"You didn't have to leave. I'm okay."

"I know it's hard for you to think about your childhood. I could feel how tense you were."

"I don't want you to leave just for me, though." I look down. "Today is supposed to be about you and your feelings."

"Jules, look at me," he whispers into the night. I slowly raise my eyes to meet his. "You've done so much for me today. It's okay that you got overwhelmed at the end of a long day. Our relationship isn't going to be even all the time. No one day is going to be dedicated to either of us, even one like today."

"I just want the best for you," I tell him. "You should get to sit around that fire all night if you want to, not worry about me."

"Would you blame me if while you were having a rough day, I started feeling emotional about losing my mom?"

I sigh. "No."

"Then you can't blame yourself for having feelings you can't control." He stares into my eyes. "Jules, you said you'd stay here all night for me, well I'm telling you I'd leave for you. Because I love you."

Tears well up in my eyes, all of my emotions swirling together and rising up like a tsunami. I thought I was moving too fast. I was afraid of scaring him away. And yet here he is, confessing the very thing I was afraid of telling him.

"I love you too," I whisper and the smile that breaks out across his face is so beautiful it hurts.

He pulls me close and kisses me like it might be the last time we ever get to. The gentle yet fierce way he holds me breaks the dam on my tears. But it's not too much for him. No, he brushes away each droplet with his lips and turns our kiss into a salty-sweet mix. It tastes like love, the raw and real kind that sacrifices.

For most of my life, I thought I had to earn love, but here in Adrian's arms, I realize I was wrong. Love isn't earned, it's given freely. And no matter what the future might bring, knowing that brings me a sense of peace I've never known.

Epilogue

ADRIAN CARTER

MJ: We're headed your way. Fifteen minutes tops.

I send a thumbs-up emoji in response to MJ's text and turn back to the task at hand: turning the trail around the lake into a place worth proposing at. When I was brainstorming where to propose to Juliette, I wasn't sure if I wanted to propose here because it seemed so mundane.

The lake is essentially our backyard, so it didn't seem worthy of being *the* place. But I realized Juliette loves Peach Hollow, and most of our memories involve this little community and the lake it surrounds. So, I decided I would turn it into a proposal fit for Juliette.

"Adrian, the trees are officially lit," Poppy says, walking up beside where I'm setting up a table.

I've lined the trail with various small tables that have photos of us and quotes from her favorite books, plus a singular sunflower. It just so happens to be August, which is sunflower season and made this part of the proposal easy on me. By the end of the trail she'll have a bouquet of sunflowers and arrive at me standing under a tree draped in twinkle lights. Then, after she says yes, we'll have croissants and tea from Peaches and Cream on my back deck which is also lined with twinkle lights. And then I'll give her the envelope that's in my pocket and hope that she doesn't get overwhelmed.

"Thank you, Poppy. I just got a text that she's almost here."

"I'll make sure everyone clears out then." She gives me a one-armed hug that I return. I'm not usually the hugging type, but Poppy is a mother figure to Juliette and has rooted for us from the start, so I make an exception for her. "You be good to my girl now," she says, but there's no threat in her tone. She knows how much I love Juliette.

"Yes, ma'am."

She pats my back before walking off to shoo away the remaining residents. I'm left alone with my thoughts as I place items on the last table remaining. Anxiety swirls in my stomach and makes my heart pound. I'm not nervous that Juliette will say no, but I am nervous that this won't be as perfect as I hope.

Maverick: You got this, man.

I glance down at the text into the group chat. My whole family knows that tonight is the night. Before I can respond, more messages roll in.

Grayson: Yeah, don't sweat it. She can't say no to a face like y(ours).

Levi: Grayson, why do you make everything about the fact that you're twins?

Grayson: It's a twin thing, you wouldn't get it.

I laugh at their bickering, shaking my head. Even though I usually hate the group chat blowing my phone up, it's nice to have a laugh today.

I spot MJ's SUV pulling into the drive and take a deep breath, pocketing my phone. Here we go.

Juliette Monroe

Adrian is going to propose this evening. I've known for a week now, and hanging out with MJ the past few hours just confirmed it. The Carter family is well versed in schooling their emotions, but they weren't able to fool me.

Butterflies fill my stomach as I step out of MJ's SUV. She tried to hide the fact that our hang out was meant to get me away from Peach Hollow, but the way she kept checking her phone and the looks she gave me when she thought I wasn't paying attention tipped me off.

I spot the trees sparkling in the setting sun right away. My breath catches in my throat at how beautiful it is. I hear a car door open and shut.

"What's that down there by the lake?" MJ asks in an inconspicuous tone that makes me laugh.

"I knew he was proposing today." Tears burn my eyes as I glance over at her. "Thank you for helping."

"Of course you did," she laughs. "I told him there was no use in trying to surprise you. I'm supposed to tell you to go down to the bench you two sit at, then walk the trail from there."

"Okay," I whisper. She hugs my shoulders then hops back in her car.

I slowly make my way down to the lake, taking in the gorgeous scenery. Even though I've lived here for years now, I've never quite gotten over the beauty of this place. And the twinkle lights only add to the magic.

There's a table by my usual bench, with a photo of us smiling on the beach in June, along with a sunflower and a note.

Jules,

I've set up tables for you around the lake. Stop at each one, take a sunflower, then meet me under the dogwood tree.

I love you,

Sunshine

My eyes are already full of tears as I grasp the first sunflower stem. When I look around the lake, I spot Adrian waiting for me. I want to run to him, but I also don't want this moment to end.

I make my way to the next table. The note there makes my breath catch.

> *"In vain have I struggled. It will not do. My feelings will not be repressed. You must allow me to tell you how ardently I admire and love you."-Pride and Prejudice, Jane Austen*

I collect the flower and walk to the next table, convinced I'm going to be a puddle of tears by the time I reach Adrian.

> *"Did my heart love till now? Forswear it, sight! For I ne'er saw true beauty till this night." -Romeo and Juliet, Shakespeare*

Another flower, another shaky step in the direction of the love of my life.

> *"You pierce my soul. I am half agony, half hope."-Persuasion, Jane Austen*

I swipe my tears away and grab the flower, pausing for a moment to gaze at the photo of us on the table. I didn't even know he took that one. I'm asleep on his chest, the glow of the sunrise filtering the photo. I bite my lip and keep going.

"We loved with a love that was more than love."
-Annabel Lee, Edgar Allen Poe

This one makes me laugh through my tears. Adrian thought this poem was too dark to be a love poem, but I argued that it was wonderfully romantic.

Final flower in hand, I rush to cross the distance between us. Adrian drops to one knee as soon as I step under the shade of the tree, making me suck in a breath. I don't even have a moment to collect myself before he speaks.

"Jules, you are everything to me. Your soul is made up of sunshine and sugar and silk. Being with you these past few months has been the greatest joy of my life. I don't have the words to express how beautiful and utterly amazing you are. If I loved you less, I might be able to talk about it more."

A breathless laugh escapes my lips at his quoting *Emma* by Jane Austen. *I love him so much.*

"I love you, everything about you. Will you do me the honor of becoming my wife?" He opens up a velvet ring box and a diamond shimmers under the lights.

"Yes," I whisper and he grins up at me. He quickly stands and slides the beautiful ring on my finger before lifting me into his arms and spinning me around. I drop the sunflowers, but Adrian doesn't seem to mind.

I squeal and giggle at his elation and then our lips collide in a kiss that makes heat rush through my whole body. His teeth graze my lip when we pull apart, sending a shiver down my spine. His gaze meets my own, pure happiness swirling in his irises.

"I love you," I say and he brushes his lips against mine.

"I love you." He sets me back on my feet and takes my hand. "Come on, I have something to show you."

"There's more?" I ask and he smiles. We set out toward our cottages. In the distance, I notice more fairy lights hanging above Adrian's deck.

"You should know by now I'd go to great lengths to give you everything you deserve. If you said you wanted a star out of the sky I'd start building a rocket."

I shake my head in disbelief. The joy coursing through my veins is unlike anything I've ever experienced.

"I don't think there's a happier woman in the world than me right now."

"Good. I hope that never changes." He pulls our joined hands up to kiss the back of mine.

We walk in a peaceful silence that I've grown accustomed to over the past few months. Being around Adrian has taught me that silence isn't bad. I grew up in a home where silence usually felt like the calm before the storm. But with him, it's just calm. True serenity.

He leads me up the steps to where there's a table set for us. A carafe of tea and a plate of almond croissants sits in the middle of it.

"This is wonderful," I say and take a seat across from him. I stare down at the ring on my hand, admiring the beautiful marquise-cut diamond. He must have talked to Caroline, she's the only one who knows this was my dream ring.

It hits me suddenly that I wish she were here. That I could celebrate with her in person. The thought makes some of the glow within me dull.

"Everything alright?" Adrian asks, pouring us each a cup of tea.

"Yes, this is amazing." I look around, smiling at the loveliness of it all. I couldn't have planned the proposal better myself.

"But?" he asks, not looking upset at all that I might be wanting something more after he went to all this trouble.

I sigh. "I'm just wishing Caroline was here. You don't have her hiding in a closet somewhere by any chance?" I ask with a laugh and his mouth hitches up in a grin.

"No, but I do have this." He pulls out an envelope and slides it across the table to me.

Inside of it are two plane tickets to California. The flight leaves in a few hours. I look up from the papers, blinking back tears once more. *He thought of everything.*

"I thought that if you were ready to go back to California, we could go see her and celebrate in person. If not, I've also bought tickets for her and Josh. They have their bags packed, ready to leave on a flight tomorrow morning."

"Sunshine, I-I don't know what to say. You've done too much."

"Nothing is too much for you, Jules. Anything for you, remember?"

I stand up and walk around the table, throwing myself into his lap and hugging him tight.

"I love you," I murmur into his neck and he rubs my back.

"I love you, too."

I pull back and meet his eyes. "I want to go to California. I'm ready."

"Then let's go pack our bags." He cups the side of my face with his strong hand. "I'm so proud of you, Jules."

And just when I thought I couldn't get any happier, I do. I have a feeling the rest of our lives will be like this. Each new day will add to the joy from the day before, just by being with each other. After spending most of my life lonely and afraid, I finally get to experience *true love*. I'm never going to let this go. I'll carry it like a torch and pass it down to our kids and grandkids. They'll know the love I didn't have as a child, and it'll be in part because of the man holding me in his arms. The man who called me worthy when I didn't feel it. The one I'll spend the rest of my days with. My future husband, *Adrian Carter*.

Keep reading for a look at the next brother in the series: Levi Carter!

"SURPRISE!" We all shout collectively when Adrian and Juliette walk into Grayson's house. Neither of them looks surprised, but they do smile and laugh.

"Told you they wouldn't be surprised," I say to Grayson, who just shrugs.

"I'm counting it as a win that Adrian even showed up."

I laugh at him and watch him walk over to bear hug Adrian. Grayson started planning this engagement party as soon as Adrian mentioned proposing to Juliette. We had to wait to have it until after they came back from California, but that didn't deter Grayson. I'm convinced nothing could deter him from having a party.

I follow behind Grayson so that I can hug the happy couple. It's surreal that one of my youngest brothers is engaged. Adrian was the last one I would have thought would get married first out of all of us brothers, but here he is, grinning like a fool down at his fiancée.

"Congrats, man," I say to him and slap him on the back.

"Thanks, Levi."

I give Juliette a hug too and then let them give their attention to everyone else. There's a long line of people waiting to give their congratulations and some of them even have presents. I'm sure Adrian wants to move through the line as quickly as possible, knowing his introverted ways.

I fade to the edge of the crowd, sipping on a glass of sweet tea and observing. There are a lot of couples here. And everyone seems to have this glow about them. It's like they're all a part of this secret happiness club that can only be obtained by way of wedding rings.

I didn't use to care about being in that club. That was, until I met Dahlia. Now, I spend every summer the same, thinking of her and recalling those days spent seaside. Maybe if I would have had the courage to tell her how I felt—to give up my life's plan for her ... maybe I'd be watching Adrian and Juliette with a more authentic smile. The kind that doesn't have even a hint of jealousy attached to it.

I down the rest of my sweet tea, wishing it was something stronger. But nothing helps me forget her anyway. Trust me, I've tried. No, every time I close my eyes I can see her windswept hair and smell the coconut lotion on her skin. It's enough to make a man lose his mind. But I have no hope of seeing her again, so I should try to move on. I can't wait around hoping that she'll show up out of the blue, and I can't track someone down with nothing but a first name and a memory to go off of.

Maybe this year will be the one that I find someone who can make me forget about her. Or at least dull the ache of regret that's taken up residence in my chest.

Preorder Levi's book: But He's My One Regret!

Want to skip into the future and see a glimpse of Adrian and Juliette's blissful marriage? Sign up for my newsletter to get a BONUS scene!

Ps. You'll also get a FREE recipe book with teas featured in the novel!

Also By Annah

Sweet Peach Series

The Love Audit – A grumpy/sunshine, enemies to more, office romcom.

One More Song – A second chance romcom with a celebrity guy and bookish girl.

Out of Office - A FREE novella about two coworkers falling in love over a road trip.

The First Taste – A childhood best friends to more, fake dating romcom.

One Last Play – A reverse grumpy/sunshine, age gap, sporty rom-com.

But He's a Carter Brother Series

But He's My Grumpy Neighbor – a grumpy/sunshine, slow burn romcom

But He's My One Regret – a second chance, opposites attract rom-com

Author's Note

Hello lovely reader,

Here we are again. Another book, another note from me. I was talking to a few of my best friends and I said that my toxic trait is I think every book I write is totally different from my other books in a scary way. But it truly does feel that way.

I know my voice is still *mine*, but if you go back to my debut novel a year ago, I truly feel like you'll see a difference. And each time I go through this process of stretching and learning and growing through a book, I get terrified that you're all going to hate it. Even when I want to be proud of it, I still get that little hitch in my breath when I send it to my editor. And then again when I send it to my wonderful ARC team. And then *again* when I publish it.

Every book so far has taken me through that process, but this one is different. The things in this book feel like they were ripped right out of me. Like someone cracked open my ribs and cut out a piece of my heart to give out to the world. My darkest struggles and deepest fears. My sweetest moments and brightest joys. It's all here wrapped up in this book covered in flowers.

Some people are going to read this and forget about it, or just say it was a cute read or–goodness I hate to write this–think it was terrible or mediocre. And I'd like to say I don't care what you think, but I'd be lying. I'm still growing in that area. But I *can* say that in the end it won't matter most. Because this book was a part of my healing process. It's the puffy pink scar after surgery. And I'm proud of myself for writing it.

Anyway, thank you for reading Adrian and Juliette's story. For taking time to escape into Peach Hollow. I hope you enjoyed your stay.

If you related to anything in this book, or you just enjoyed it, please come find me on socials and tell me! My heart melts every time a reader message comes into my inbox. Spam me with all your reactions. Tell me which brother is your favorite. Anything and everything!

IG: @authorannahconwell

annahconwell.com/contact-me

Happy reading,

AC

Acknowledgements

Jesus, thank you for healing me. All glory and honor to you.

To my husband Ryan, thank you for being my Adrian. For loving me with such care and tenderness, yet with a wild intensity and devotion that no one else could ever understand. And for calling me worthy of such love when I felt no worth at all. My single friends jokingly say you're the standard, but it's true. You're not trying to live up to the fictional men I write, they're trying to live up to you. I adore you, love of my life.

To my best friends, my ladies in waiting, my sisters in Christ: Baylie, Kathryn and Beth, thank you for being there for me when this book felt hard and scary. For encouraging me whenever I was worried it would flop. You're true friends. I love y'all!

To Dulcie, thank you for reading everything I write and encouraging me to keep going! This author life is hard. I'm grateful I have you!

To Amanda, I'm so glad I got to meet you. Thank you for being my friend and for your part in making this book better!

To my assistant and bestie Beth, thank you for joining me on this journey and learning everything you can along the way. I couldn't do so much of this without you! You're a rockstar.

To my editor Caitlin, each time I get to work with you I become more and more grateful to have you on my team. You make my books so much better and your kind encouragement spurs me forward in times of anxiety. Thank you!

To my cover designer, Stephanie, thank you for creating a cover that people will beg to have on their shelves. I'm convinced people will buy this book just to look at the cover, even if they never open it up.

Lastly, thank you to my ARC team and all my readers. It blows my mind that you want to read what I write. I'm brought to tears often by your love and support.

About the Author

Annah Conwell is a sweet romcom author who loves witty banter, sassy heroines, and swoony heroes. She has a passion for writing books that make you LOL one minute and melt into a puddle of 'aw' the next. You can find her living out her days in a small town in Sweet Home Alabama (roll tide roll!) with the love of her life (aka her husband), Ryan, and her two goofball pups, Prince and Ella. Most of the time she's snuggled up under her favorite blanket on the couch, reading way too many books to call it anything other than an addiction, or writing her little hopeless romantic heart out.

Find out more on her website: annahconwell.com

Made in United States
Orlando, FL
26 September 2024

51997681R00169